I0824993

THE DELIVERY

THE DELIVERY

A MERCURY CARTER ADVENTURE

ANDREW
WELSH-HUGGINS

THE MYSTERIOUS PRESS
NEW YORK

THE DELIVERY

Mysterious Press
An Imprint of Penzler Publishers
58 Warren Street
New York, N.Y. 10007

First edition

Interior design by Maria Fernandez

Library of Congress Control Number: 2025942860

ISBN: 978-1-61316-717-5
eBook ISBN: 978-1-61316-718-2

10 9 8 7 6 5 4 3 2 1

Printed in the United States of America
Distributed by Simon & Schuster

In memory of Barbie Herman and Stjepan Vlahovich,
inspirational readers and the most supportive fans
a writer could ever dream of having

"Playing shortstop is 75 to 80 percent anticipation, knowing the hitter and the pitch being thrown."

—Lou Boudreau, Major League Baseball All-Star player, credited as the inventor of the infield shift

ONE

Carter eyed the woman in the wrecked car, guessing from the blood on her face and the fact she wasn't moving that she didn't have long without his help.

Then he looked at the man walking toward him in the pouring rain with a large handgun leveled at Carter's chest.

That's not good.

"Get away from that car," the man yelled.

Not good at all.

It was three minutes past 10 P.M. on a Wednesday in late September. The rain was cascading like spring melt over steep falls, raking the slick asphalt, pooling in the roadway, silting sand and gravel across the bend in the road in Pawtucket, Rhode Island. The bend that the woman lying unconscious in the car hadn't negotiated. Instead, as far as Carter could tell, she'd hydroplaned straight through it and collided head-on with a utility pole that sheared the car's front as effortlessly as a buzz saw biting into a two-by-four.

Even with that much damage to the vehicle, Carter almost missed the wreck, preoccupied as he was by the storm, the extra innings Jays–Nats game on SiriusXM, and anticipation for the delivery he was slated to make tomorrow. A delivery that was tempering the disappointment he felt at spending the past three days on the mother of all wild goose chases. Though not by much.

What saved the day was the rain.

He'd slowed to twenty miles per hour at the curve, afraid of fishtailing despite the weight of the Suburban, glanced over, spied the woman's sedan, and eased onto the berm ten yards ahead of the crash.

"Ma'am," Carter called out when he reached her vehicle, tapping gently on the driver's side window. Hoping against hope she was alive. Worrying about the acrid electrical smell coming from inside the vehicle. "Ma'am, can you hear me?"

Even with the brim of his Rochester Red Wings ball cap pulled tightly over his brow, Carter had to pause to remove his glasses and wipe his face, so hard was the rain coming down. Which, gesture complete, was the moment he saw faint movement inside. The woman's lips parted and her head shifted an inch to the left.

"Hang on, ma'am," Carter said, spinning to return to his Suburban to dig out a crowbar in hopes of prying the door open and freeing her before shock set in or her injuries passed the point of no return. Or that acrid smell further compounded the danger the woman was in. He figured he could call 911 as soon as he had her out and comfortable.

Crowbar in hand, Carter was hustling back when he saw a vehicle roll up behind the woman's car and park, brights on. At first, blinded by the lights, Carter mistook the van for a rescue vehicle and relaxed, thankful the experts had arrived. Then a thick-waisted figure emerged from the driver's side and Carter realized that the man's sneakers, jeans, faded Pats jersey, and handgun weren't standard EMT issue. The man's demand that Carter get away from the wrecked vehicle was also off-brand.

"Sorry?" Carter said in response.

"You heard me. Beat it."

"Woah," Carter said. "I'm trying to help here. That lady's trapped and hurt. Pretty bad, I think."

"Now." The man raised the gun.

"Okay, okay." Carter backed up a step, his heart racing. "It's all good."

"Stop," the man said.

Carter stopped.

"Turn around."

The rain beat down, water streaming off the brim of Carter's ball cap. He shot a glance at the woman and saw she'd gone still again. Shock was setting in. She didn't have much time.

"Did you hear me? I said, turn around."

Carter thought about next morning's delivery. He'd been looking forward to it, even beyond the payday. It wasn't every day he got to hand over something meaningful both to the recipient and to Carter as well. He adjusted his cap. Looked like the Red Wings would miss the Governors' Cup playoffs again, but there was always next year.

Carter took another step back and said, "Probably not."

"What?" the man said, disbelief painting his fleshy, unshaven face.

"I mean, maybe we could work things out? I help this lady, you go your way, no harm, no foul?"

"Turn the fuck around."

"No thanks," Carter said, and underhanded the crowbar with a single, smooth upthrust, arcing it with the slightest forward lift at maybe thirty, thirty-five miles per hour. Not even close to his record. No matter. It struck the man on the bridge of his nose with a wet smack like a melon hitting pavement. The man grunted and staggered back, dropping the gun as his hands rose to his face. A second later, recovering, he knelt for the weapon, but it was too late. Carter covered the gap in two seconds, made his calculations, and kicked the man square in the face.

Which was Carter's first mistake. Don't get him wrong. The blow from his gray nylon hiking boot landed true, splintering the cartilage in the man's nose, eliciting a howl of agony as the man fell back. What Carter hadn't anticipated was that the man would have the wherewithal to grab Carter's right foot and tug hard even as the man collapsed to his side. Carter hop-hopped on his left foot, trying unsuccessfully to stay upright before he too went over. Carter flailed with his left hand, trying to find the man's gun where it had fallen, which was his next mistake.

He should have gone for the crowbar, which was now in the man's right hand and headed for Carter's left shoulder. Carter yelped as the crowbar hit home. He scrabbled in vain for the tool, hoping to wrest it free, but the man was too fast, whipping it back for a second blow. Which landed on Carter's left shoulder blade as he tried to roll away. He yelped again, feeling the pain shoot down his back.

"You little fucker," the man said, rising to his knees, his voice nasally from his shattered nose.

Reversed, stomach down, Carter had no hope of grabbing the crowbar back from his assailant. Instead, taking a breath, wincing at the ache in his shoulder, thinking about the woman in the car, he pulled his right leg forward by five inches and kicked out hard and fast, slamming his boot into the man's chest. It was like brushing a cedar chest with a feather duster. Carter absorbed the blow up to his knee, feeling a new pain as his leg nearly buckled.

But cedar chests serve their own purpose. Because every action has an equal and opposite reaction. Connecting with the man's immovable bulk propelled Carter two inches forward. Just far enough that, as the man recovered and raised the crowbar again, Carter reached his right hand out—straining, straining—and grabbed the gun glistening in the mud. He flipped himself around and crouched.

"Drop it," Carter gasped, aiming the gun between the man's eyes. "Do it now."

The man's expression morphed from fury to shock to bewilderment. He was frozen on his knees, crowbar held above his head like a torch in a sculpture's hand.

"I said now."

Scowling as if Carter had asked him to remove an appendage, the man dropped the crowbar.

Carter slowly rose, feeling his knees crack and pop. He kept the gun trained on the man.

"What's going on? Who is that lady?"

"Fuck you."

"Answer the question."

"Or what?"

Carter ignored the man's sneering tone. He didn't have time for this nonsense. Not with the woman's condition no doubt worsening, if she was even alive at this point.

Instead, he took a step toward the man, bobbed his head, and fake-punched, then raked the left side of the man's face with the side of the gun. Not full strength, though. Enough to send a message.

"Or I keep doing that until you answer the question."

The man fell backward with another grunt, touched his face, and looked in disbelief at the rain-washed blood streaming through his fingers.

"Help."

The woman in the car.

The man rose slowly to his knees, righted himself, and saw in Carter's eyes the desire to help the woman instead of finishing the fight.

"You're dead, asshole," he said. And stumbled back to his van.

He was gone a moment later, drenching Carter in a spray of water as the vehicle raced past him.

Carter waited until he was sure the man wasn't pulling a U-ey around the corner and barreling back. Satisfied, he set the man's gun on the ground, picked up the crowbar, limped to the woman's car, and jammed the bar into the gap between the driver's door and the bent frame. He pushed, leaning hard for leverage. Nothing happened. He smelled gasoline and, from inside the car, the caustic odor of an electrical fire. He took a breath, relaxed, and pushed again. The door gave with a crack and he dragged it open.

"Ma'am? Hang on, now."

He tried freeing her but her seat belt was jammed. Carter reached into the left lower pocket of his utility vest and retrieved a box cutter. It took him three slashes to cut the woman free. He examined her, checked out her pupils, decided he wasn't seeing a neck or spinal cord injury. Based on his experience. He put his arms around her and pulled her free of the car. As he did she stirred, awoke, and panicked. Her hands clawed at his waist, and tugged at his vest, as she cried out.

"It's all right," Carter said, easing her onto the ground. From there, still keeping an eye out for Pats Jersey, he maneuvered her away from the sedan and toward his Suburban. Slowly, careful not to jostle her. Finally, on the far side of the SUV, the Suburban between them and the sedan, Carter laid her down on the wet grass, the rain pounding even harder now.

He rose, retrieved his phone, shielded it from the weather with his hand. He had just managed to dial 911 when the first flames erupted inside what remained of the front half of the woman's car.

The explosion came half a minute later.

TWO

Carter stayed on scene for nearly ninety minutes, reasoning with the cop who took the call.

It wasn't that the officer wasn't buying Carter's story. A man with a gun. A confrontation in the downpour. The guy's hurried departure. He just had a lot of questions. Carter didn't blame him. He'd been in his shoes once. At the same time, Carter wanted to be on his way. He had a delivery to make.

"Listen, Mark," the Pawtucket cop said. Dark uniform soaked, body angled to look at Carter in the back of his cruiser. "You sure he didn't say anything else? This guy?"

"It's Merc, not Mark," Carter said. "Short for Mercury. It's okay. I get that all the time. Yes, I'm sure. 'Get away from that car.' That's as far as he went. Oh, and, 'You little fucker,' and 'You're dead, asshole.'"

The cop stared at Carter, the look plain: was Carter messing with him? No, Carter wasn't. He was being straightforward. In hopes of getting on the road and out of his sopping tan cargo shorts, gray T-shirt, and brown utility vest, all of which were currently dripping puddles in the back seat of the officer's white cruiser.

Dissatisfied, the cop held up Carter's license. "Rochester, New York. Long way from home."

"Not that far. Three hundred and eighty-four miles. Under six hours."

That earned another stare. Carter once again didn't blame him. He wasn't trying to be funny. He kept exact mileages in his head. A habit he developed at his neurologist's suggestion. Helped keep the headaches at bay. Distances, state capitals, the names of all fifty vice presidents. That kind of thing.

"You're a mailman?"

"Strictly speaking, a freelance courier. Independent, is my point. But technically, yes, a mailman."

"And you were making a delivery up in Lynn."

"Not exactly."

The cop sighed. "What, then?"

Carter went over it. Reluctantly, but what was he supposed to do at this point? A couple of calls and the cop, or one of his dayside colleagues, would have the truth sooner rather than later. He took it slowly. The murder several years back of Carter's father, Danny Carter, a postman in Rochester ambushed in his truck near the end of his route. His father as collateral damage in a gang war. Carter's decision to become a US Postal Inspection Service agent in the aftermath of the disaster.

Years later, Carter's on-the-job discovery that his father's mailroom supervisor, Earl Madden, had orchestrated the robbery that led to Danny Carter's death. Madden's hiring of a hitman to silence Mercury when he realized Mercury had stumbled upon the truth. Carter's survival despite the bullet that had passed through his skull, miraculously missing vital brain tissue and major arteries, but which left him with a traumatic brain injury. Carter's new career as an independent mailman. He left out the fact that he'd never missed a delivery.

"Okay," the cop said when Carter was finished. "I've got all that. It's quite a story. I'm sorry for your loss. But what's Lynn, Massachusetts, have to do with any of this?"

Carter continued, explaining how a body had been found on the first floor of a burned-out triple-decker in the small Massachusetts city, with evidence spread across the room suggesting that the victim was Earl Madden.

Except it wasn't Madden. Madden was a Johnnie Walker guy, always had been.

The empty Dewar's bottles arranged around his scorched remains didn't track. A dead end, Carter said, meaning a return home empty-handed.

The cop took a few more notes, nodded, and said, "Pawtucket's not exactly on the way home to Rochester from there."

"Correct. I was making an actual delivery here. Well, Providence. As long as I was in this neck of the woods."

"What kind of delivery?"

"The nature of my deliveries are confidential, sorry."

"Confidential or illegal?"

"I resent that question. I'm a former federal agent."

"In that case, mind if I search your vehicle?"

"Be my guest."

The cop poked around inside the Suburban. Carter wasn't sure about Rhode Island law, but he informed him of the Beretta 92D in the glove compartment anyway. Standard issue from Carter's USPIS day, and he couldn't see a reason to switch when he went private. The cop took his time examining Carter's license for the gun. Carter thought they were finished when the cop tapped the locked metal box underneath the middle seat.

"What's in there?"

"Usual stuff. Granola bars. Change of clothes. Hand grenades."

The cop squared his flashlight in Carter's face.

"Kidding," Carter said. "About the grenades."

Mostly kidding.

"Mind opening it?"

"Yes."

The cop looked surprised. "I could get a warrant."

"Go ahead."

Then, because he wasn't trying to be difficult, Carter gave him the number for Marcus Washington, USPIS Inspector in Charge for Rochester. Washington, the agent who oversaw the investigation of Carter's father's murder and later Earl Madden's disappearance. Who wasn't thrilled, apparently, to be awakened by a Pawtucket police officer after eleven at night but was good enough to confirm Carter's story.

Eventually, close to midnight, the cop cut Carter loose with a request to keep his phone handy in case a detective needed to reach him. Which was almost certain, given the seriousness of the injuries of the woman in the crash along with Carter's story of the confrontation with the man in the Pats jersey.

"You staying here tonight?"

Carter confirmed he had a hotel a couple of miles down the road.

"First time in Pawtucket?"

"Second. My dad and I drove to McCoy Stadium to see the Pawtucket Red Sox play. April 2002. Really cold day. Before they moved to Worcester."

"Shame about that. Hang on. You drove all this way to see a Triple-A game?"

"Sure. Wouldn't you?"

The cop didn't have an answer for that. He also didn't have an update on the condition of the woman in the wreck, other than it was serious. The woman whose life Carter saved. Maybe twice—from the crash, and from the man wielding the large handgun. Carter knew the woman's name, Linda Stauch, a fact he'd gleaned from checking her wallet, which he found in her coat after laying her out by his Suburban. That was all. He wasn't even sure what hospital she'd been taken to.

It was almost 1 A.M. by the time Carter checked into the Motel 6 by the airport. He thought about calling his uncle to let him know what happened but decided it was too late. He texted Tomeka, who wouldn't see the message until she got up, but he knew his wife would be put out if she learned the details of this encounter after the fact. Not that he could blame her.

Carter hung his socks and cargo shorts and T-shirt and utility vest on hangers in the shower to dry. He tried reading up on the Red Sox–Guardians results and a couple other games, but his eyes were drooping. He plugged his phone into the charger, turned off the light, rolled over, and almost immediately fell asleep.

He awoke seven hours later, groggy and sore from his run-in with the crowbar. The first thing that came to mind was that it had been a mistake to hang up his wet utility vest fully loaded. Some of the things in the multiple pockets, like the twenty-four-inch heavy-duty zip ties, would be fine. Others, like the flashlight, the pliers, the extra Beretta magazine, the pepper spray, not to mention the box cutter, not so much.

Carter used the restroom, slipped the vest off its hanger, and set it on his bed. Methodically, he emptied the pockets, placing the items one by one on a towel to dry.

He found the envelope in the bottom right-hand pocket. Where Linda Stauch had grabbed him, startling awake as he pulled her free from the car. She must have slid it inside without him noticing.

Carter used the box cutter to gently slice open the envelope, which looked like something you'd use for bank deposits if you still banked that way. He palmed the small ruby ring that fell out. He set it on the towel and lifted out a damp business card. The card belonged to someone named Jason Schulte, a Barrington, Rhode Island, banker. Carter turned the card over. Someone had written two things on the back. The first thing was a phone number with a local area code.

The second was a single word.

Help.

THREE

Even as a little girl, Monica Carmichael had appreciated the utility of an object over its shape or form, regardless of how pretty it was.

Farmer Barbie, for example. The doll's stiff legs, when gripped in Monica's tightened fist and jabbed fast and hard, left bruises on the arms, stomachs, and thighs of any girl who dreamed of teasing her about her drab clothes, unwashed hair, or ragged nails.

Later, in high school, Monica's lavender backpack wasn't solely a receptacle for the usual stuff—schoolbooks, notebooks, pens and pencils, makeup, tissues, gum, a hairbrush, tampons, loose change, and condoms. It was a mobile pharmacy, an emporium of goods from Ritalin to benzos to mollies to whatever else was in short supply at school that week. Guess who was the center of attention now?

A few years later, people went gaga for Monica's red BMW convertible even as they asked themselves privately how she afforded such a car on her prison nurse salary. Monica couldn't care less about the car's aesthetics. What mattered to her was the surprisingly roomy trunk and the speeds it reached as she burned up Route 1 after emptying yet another vacation home of its belongings based on the latest tip from an inmate who asked to see her in the Rhode Island Department of Corrections medical clinic, "because I just ain't feeling right."

Or as now, rocking atop Vickers, her left hand on her left nipple, right hand touching herself as she leaned forward to receive him fully inside. Monica wasn't trying to kid anybody. Vickers had the muscular thighs, taut belly, and ripped arms any girl would appreciate. Beyond that he was a certified looker, with his close-cropped blond hair, carefully maintained three-day stubble, and cornflower-blue eyes. He also had ambition, something Monica prized above all else. For all those attributes, though, he was little more to her than her latest tool—today's equivalent of the Barbie, of the backpack, of the BMW. He also got her off, which more and more recently was a necessity she had to outsource with her and Randy nitpicking at each other all day long.

Which was why the first fuck was always for her.

She came a few seconds later in a loud, long crescendo wave. Collapsing atop him, she bided her time—he was done in a few seconds—and rolled onto her back. She'd give it a few minutes and then get down to business. The second fuck—the leftovers—was always for Vickers.

Or more to the point, her down payment for the job she needed him to do sooner rather than later.

Except that didn't happen today. At that moment, Vickers's phone buzzed.

"Shit," he said, examining the screen.

"What?"

"Your husband just texted."

"And?"

"We've got a problem."

Carter's first move was to let the police know about the ring and Jason Schulte's business card. The faster he turned them over, the better. He had a delivery to make—one he was still looking forward to—and then a 384-mile drive home to Rochester. He found the number for the Pawtucket Police Department and asked for the detective handling a bad wreck the night before on Armistice Boulevard. The dispatcher said she'd have to take a message. Carter left his details and added that he might swing by to drop the items off.

Except now Carter was stuck. He hadn't been a cop for several years. He was a mailman now, albeit a freelance one. That part of him was intrigued by an envelope. Never failed. Meanwhile, the ex-cop in him was bothered by the word *Help* scrawled on the back of the business card inside the envelope. No way around it.

Result: He was both curious and worried. Against his better judgment, he picked up his phone again.

One ring, two, three, before a man answered.

"This is Mercury Carter calling. Sorry to bother you. I'm trying to reach"—he glanced at the business card he found in the envelope—"someone named Jason Schulte?"

"Who?"

Carter repeated the name.

"Sounds like you've got the wrong number." Matter-of-fact, but not unfriendly. Broad New England accent. *Gawt the wrong numbah.*

"Sorry about that. One other thing."

"Yeah?"

"Whoever Jason Schulte is, this number was handwritten on the back of his business card. The card was in an envelope along with a ruby ring." Carter described it, including the intertwined gold strands constituting the ring's thin band.

A long pause.

"Who did you say you were?"

Carter said his name again.

"And how is it that you have that ring?"

Carter recalled the guy with the fleshy, unshaven face in the faded Pats jersey carrying the large handgun. He said, "It was passed on to me. I thought I'd try to find the person it belongs to."

Carter couldn't be sure—the heater in the motel room came on just then, blowing loudly—but he thought he heard the man choke up.

"Belonged," the man said. "If it's the same ring, that belonged to our daughter, Terri."

Jim and Valerie Watkins lived down the road in Cranston in a one-story gray clapboard bungalow on Kole Street. A seasonal display of pumpkins and cornstalks crowded the front door. Carter pulled up to the house at ten thirty that morning after an hour on the phone. First with Uncle Dean, reviewing the events of the night before. Like Tomeka, Carter's uncle didn't appreciate being left out of the loop. Both as Carter's business partner, handling the administrative side of Carter's deliveries, but also as his relative who shouldered the shared grief over Carter's slain father—Dean's brother. A quick call to Marcus Washington at USPIS to smooth things over.

Then, with Tomeka.

"Assuming you won't be home for dinner?" she said after he explained everything that happened since he left the Boston suburb of Lynn and arrived in Pawtucket the night before.

"I'm just dropping the ring off. It won't take long."

"Where have I heard that before?"

"How about I pick up root beer floats on the way in?"

"That would help."

"Done. But I won't be that late. Promise."

"Mm-hmm."

As Carter walked up the drive, a chocolate-and-white spaniel with ears on independent flight paths shot out the Watkinses' front door, traced a double circle in the small front yard, watered a line of marigolds, investigated Carter's boots, and ran back inside.

"Jim Watkins," the dog's owner said, extending his hand. "Please excuse Daisy."

"No problem. Cute dog. Mercury Carter. Thanks for letting me stop by."

Inside, Watkins introduced his wife, Valerie, a heavy woman with tired eyes who nonetheless looked shocked at Carter's appearance at the door, as if his earlier call had been a prank. Picking up on her reaction, Carter saw no reason to delay the inevitable.

"Here it is," he said, withdrawing the ring from a pocket on the left side of his utility vest. He'd stopped by CVS on the way and purchased a birthday card to have a fresh envelope to store it in.

Valerie cupped her right hand to her mouth and burst into tears. Jim Watkins's face was a stone, his mouth set in a grim line.

"Why don't we sit down?" he said.

Jim settled Carter in a cherry-stained straight-back chair in the living room. Watkins and his wife sat together on a beige couch opposite Carter, Daisy between them.

"Please tell us what's going on," Valerie said, wiping her eyes. "I don't understand."

It wasn't the most difficult conversation Carter had ever had. But maybe top five. He eased into things, double-checking that they didn't know a Jason Schulte.

"Never heard of him," Jim Watkins said.

Now came the hard part. Carter gave them the basics: freelance mailman, happened to be making a delivery in Pawtucket, came across a woman in a wreck. His gut told him to leave out the man with the gun for now.

"Linda Stauch?" Valerie said. "I have no idea who that is. How would she know Terri?"

"I'm not one hundred percent sure she did. When did your daughter—"

"We haven't seen Terri in, well, for a while," Jim said. "I know how I made it sound on the phone." He took a breath. "She might be dead. But maybe not. We have no idea either way. Which makes it all the harder."

"When did you last see her?" Despite himself, Carter was curious. Once a federal agent. He wouldn't mention this part of the conversation to Tomeka.

Valerie began crying again, so softly Carter didn't realize it at first. Daisy raised her head, looked at Valerie, and put her head in her lap.

"I'm sorry," Valerie said.

Jim rested his hand on his wife's knee. He said, "Mother's Day, last year. What's that, almost sixteen months? My mom was still alive, and we all went over to the home for a visit. Afterward, the five of us went out to dinner—our son, Nate, was in town. We went to Marchetti's. My mom's favorite place. She loved their penne. It was a good day, mostly. Until . . ." He went silent, his face a mask.

Carter gave it ten seconds. "Until?"

"Until Terri asked for money. Again. We realized that was the only reason she'd agreed to visit. That and the free meal. We had an argument at the table. I lost my temper, big-time. Terri yelled and Nate yelled back. Terri stormed out. It was pretty bad. The whole restaurant was staring."

"What about the ring?"

"Terri struggled in high school," Valerie said, voice still soft but regaining strength. Her face was blotchy and red, as if hives had come on suddenly. "Bad grades, ran with a tough crowd, never listened." She sighed deeply. "She was a handful. Half the time she holed up at Dottie's—that's Jim's mom—especially after we fought, which was a lot. Somehow, Terri's senior year, she pulled it together enough to graduate. Dottie gave her the ring for graduation, to show how proud she was. The ring was *her* mom's. An heirloom."

"Quite the gift," Carter said.

"Foolhardy," Jim said. "We tried to talk my mom out of it. We knew by then Terri had a drug problem. Figured she'd sell it first chance she got. Somehow she hung onto it. Terri robbed us blind over the next few years, but she always had the ring on."

"Robbed how?"

"Silverware, electronics, cash from our wallets the second we turned our backs. Two different TVs—we just came home and they were gone. You name it. We had the locks changed twice and installed a bedroom safe."

Carter nodded in sympathy. It was a familiar story. He encountered versions of it again and again when he was on the job. And off. Tomeka had a nephew who landed in prison after drugs took over. Carter had a cousin in Syracuse who fatally overdosed. He got it. He said, "After that Mother's Day?"

Valerie shook her head. Jim stared out the living room window. Thin, brown hair receding from his forehead. Face gaunt and pinched as if perpetually straining to lift a box of encyclopedias. Dressed in jeans and a button-down blue work shirt; the look of a man who spent a lot of free time in a garage workshop.

Jim said, “Nothing. We knew things had gotten bad. She was working the streets for a while. Turning tricks. Before that blowup, we got her in a program a couple times but she relapsed almost immediately.” His face turned hard. “No refunds from those places, by the way.”

Valerie took his hand, frowning. Jim said, “After the scene in the restaurant, hearing nothing, knowing what we did . . . You just figure, after a while. There’s a reason it’s easy to fear the worst.”

Something occurred to Carter. He reached into a left side pocket of his utility vest and retrieved the envelope that Linda Stauch put there. He showed Jim Watkins the back of Jason Schulte’s card.

“Yes,” he said after a second. “That’s Terri’s handwriting.”

Valerie gasped. “That could mean . . .”

“It could mean anything,” Jim said. “Who knows when that’s from? Could be something she wrote after seeing a, you know, *client* months ago.”

An interesting thought, Carter said to himself, recalling the unshaven man in the Pats jersey.

“What do you think?” Valerie said, directing the question at Carter. The voice of a teacher wanting an answer from a reluctant student.

I think I want to make my delivery and get home, Carter thought.

He cleared his throat and said, “Based on my experience, and the circumstances, I’m thinking Terri wrote that recently.”

“What do you mean, the circumstances?” Jim said, leaning toward Carter. “You still haven’t explained how you got that ring. ‘It was passed on to’ you? What the hell is that about? How do we know she didn’t give it to you personally? Maybe you’re one of her clients?”

Carter kept his cool. “It’s a fair question. I’m not one of her clients, trust me.” He wrestled with what to say. His eyes drifted to a black-framed family photo on the wall by the dining room entryway. A much younger Jim and Valerie, with a pair of elementary school kids by their side, boy and girl. The girl, presumably Terri, grinning at the camera a little too hard.

He decided to come clean. It was the right thing to do. It would raise more questions than it would answer, but he couldn't help that. It was what it was.

"Dear God," Valerie said when he finished describing the events of the previous evening. "That poor woman. She must have been terrified. Do you know how she is?"

Carter shook his head. "She was stabilized by the time she left in the ambulance. She was pretty banged up but my guess is she'll make it."

"What about the man?" Jim said.

"He was a little worse for wear. Still able to drive, though."

"What are the police saying?"

"I'm not sure. I know they're looking into it. There wasn't a lot of evidence at the scene."

"What would that man want with this woman, Linda Stauch?" Jim said. "Was she a you know—like Terri?"

Carter summoned an image of Stauch, a middle-aged woman in business casual dress—dark slacks, cream blouse, light blue sweater—in her newer model Camry.

"I wouldn't think so, no. As for why the man warned me off from her, I can't answer that." He paused. "I'm sorry to dump all this on you. I just got curious, thought I'd call. As soon as I get the name of the detective handling the case I'd be happy to put you in touch."

Jim sighed as deeply as his wife had, a man with the weight of the world on his shoulders. "We'd appreciate that. It's distressing, I'm not going to lie. And strange. At least we have something to hold on to, for now."

Carter nodded his agreement. He patted his right-hand shorts pocket for his keys and rose from his chair.

"All right," he said. "As soon as—"

"A mailman."

Carter looked across the room.

Valerie had spoken.

"I'm sorry?" Carter said.

"You're a mailman. Isn't that what you said?"

"That's right, yes. A freelance courier."

"What kinds of things do you deliver?"

Jim turned to his wife, his eyes questioning. She shook her head at him. "Well?"

"All kinds of things, I guess."

"Like what?" Her voice was stronger now, insistent.

"Like things that people don't want going through regular channels. Postal service, FedEx, any of that."

"Can you be more specific?" Insistent verging on impatient.

Carter reviewed some of his recent deliveries. "Paintings, family heirlooms, jewelry like that ring. Occasionally pets. Sometimes I deliver information. Very rarely, people."

"People?" Jim said. "Like who?"

"Like people who need to get from Point A to Point B, and are, well, nervous they might run into unexpected encounters along the way."

"Bad guys?" Jim said. "Drug dealers? Like who?"

Carter recalled the patrol officer's question along the same lines the night before.

"I chauffeured a pharmacist once on his way to testify in a pill mill case. That's as close to drugs as I get. Nothing illegal. Not my thing."

"So you protect people," Valerie said.

"In a manner of speaking."

"Funny way to make a living, working under the radar like that," Jim said.

"It's not the most orthodox occupation, I'll grant you. But it suits me. Listen, I don't want to keep you any longer—"

"I want to hire you," Valerie said.

Carter and Jim stared at her.

"Excuse me?" Carter said.

"I want to hire you to deliver this ring to Terri." She held it up as if it were a rare shell found beachcombing. "Or get it back to her, if she had it recently. Either way."

"Val," Jim said. "What are you doing? He doesn't know where Terri is. Do you?"

Carter said that he didn't.

"Does that matter?" Valerie said. Her voice was stronger now, and she was sitting up straighter. She looked younger than she had when Carter walked in. Some of the despair and fatigue had dissipated, softening her features, replaced by the faintest trace of hope in her eyes. Hope and steel.

"Well . . ." Carter said.

"Well, what?" Valerie demanded. "Does it matter whether you know where Terri is, or not?"

"The thing is, most of my deliveries are pretty straightforward. Even the ones involving people. Their fears turn out to be unfounded and they end up paying a little bit extra for a quiet trip across the country."

"But?" Valerie said.

Carter hesitated. "Sometimes things come up that, let's say, impede my ability to make a delivery. Occasionally—rarely—the original destination shifts while I reroute things. When that happens, it's true that I don't always know exactly what's happening next, or who I might be dealing with." He paused. "Or where the recipient is."

"Do you have a gun?"

"Yes."

"Have you ever used it?"

"Val," Jim said.

"Occasionally," Carter said.

Jim stared at him.

"What do you charge?" Valerie demanded. "For a normal delivery. Returning one of those heirlooms you mentioned."

Carter hesitated, told her.

"That's not cheap," Jim said. "You could mail something certified with full insurance for a fraction of that."

"You could," Carter said. "I can't disagree with you."

Valerie walked out of the room without speaking. She returned a minute later with a small velvet ring box, the ruby ring visible inside it, and said, "How many times have you missed a delivery in your career? Give or take. Failed to get something or someone to where it's going?"

Carter dug his hands into his pockets. He felt a headache coming on. The morning was not unfolding as he'd imagined or hoped. Not to mention the past twelve hours.

He said, "I think the police are your best option here, Mrs. Watkins. They've got the resources to look into this stuff. I'm a sole proprietor. Also, I'm not from here. I don't know the lay of the land."

A sour look darkened Jim's face. "The police, yeah. Because they've looked so hard already."

"This might be different," Carter said. "Given the circumstances."

"You didn't answer my question," Valerie said.

"Sorry. Could you repeat it?"

"Have you ever missed a delivery? Yes or no?"

Carter sighed.

"No," he said.

FOUR

"What kind of problem?"

Vickers, sitting on the side of the bed, still unclothed, his muscular, bare back to Monica, said, "Chuck Gibbons is dead."

"What? What happened?" Monica pulled a sheet around her and reached for her phone.

"Not sure. Randy says he was found unresponsive in a motel room in Pawtucket."

"When?"

"Three days ago. Explains why we haven't heard from him."

Messages app open, Monica read the text from Randy.

"Fuck," she said. "This is all we need."

"Let me make some calls. See if I can find out what happened."

"Yes. You do that."

He swiveled to look at her.

"What's that supposed to mean?"

She watched his eyes trace the outline of her body beneath the sheet. She hardened her face. *No seconds today for you, bubs. Sorry.*

"It means Chuck is your responsibility," she said. "Was your responsibility. It's on you to find out what's going on. So the whole thing doesn't go to hell."

"We're in this together, last time I checked."

"Don't assume—"

Monica was interrupted by their phones buzzing simultaneously. A new text from Randy in the chain.

Anybody know where Chuck's laptop is? It's not here.

"Shit," Monica said. "Shit. Shit. Shit."

Great, Carter thought. Now he had a job. Another job, besides the delivery he was supposed to be making at an elderly Providence man's home at almost this exact moment. The one he'd been looking forward to, since anything baseball related was a professional bonus.

Okay. Not to worry. A delivery was a delivery. The question was, what next? Try to reach Jason Schulte, whose business card was used to send a message for help. Or hunt down Linda Stauch and figure out why she had an envelope with that business card and the ring in her possession when she wrecked in the driving rain on Armistice Boulevard in Pawtucket, possibly as she lost control fleeing a guy with a gun. One or the other on the chance that either could lead him to Terri. But who first?

Carter didn't drive far after leaving Jim and Valerie's house. Straight to the nearest coffee shop, in fact. Medium tea. Surefire way to calm his nerves. He patted the ring box in the upper left pocket of his utility vest. He glanced at the paper receipt sitting in the passenger seat of the Suburban, the carbon copy of the one he left behind, confirming his acceptance of the Watkinses' down payment on his fee. Confirming, and binding him to his word. That the delivery would happen no matter what. Carter carefully placed the receipt in the manila envelope in the glove compartment he reserved for important papers, just under his Beretta, and went over his conversation with Jim Watkins in the front yard after Watkins showed him out.

"I need you to promise me something."

"If I can," Carter said.

"If you find Terri and she's, well, if she's dead, call me first."

"I think we've established there's a good chance she's not dead."

"I pray to God you're right. That doesn't change what I'm asking. I need to be the one to tell Val. She came on strong at the end, but this whole thing has devastated her. She's a different woman."

Carter didn't say anything.

"I mean, she's the best cook in the world," Jim continued. "But ever since . . . it's nothing but frozen meals. That's just the tip of the iceberg. You know what I mean?"

Carter nodded. He knew. Once upon a time, if there were a more devout Catholic than his mother, Carter hadn't met them. But after Carter's father's murder, she attended Mass only irregularly. After they learned that Danny Carter's own supervisor, Earl Madden, was behind the killing and tried to have Mercury killed as well, she stopped going altogether. Hadn't been back in more than a decade.

"It's all fairy tales," she said, waving off Carter's and his uncle's repeated efforts to get her to rethink her decision.

"I'll call you first," Carter said to Jim Watkins.

"Thank you," Watkins said.

Carter brought himself back to the moment. Decision time. Jason Schulte or Linda Stauch. Stauch or Schulte.

He picked up the phone and called his uncle back. The line opened after a single ring.

"Dispatch."

Carter couldn't remember exactly when he gave up trying to persuade his uncle he didn't need to answer Carter's calls like a trucking company switchboard. Sometime between a couple of his more memorable deliveries. The first, chauffeuring a hundred-year-old handwritten fruitcake recipe from a great-aunt in Des Moines to a great-niece in Albuquerque. The second, shepherding a ceremonial Lakota eagle feather headdress from Toledo to Pine Ridge, South Dakota. The latter involving one of those "occasionally" times, gun-wise, that he'd mentioned to Valerie Watkins. Someplace in there. He'd decided to let it go.

After all, recovered from the gunshot that nearly killed him, Carter owed his new direction in life in large part to his uncle. He'd found Carter his first job and then quit his own to be Carter's backup when, to their surprise, the freelance courier business took off.

If Uncle Dean's approach suited him, and helped him with his own long recuperation from the murder of his brother, so be it.

If he was being honest about it, Carter liked the affectation at this point.

Carter reviewed the conversation with Jim and Valerie Watkins and his quandary over where to start.

"Where's the banker's office?" Carter's uncle asked.

Carter examined the card. "Barrington. It's a Providence suburb."

"Guessing that lady, Linda Stauch, is in a Providence hospital. Each are about the same in terms of distance."

"What I was thinking."

"I'd call the banker, set up an appointment on some kind of pretext. Then go to the hospital in person."

"What about my other delivery? Or the fact I took this one on at all? The ring, I mean."

"The other one can wait. What's his name? Pellegrini?"

"Pellegrino. Lenny Pellegrino."

"Right. It's not like he's going anywhere."

"I guess not. He's pretty old. Though he sounded fine over the phone."

"Must be old if he played with Lou Boudreau."

"Watched him play," Carter corrected. "He'd be a hundred something if he'd been a teammate."

"Gotcha. Okay, as far as the ring," his uncle said, "think the cops have any interest in finding this lady, Terri Watkins?"

"Depends. If finding her helps them find the guy who was chasing Linda Stauch, sure."

"You find her first, you going to keep any of that from them?"

"Obviously not. As long as I make the delivery—find Terri and give the ring back—why would I?"

"Good to hear. Let me know how it goes."

Carter took his uncle's advice and called the banker. Ended up leaving a voicemail on Jason Schulte's cell phone. He asked him to call, keeping it vague, mentioning a need to set up a business account separate from personal.

He and his uncle split up the calls on Linda Stauch. It would be tricky with all the privacy rules and regs. But there were ways around those. People still had a right to call and ask if someone had been admitted. Ask their condition? Forget about it. Fortunately, that's not what Carter needed.

He was draining the last of his tea when his uncle texted. He'd found her. Providence Memorial Hospital off Exchange near downtown. No other information available. But that was enough.

Carter considered his parking options and decided to go with a meter on the street. Too many cameras in garages. He located the lobby, skipped the information desk, gambled on Intensive Care Unit, Third Floor, and headed up.

He hit his first roadblock at the nurses' station. The nurse in charge, a Black guy in scrubs who looked like he'd be as comfortable taking your blood pressure as bench-pressing his weight in an NFL locker room, made it clear only family members were allowed back.

"I'll wait," Carter said, nodding at the room with pastel chairs and couches and a TV tuned to CNN that he'd passed on his way from the elevator.

"Suit yourself."

Carter didn't intend to wait. He intended to sit for five minutes and plan his next move. Maybe sneak past the linebacker nurse. Maybe motor over to Jason Schulte's bank in Barrington to try an in-person conversation. Maybe head back to the scene of the previous night's confrontation. He figured something would shake loose. It usually did.

Three minutes in, as Carter read the captions on a commercial for a prescription drug whose side effects seemed guaranteed to kill you first, something shook loose.

A someone.

A woman entered the waiting room from the direction Carter had just come, eyes red, face drawn. Shoulder-length hair that looked as if it might normally be put up with a hair band or braid, but was now hanging in undisciplined strands like a tattered shroud. She wasn't Linda Stauch's twin. But if she wasn't related, Carter was a Blue Jays third baseman.

He gave her a minute as she sat heavily and looked at her phone, answering a series of texts. Finished, she placed the phone in her tan, faux-leather purse, and stared at the wall where the TV hung.

Idly, pretending to watch the CNN crawl, Carter said, "Excuse me."

She looked up, wary. "Yes?"

"Are you by any chance here for Linda Stauch?"

Her eyes refocused. “Yes,” she said, suspicion straining her exhausted face. “Who are you?”

“My name’s Mercury Carter. I’m the person who found her last night. In her car. I wanted to be sure she was all right. I couldn’t get any information by calling, or at the desk.” He gestured in the direction of the nurse’s station.

“Oh my God. You’re the one?”

“That’s right.”

“The police said . . .”

Carter waited.

“They said you pulled her free. And there was a fight or something? Someone trying to stop you?”

“It got a bit confusing. It turned out okay in the end. Right time, right place, I guess. How’s she doing?”

The woman’s eyes brightened. “She’s alive, thanks to the airbag. And you, apparently.”

Carter nodded his acceptance of the compliment.

“But she’s really banged up. Two ribs are broken. She might have a concussion.”

“Sorry to hear that. Are you a sister? I don’t mean to be forward, but you look just like her.”

The woman nodded. “I’m Abigail. Abigail Shipley. What did you say your name was again?”

Carter told her. She reached out and briefly grasped his left forearm.

“Thank you so much for helping her.”

“My pleasure.”

“This fight,” Abigail said, as if the thought had just occurred to her. “What happened? Who was that guy?”

“What did the police tell you?”

She said the officer who reached her after midnight explained there'd been an accident. When Abigail arrived at the hospital, the officer told her about a Good Samaritan who had said something about a man with a gun. The officer asked if she knew whether her sister might have known someone who wanted to hurt her. An ex-husband or boyfriend.

"And?" Carter said, keeping his voice as even as possible.

"No one," Abigail said. "She divorced Carl last year after his second affair. He was a piece of work, but never violent. This guy last night—what did he look like?"

Carter described him.

"That's nothing like Carl. I have no idea who that would be."

"Who knows. Maybe a road rage thing. I'm glad she's okay." He paused, giving it a count of three. "By the way, does the name Jason Schulte mean anything to you?"

"Who?"

He explained about the business card he found in his utility vest in an envelope he was pretty sure her sister slipped into a pocket as she came to.

"I have no idea," Abigail said, confusion in her eyes. "That's not even her bank, as far as I know. She does everything at a credit union. Why would she have his card?"

"I'm not sure. How about Terri Watkins?" He kept it vague, leaving out the ruby ring and the word scrawled on the back of Jason Schulte's business card.

Help.

"I don't know who that is either. These names were in an envelope Linda handed you? That doesn't make any sense. The police didn't say anything about this."

"I only found it this morning, after I woke up. It might be nothing."

"Why would she hand the envelope to you?"

Good question. Carter said, "I don't think she was in her right mind at the moment. Shock was setting in. It might have been accidental."

Abigail frowned and shook her head like someone ridding herself of a buzzing mosquito. Carter felt bad. He'd made a traumatic event more worrisome, if that were possible. The fact the names meant nothing to Linda's sister was problematic, but no worse than the man with the gun who told Carter to get away from the wrecked car. Seeing another question forming on Abigail's lips, Carter decided on a gambit.

"That wasn't a rental, was it? Maybe the envelope was something she found inside?"

"A rental? No—that was her car, at least according to the police. A Camry. Brand new last year."

"Any idea where she was headed?"

Abigail looked surprised at the question. "Home, I assume. She wasn't that far when it happened."

"How far?"

"Not twenty minutes away. The terrible thing is, she shouldn't even have been there. On the road."

"Why not?"

"She stopped for gas. The police found a receipt in her purse. She filled up a few minutes before she crashed. I don't know what possesses her to work so late. It's been that way since Carl left."

"The officer told you that? About the receipt?"

"No—a detective. He came by this morning. Here, I mean." She dug in her purse, produced a card, and handed it to Carter. He read the name on it.

Detective Gus Papaleonardos, Pawtucket Police Department

"Do you mind?" he said, pulling out his phone, and when she shook her head, he took a photo of the card.

"Thanks," he said, handing the card back. "Was it close by?"

"Was what?"

"The gas station where she stopped."

"Not far. Narragansett Get 'n Go. She always stopped there."

FIVE

Monica departed out the back of Vickers's Thayer Street apartment, as always, walking the length of his squash court–sized backyard and undoing the latch on the fence at the end. She strolled around the corner, turned left, and walked the block and a half to her red BMW. The previous night's storm had given way to an almost cloudless blue sky. The temperature had dropped and a breeze lifted the yellowing leaves of a locust tree at the end of the block.

The day had begun so promisingly. A chance to toast successes. To permit herself to appreciate what she and Vickers had been doing twenty minutes earlier. To hope that their second time between the sheets would ensure his cooperation for what was coming down the road.

Except that didn't happen. The morning was unfolding very differently. From rainbows and flowers to shitstorm in the blink of an eye. In the arrival of a text. Now she had to pivot, and fast, to figure out why Chuck Gibbons was dead and where the hell his goddamned laptop was.

Reaching her car, Monica glanced up and down the street to be sure she hadn't been followed. The only person she spied was a woman who might have been her mother's age—if her mother had lived so long—bent over a leash at the end of which trotted a West Highland terrier. Monica paused for a few moments, her eyes lingering on the woman and her frail, arthritic gait, before climbing into the Durango and driving away.

She headed down the hill, angled through downtown to Broad Street and then over to Olneyville. Thirty minutes after she'd sat wrapped in one of Vickers's bedsheets examining her husband's panicked text message, she was parked at the rear of the office building in the space with the sign that said *Reserved, Mrs. Carmichael.* She admired the beds of yellow mums and ornamental purple cabbages vibrant against the chocolate of the newly laid mulch. Twin beds to the ones out front. The two-story brown brick building that housed Second Act Staffing Solutions, with its power-washed façade, new double-pane windows, and sharp signage, stood out in this neighborhood like a yacht in a sea of dinghies. Which is how she—how she and Randy—wanted it. Gawk all you want; we have nothing to hide.

She bypassed the large, first-floor room where Chuck and Aiden spent most of their time—they'd given it the eye-rolling name of *The Bunker*—and took the rear stairs to the second floor. No point in running the risk, however slight, of encountering Aiden. Good ol' Aiden. If anyone could appreciate the value of a man on the edge of society, the usefulness of an outcast, it was Monica. But even she had her limits, especially when it came to someone like Aiden, a Johnny One Note IT whiz who seemed satisfied to play second fiddle in the Second Act operations to a much bigger wizard like Chuck Gibbons. A real winner, Aiden. Basic hygiene, anyone?

Yes, better to avoid that scene altogether.

Monica found Randy in his office, studying his monitor with a frown, bald pate shiny with sweat.

"Anything?"

Randy shook his head.

"Where the hell's Vickers?" Monica said, carefully calibrating the amount of outrage in her tone.

"He better be at Chuck Gibbons's house, seeing what his wife knows."

"Anything more?"

"Just this." Randy rubbed his beardstache, which was still more red than gray and stabbed a forefinger at the monitor. Monica walked around his desk and leaned in.

OVERDOSE SUSPECTED IN PROVIDENCE MAN'S DEATH

A barebones *ProJo* brief offered a few details, including the name of the motel—Lighthouse Inn—where Gibbons's body was found, the fact it was a frequent source of complaints to police over prostitution and drug activity, and Gibbons's age: thirty-eight.

Nothing about a laptop that could mean a federal indictment if word of its contents got out.

"He was whoring," Monica said, shaking her head in disgust.

"Looks like it."

"With the laptop with him."

"We don't know that for certain."

"Where is it, then?"

"It's a good question. One I'm hoping Scott can answer sooner rather than later. I'm not sure what's taking him so long."

Monica studied her husband out of the corner of her eye, trying to decide if he was insinuating something. She didn't think so but couldn't be sure. Nor could she take any chances.

At home, at least when they weren't arguing, Monica gave Randy no reason to think she might be seeking relief elsewhere. Sure, they weren't quite as frenetic as their first days together. Amazing they didn't knock down the walls in the RIDOC nurse's office back then. Marriage lowered the temperature a little, as it always did; she should know, this being number three and all. Plus, Randy's stress over his daughter and what the upcoming heist meant for her was sapping his staying power, just a little.

Nevertheless, as far as Randy knew, they were still a team, happily married in all the ways that implied. They were personal and professional partners. For now, life was still good.

Unless Chuck's laptop was really missing.

In which case, life might be very, very bad.

Monica and Randy's phones both buzzed with an incoming text. They reached for them and read the message at the same time. From Vickers:

> **I'm here. Stacy's clueless. No sign of it—laptop's definitely gone**

On the way to the gas station, Carter stopped first at the scene of the wreck the night before. As he guessed, there was nothing to see other than a Rhode Island Energy van parked by the remains of the utility pole that had cleaved Linda Stauch's Camry almost in two. Four guys, including one a story up on a cherry picker, worked on repairs.

He proceeded on to Narragansett Get 'n Go. As Linda Stauch's sister suggested, the station was basically around the corner. A five-minute drive up Armistice when it wasn't raining like an overdue monsoon. The business occupied a lot on the corner of a busy commercial street and a nondescript side street. Kitty-corner on the side street, a cinderblock DIY carwash sported a For Sale sign. On the main street, a gravel lot more scrub than gravel sat between the station and a small used-car lot. The lot looked to specialize in blue and gray two-door beaters that hadn't seen under a hundred thousand miles since Obama's second term.

The gas station featured four pumps under an awning, with an air machine at the side next to a dented ice machine. It was hard to call the facility isolated given the nearby businesses and the traffic on the main street rushing past in either direction. But it wasn't a convention center, either.

Carter stopped at the pump closest to the street and filled up. Finished, he backed the Suburban into a space at the side of the station by the restrooms. Rather than go inside right away, he retrieved his phone and checked his messages. His uncle had texted, looking for an update. Rochester USPIS Inspector in Charge Marcus Washington had called without leaving a message. Tomeka had also texted, sending him a clip of a diving catch by a Cincinnati Reds outfielder that appeared to defy gravity. Carter had already seen it at least five times but sent a "thumbs-up" anyway. Satisfied he was caught up, he bypassed Jason Schulte's cell and called the number for the bank in Barrington.

He didn't get through right away, of course. He waded through three levels of automated phone prompts first. No one called a business anymore expecting a human to pick up unless you were talking about a mom-and-pop butcher store or maybe a head shop. People worried about the AI future, but the fact was, the bots were already in charge and they had you on hold. It was one of the reasons Carter suspected his services were in demand. People craved the personal touch. He or his uncle always answered by the second ring.

Finally, three minutes in, a woman's voice, professional and courteous.

"Barrington branch. How may I direct your call?"

Carter asked for Schulte.

Silence.

"Hello?" he said at last.

"I'm afraid Mr. Schulte isn't available. Is there someone else who could assist you?"

Something in the woman's tone followed by her silence at the mention of Schulte's name got Carter to thinking. Specifically of an unshaven man in an oversize Pats jersey wielding a large handgun.

"I'm sorry, but no. I specifically need to speak to Jason." Carter turned ideas over in his head as he thought about what to say next. "He was arranging a loan for me . . . on an expedited basis and asked me to dig up several pieces of information. I've got all that now and need to pass them along."

More silence.

"Ma'am?" Carter said.

"What did you say your name was?"

Carter thought back to the video clip that Tomeka sent him. The Reds player levitating toward what might have been a run-scoring triple before reaching out and snatching up the ball like a Cooper's hawk nailing a low-flying sparrow.

"Sam Spofforth."

"Well, Mr. Spofforth, I'm sorry to have to tell you"—a catch in her voice—"that Mr. Schulte has tragically and unexpectedly passed away."

"He's dead?"

A pause. "That's correct, yes. Perhaps if you could stop by, we could make other arrangements?"

"How did he die?" Carter said, unable to help himself.

"I'm afraid I can't divulge that at the moment. As I said, we'd be happy to talk about alternative assistance."

Carter recovered, thanked her for her help, expressed his condolences, and said he'd try to come in later. Call disconnected, he Googled Schulte's name but came up blank other than a couple of bank-related mentions and a LinkedIn profile. He stared at a photo of a smiling man in his late thirties or early forties with wide cheeks, a receding forehead, and a neatly trimmed mustache.

Tragically and unexpectedly passed away.

Meaning what?

Carter did the math. If Terri Watkins, an addict with a history of prostitution, encountered Schulte the night before, presumably before Schulte died, his death was unlikely to be online yet. Unless he'd been violently murdered, in which case there ought to be something out there by now. That absence, plus the fact the woman at the bank knew of his passing, had Carter thinking accident or natural causes.

Except for the events of the previous evening.

Could Terri have killed him? Was he a john she had to fight off? Is that what her message—*Help*—meant? If that were the case, how did either Linda Stauch or Stauch's presumed pursuer, the man who pulled up behind her wrecked car, fit into the picture?

"It's me," Carter said, reaching his uncle. He filled him in.

"That's odd. Yeah, I agree, probably not a coincidence. I mean, the fact he's found dead the same night you find out about Terri and there's this car accident. Let me see what I can find out."

"Thanks."

"What are you going to do now?"

"What do you mean?"

"What's your next move?"

Carter glanced to his left.

"I'm going to buy some tea at the Narragansett Get 'n Go."

SIX

Fuck climate change. It's fucking cold. In fucking September.

Terri tried unsuccessfully to sit up. Her right hip wouldn't cooperate. It ached from colliding with the corner of the desk after Donny backhanded her. After he had walked inside the motel room and saw the look on her face. The look that said, *Thirty seconds later and I would have been gone, asshole.*

Despite the pain she was in, the ache in her hip, the stiffness in her bones from the cold, her dry mouth, and her pounding headache, Terri permitted herself a small smile. A smile because Donny hadn't thought things through. Per usual. Normally, he had no need. At close to three hundred pounds, more of it muscle than fat, with arms like bridge cables and a temper like a hungry mastiff, a guy his size running a girl like Terri was like a zoo gorilla palming a baby doll in its leathery mitt. Hurricanes don't think things through. They just hurricane.

Except last night. Oh, he thought he had everything under control. Dragging Terri from the motel room so hard he left bruises on her arm. More bruises. Forcing her into the van. A few minutes later, yanking her into the gas station, unwilling to let her out of his sight for even a second while he scooped up his nightly Monster Energy.

He hadn't counted on the Diet Dr Pepper. A two-liter bottle. One of the big boys. Terri grabbed the bottle as soon as she passed the counter. She figured she only had one chance.

"The fuck you need that for?" Donny said, reaching for it. Which was when she hit him. More accurately, swung the bottle as hard as she could between his legs. Heard him shout, didn't wait to see what happened next, but ran for the door. Outside, into the rain. Which is where she saw the woman.

Nothing stood out about her. She was a regular lady filling her car under a gas station awning in the middle of a downpour. Maybe that was it. Regular. Not mean looking and not happy looking. Just looking. Not a whole lot of people like that in Terri's life recently, that was for damn sure.

"Take this, please," Terri said, rushing up to her, holding out the envelope she'd prepared right before Donny walked inside the motel room thirty seconds earlier than expected.

"What?" the woman said, startled.

"Here—please."

Momentarily speechless, the woman reached out reflexively and took the envelope from Terri.

"I'm here," Terri gasped.

"What?"

Terri glanced behind her and saw Donny stumbling bowlegged through the gas station door and into the rain.

"I'm here," she repeated, gesturing around her. "Here." What she meant was, *Here, in Pawtucket.* A clue to her whereabouts. None of that came clear. Now it was too late.

Donny was running toward them, splashing through puddles, screaming her name. A guy his size, he rocked comically back and forth as he charged, feet pounding the wet pavement, arms cartwheeling. The blow to his junk probably not helping. He still moved toward Terri inexorably, a truck headed downhill without brakes.

Terri ran.

Now, ten, twelve, who the fuck knew how many hours later, she was still here. Hidden in a thicket of trees and weeds next to a river or some shit. Cold, because she'd lain down soaking wet and awakened just as soaking wet except with the temperature a whole lot lower. Her and twenty dollars she'd somehow hidden from Donny. And literally nothing else.

But alone.

Not in a motel room, panties around her ankles.

Not a baby doll palmed in a gorilla's mitt.

She permitted herself another smile.

And froze at the sound of a branch snapping three feet in front of her.

She looked ahead of her. And then up. And up.

"Terri," Donny said. "You little bitch."

Carter side-eyed the clerk behind the counter as he pushed through the gas station door and walked inside, but didn't approach. Gave him a nod instead, walked down the first aisle, and perused the snack offerings. He studied the Hostess cherry pies and the bags of Fritos, but it was all for show. He was a Twizzlers man first and foremost. Give him a large black tea and a bag of strawberry extra-longs and he'd give you Nashville to Fort Worth in under ten hours. Including breaks. Had, in fact. More than once.

He grabbed a package of the red licorice and headed to the hot water dispenser. He selected a Lipton's bag and filled his travel mug with hot water. He walked to the counter, set down the candy and the tea. The clerk was glancing through the front window and didn't engage right away.

"Excuse me," Carter said.

The clerk stared out the window a full two seconds longer before turning his attention to Carter. Carter followed his gaze and saw a gray pickup truck, maybe Ford F-150, possibly a Ram 1500, parked by the entrance closest to the DIY car wash. It occurred to Carter that the truck was blocking anyone from pulling into the filling station off the main street.

"Friends of yours?"

"What?"

"Guys in the truck."

Worry pinched the clerk's eyes. "No, no. Nobody. It's all good." He looked at Carter's tea and scanned the candy. "That'll be $4.05."

Carter handed him a five-dollar bill and a nickel, and said, "Were you working last night, by any chance? During the storm?"

"The storm?"

"All that rain we had. Heck of a gully washer. Wondered if you were on duty."

The clerk was back to staring at the truck. Maybe early thirties, strained face to go with the worried eyes, brown skin, oversized gray Providence College hoodie and jeans. His name badge read *Nelson*. And nervous—no, scared. No doubt about it. On the counter, a small, mostly blue flag jutted out of a cup holding pens. Carter studied it, came up with the answer a moment later. Cape Verde. Flags of the world—another of those brain exercises to help with the TBI.

"Are you from Praia?"

"What?" the clerk said.

"Praia—capital of Cape Verde."

The clerk stared at Carter as if he'd begun rapping in Portuguese. "No. My grandparents were. I'm from here."

"Got it. Anyway. Last night? Were you working?"

The clerk studied Carter a moment. "Yes, right. Yeah, I was here. Feels like I'm always here. Why?"

"A woman filled up about ten o'clock. Toyota Camry." Carter described Linda Stauch. "After she left, a man in a van followed her. Any of that ring a bell?"

The clerk's eyes shifted to the truck outside and back.

"Not really. It was raining so hard. Tough to see."

"It was bad, yeah. Got stuck in it myself," Carter said. "Any chance you might have security footage from around that time?"

Finally, he had the clerk's attention.

"Uh, maybe? But who are you? Are you, like, a cop?"

Carter didn't like to dissemble. Honesty, best policy, etc. But there was a time and place for everything.

"I can't really go into that," Carter said, lowering his voice. "The thing is, the woman who filled up, the one in the Camry, was in a bad wreck. It's important I figure out what happened." He described the large man in the Pats jersey. "See anybody like that?"

A twitch at the side of the clerk's mouth.

"Like I said, it was raining so hard."

Carter glanced at a fish-eye camera in the ceiling behind the clerk. "Security video?"

For just a minute, Carter thought he had him. The expression on the clerk's face like anything would be preferable to worrying about whatever was going on with the truck outside blocking the entrance. Then a sound distracted him. The pickup truck's doors had opened and closed. Carter made two guys strolling toward the door.

The clerk swallowed, handed Carter his dollar change, and said, "I'm kind of busy right now. Sorry."

"What if I came back later? When you're less busy?"

"I'm busy all the time. You should . . ."

"I should what?"

Behind them, the door opened as the men entered the gas station. They could not have looked more confident had they strolled into a Dodge City saloon donning ten-gallon hats and matching six-shooters.

"You should go," the clerk said.

Carter turned to look at the pair.

"Too late," he said.

SEVEN

The smaller guy had a vibe like Tweedledum missing his twin. Shorter than Carter, but unlike Carter he was round on his way to enormous, like a cartoon fireplug swelling with backed-up water. Baseball cap on backward—*really*?—patchy goatee, mirrored Ray-Bans hiding his eyes. Maybe Hispanic, or possibly Laotian. Direct from a Central Casting "ethnic muscle" call. Significantly—where Carter was concerned—the sag in his waistband suggested a handgun. Which had Carter thinking about his Beretta in the Suburban's glove compartment and why leaving it there might have been a bad choice.

The lead guy, on the other hand, the alpha, was UFC lean with tattoos running down ropy neck muscles, bare arms rippled and taut, and a gait that suggested frequent use of his fists and feet, one after the other. White as a Viking on the shortest day of the year, the blue squiggles and shapes inking his face notwithstanding. UFC wasn't packing, unless you counted the sheathed knife holstered to his right hip that looked long and wide enough to field dress a moose.

"'Sup," UFC said, eyes drilling Carter.

"How's it going?"

"Beautiful day."

"Little chilly. At least it stopped raining."

"Ain't that the truth. Anyway, my man, we've got some business to conduct with Nelson here. If you're wrapping up?" UFC glanced at Carter's tea and candy.

Slowly, telegraphing the motion, Carter reached for the Twizzlers and pocketed them in his cargo shorts. Just as slowly, he picked up his to-go cup of tea. Twenty-ounce cup. Carter liked tea.

"On my way."

"Excellent—"

"Except for your truck."

"What's that?" UFC narrowed his eyes—antifreeze blue—and cocked his head as if he hadn't heard correctly.

"Your truck." Carter inclined his head toward the parking lot. "It's blocking the exit."

UFC turned around as if he hadn't parked the truck there two minutes earlier.

"Whaddya know. Guess you got a point." He paused as if pondering the dilemma. He said, "There's still the other way," and pointed at the second exit, the narrower one by the used-car lot.

"Sure. Except that's not the way I want to leave."

UFC laughed. "It's all the same, though, right?"

Carter met the laugh with the smile he reserved for puns; the ones he got, anyway.

"Thing is, I want to head east. But that way"—Carter gestured at the car wash exit—"takes me onto the north-south road. I'd have to turn right to get the direction I'm going. Which I don't want to do."

He was describing a maneuver that would have taken him no more than ten seconds.

"Funny guy," UFC said. "And *thing is,* my man," he said, mimicking Carter, "it's not my problem. It's still a way out. Which I suggest you take. So Nelson and me can conduct our business."

Carter glanced at the clerk. His face shone with perspiration. Even across the counter, Carter could smell the rank odor of fear rising off him.

Carter said, "Regardless, I need you to move the truck. That's the way I want to leave." Carter was growing frustrated, thinking about the job before him, delivering the ruby ring to Terri Watkins. Which meant finding her, which meant figuring out how Linda Stauch came by the ring, which meant looking at the store's security video for clues. These guys weren't helping matters.

"*Regardless*?" UFC said.

The clerk cleared his throat and widened his eyes at Carter in supplication.

"Please," he whispered. "Just go."

"Good advice," UFC said, winking at Nelson as if they were best pals.

"Sure thing. As soon as you move your truck."

One thing UFC had going for him was consistency. He'd smiled throughout his conversation with Carter. Smiled like a shark detecting chum, but a smile nonetheless. He continued to smile as he pivoted slightly and nodded at Tweedledum. The companion returned the same smile, but with a knowing glance that suggested a crocodile to UFC's shark. As Tweedledum took three steps back and turned the lock on the gas station door, Carter resisted the urge to flip the man's baseball cap around. Finished with the door, the man shifted his right hand behind his back with a practiced air, his confidence that of someone who'd been to more than one rodeo. Which was an error in judgment. It's not like this was a fable. Slow and steady didn't always win the race.

Carter clapped his left hiking boot on the linoleum floor. Tweedledum and UFC jumped at the sound of the slap. Just a little, but enough to put them the slightest bit off balance. Which gave Carter the fraction of a second he needed to hurl the contents of his to-go mug of tea into Tweedledum's face—twenty ounces of hot water, minimum temperature 180 degrees. Or so. The man howled, hands rising to his scalded nose, lips, and cheeks as he staggered back, knees buckling. No time to waste. Carter rushed UFC, hurling his wiry frame against the young man's bulk with enough force to send him reeling backward and into Tweedledum.

"The fuck," UFC said, recovering faster than Carter thought possible and slashing his blade at Carter. UFC cursed as the weapon met air occupied just seconds earlier by Carter's torso as Carter rolled himself over and behind Tweedledum. As UFC turned for a new attack, Carter grabbed the scalded man's gun from his waistband and tried swiveling into a firing stance. Too late. UFC's right foot lashed forward, caught Carter's elbow, and forced him to drop the gun as he pushed himself backward to avoid another kick. He was in the clear only a second as UFC, moving with practiced speed, thrust the knife toward Carter's left arm. The knife moved in a blur of back-and-forth thrusts so fast Carter nearly couldn't tell the weapon's point from its hilt. Carter backed up madly, grabbed a sunglasses display tree, and brought it down on UFC's knife hand, sending the weapon clattering to the floor.

"Gun," Carter yelled to Nelson.

Nelson, watching the melee with the helpless gaze of a sailor aboard a sinking ship, didn't or couldn't move.

Carter stood as UFC tossed the display stand to his left and charged. Carter reared back, which meant UFC's lightning-fast left fist brushed his jaw instead of breaking it. Carter barely had the count of "one one-thousand" to feel relief when UFC's right fist connected with his shoulder, still sore from Pats Jersey's crowbar strike, and Carter collapsed to the floor. He found himself lying on his side staring at a bottom shelf display of Pringles and something else and running his tongue around his teeth. Carter was dimly aware that UFC had retrieved the knife and he was thinking he should do something about that fact when he felt a pair of hands grip his heels and drag him into the open.

"Big mistake, asshole," UFC said, kneeling over him with the blade raised high.

"Don't," Carter said, leveling his own retrieved weapon—Tweedledum's gun—at UFC's chest.

UFC's blue eyes widened briefly, which gave Carter the split-second he needed to snap his right leg forward, kicking UFC in the left knee. Directly on the left kneecap, to be precise. The crack of the bone as audible as a triggered mouse trap. As UFC screamed and wobbled off-balance, Carter stood and trained the gun on UFC.

"I said, don't."

UFC nodded, appearing to acquiesce, but as he did he snuck a glance at the knife, still in his right hand. That was enough for Carter. He hooked his right foot behind UFC's left calf and yanked, sending the tattooed fighter and his shattered left kneecap to the floor with a cry of pain. Moving quickly, Carter stomped his boot on UFC's hand until he released the knife. Carter grabbed the hand, jerked UFC off his back and onto his stomach, and knelt atop him. He reached into his vest, retrieved a pair of zip ties, and bound UFC's hands behind his back, ignoring the man's shrieks of rage and pain. Finished, Carter set UFC's knife and Tweedledum's gun on the counter beside the cup of pens and the Cape Verdean flag, caught his breath, and surveyed the damage.

UFC, temporarily out for the count.

Tweedledum rocking on his knees as he moaned, his face looking as if he'd thought it a good idea to pull a paper bag of yellow jackets over his head.

Nelson, the clerk, stunned into silence.

"You okay?" Carter said.

Nelson didn't speak right away.

"Hey—you all right?"

Nelson nodded.

Dissatisfied, but knowing he had to move fast, Carter retrieved an additional pair of zip ties and bound Tweedledum's hands, ignoring his cries of pain as he worked.

"Should . . ." Nelson said.

Carter looked at him.

"Should we call 911?"

Carter didn't respond, but instead fished the keys to the pickup truck out of UFC's pants pocket, rose, and placed them on the counter.

"We'll get to that in a second. For now, I need you to turn off the security cameras and back their truck up to the door."

Nelson made an indecipherable sound in his throat.

"What's that now?"

The clerk cleared his throat. "They're already off. That's the deal. When they show up, I have to deactivate them."

Carter thought about the scene from the night before that he was hoping a camera had captured. Linda Stauch gassing up. The man in the Pats jersey in the van. Had this been a fool's errand?

"In that case, just move the truck. I need you to do it right now. Also, you got a mop in this place?"

EIGHT

Five minutes later, sweat pouring down his face, Carter had the two men inside the pickup truck in the back seat, leaning against each other like sacks of feed corn. If feed corn sacks had hands that were zip-tied to seatbelt buckles. Tweedledum, his face a map of red splotches, glared at Carter. UFC was in and out, but mostly out. Assured they weren't going anywhere, Carter drove the truck to the DIY carwash and parked the vehicle in the last stall on the end. Like every other stall in the business, it was currently unoccupied. Carter walked back to the station and went inside.

"Who are those guys?"

Nelson stared at Carter as if seeing a ghost.

"Answer the question, please. We don't have a lot of time."

Nelson swallowed. "They're uh, they're guys that, I, well, we, owe . . ."

"Who's we?"

He looked away. "My sister and me."

"What do you owe?"

"It's mainly my sister. She owes them money for drugs."

"How much?"

Nelson hesitated. "Five hundred."

Carter's eyes widened. "Five hundred thousand?"

"No, no. Just five hundred. Five hundred dollars."

Carter glanced at Nelson, who looked as threatening as a hare in a den of Kodiaks, then considered the show of force UFC and Tweedledum brought into the gas station. All that, for five hundred dollars?

"Where's your sister?"

Nelson shook his head.

"Nelson?"

"They have her." His eyes brightened. "They're going to kill her if I don't come up with the money by tomorrow."

"Do you have the money?"

"No," he said, so quietly Carter almost didn't hear him.

"Do you know where your sister is?"

He shook his head again.

"What's her name?"

"Fernanda. Fernanda Ramos."

"You're Nelson Ramos?"

The clerk confirmed it.

"What's the name of the head guy, the one with the tattoos and the knife?"

"Cody."

"Cody what?"

Nelson thought for a second. "Washburn. Cody Washburn."

"Got it. One more question."

"Okay," Nelson said uncertainly.

"How much was the tea, again?"

Two minutes later, Carter was back in the car wash stall. He opened the pickup's door, slid into the driver's seat, placed Tweedledum's gun—absent its ammunition—on the dashboard, turned to face the two men behind him, and took a sip of tea through the opening in the plastic lid. A small sip. It was hot.

The interior of the truck smelled of sweat, urine, and blood.

"Cody."

Cody half opened his eyes.

"Where is Fernanda? Nelson's sister?"

Cody shut his eyes, head lolling to the side.

Carter turned to Tweedledum.

"Fernanda's sister. The address."

"Fuck you, man," the man replied, but it felt to Carter as if his heart wasn't in it.

Carter took another sip of tea, mimed burning his tongue.

"How's your face, anyway?"

A second passed. Two. Five. Carter pulled the lid off the tea.

Tweedledum shot a murderous glance at Cody, then shouted out the house number and street name.

"Good man."

Without waiting for a response, Carter searched the glove compartment. He wasn't surprised by what he discovered there. He left it in place and shut the compartment door.

"Back in a flash," Carter said.

Neither man said anything.

Inside the gas station once more, Carter found Nelson mopping up Cody's blood. The floor was nearly clean.

"Any chance you could show me that video from last night now?"

Nelson stared at him, apprehension in his eyes.

"Who are you?"

It's a fair question, Carter thought. Just one he didn't care to respond to. He did anyway.

"My name's Mercury Carter. I've been hired to deliver a piece of jewelry to a woman named Terri Watkins. She's in trouble, as far as I can tell. Problem is, I don't know where she is. Seeing the video from last night might provide some clues to help find her." He paused. "I'm hoping it's convenient to show me now that you don't have any distractions."

"What about Cody? And my sister?"

"Cody you don't have to worry about. Fernanda is at the top of my to-do list. I'm just hoping to see the video first."

It took a little more convincing, but five minutes later Carter was behind the counter examining black-and-white footage from the night before. He saw right away that he had caught a break. Two cameras monitored the pumps. One, mounted on the corner of the store, was virtually useless. Thanks to the sheets of rain and the run-off from the awning above the pumps, it was like looking at something through a steamed-up glass shower door.

A second camera, though, was positioned under the awning. It showed the van Carter saw the night before, the one that rolled up on the wreck a minute or so after Carter. He saw the big guy in the Pats jersey get out and pump gas. Three minutes later, the man opened the side of the van, reached inside, and pulled out a thin woman with hair pulled back in a sloppy ponytail, her face pinched with exhaustion and something else. Something more disturbing. Resignation. The face of a woman with little left to lose.

Terri Watkins.

"Pause, please."

Nelson paused the video. Carter took three photos of Terri.

"All right."

Nelson resumed the video. A minute in, Linda Stauch pulled up, got out, and filled up. Two minutes later, right after Stauch finished and was replacing the nozzle, Terri emerged from inside the gas station, face twisted in fear. She trotted to Stauch and thrust something into her hands. Stauch, startled and afraid, refused. They appeared to have words. At last, glancing behind her at the gas station door, Terri succeeded in making her point. Staunch took the envelope and tucked it distractedly into her jacket pocket. Right on cue, Pats Jersey ran outside like a bear awakened by fireworks.

Terrified, Terri took off running toward the main road, splashing through the rain. Pats Jersey looked at her, and then at Stauch. Making some kind of decision, he made for Stauch, shouting at her, demanding something. He grabbed her arm. She screamed and pushed him away. Whether because of his size, or the concrete made slick from gasoline mixing with rainwater, or some combination of the two, he lost his balance and fell. Hard, like a bag of Quikrete dropped off a loading dock. Stauch jumped into her car and raced away. A minute later, the man was in his van and in pursuit.

"That guy," Carter said. "Any idea who he is?"

Nelson shook his head. "I think I've seen the lady before. Not him. I'd remember a guy like that. Also . . ."

Carter waited.

After a moment's hesitation, Nelson described what happened inside the store before Terri ran out. The way she clocked the man, who was about to buy a can of Monster Energy, between the knees with a bottle of soda.

So Terri had moxie, Carter thought, *even in a moment like that. Good to know.*

"Do you know how he paid for the gas? Cash or credit?"

Nelson thought about it. "Credit card."

"Can you show me that transaction?"

Nelson hesitated. Carter saw the uncertainty in his eyes. The look of a man baffled by Carter's presence, unable to process why he—Nelson—was answering questions from a slight man wearing a Rochester Red Wings ball cap while a few feet away smudges of blood stained the gas station floor despite Nelson's best efforts at mopping. Blood the guy in the baseball cap was responsible for. Carter got it. He'd seen the look before. He repeated the question.

"Sure," Nelson said.

The name on the credit card was Shaun V. Volpe. Total cost of the fill-up: $47.55.

Carter pulled out his phone and Googled the name. Stared at the result. Realized with a sinking feeling that the delivery he was trying to make—returning the ruby ring to Terri—just got more complicated.

Shaun V. Volpe, the link read.

Visitation & Funeral Information.

NINE

Carter almost felt disappointed. Almost. For all of Cody's blustery attempts to come off as some kind of kingpin, he showed a disappointing lack of imagination. Not exactly a mastermind of wickedness. No, Cody was on the other end. All bravado, no brains. Bargain badness. Family Dollar evil.

Case in point: the tough-talking drug lord wannabe had dragged Nelson's sister, Fernanda, no farther than the basement of Cody's girlfriend's grandmother's house.

Carter had Nelson follow him to the triple-decker off Admiral Street in Providence in Nelson's beater Civic.

"Wait here," Carter instructed after they parked and stood at the front steps.

"I can help," Nelson said.

"I don't doubt it. I still need you to wait. We don't know what we're looking at in there."

The woman who answered the door after three knocks fit Tweedledum's description to a T. The recitation of her features coming slow but sure as the henchman eyed Carter's cup of tea back in the DIY carwash stall. A paunchy woman, eyes rimmed with liner and mascara, skin the color of refrigerated chicken fat. A tattoo of what appeared to be an infant's face decorated her left shoulder, an intricate floral design painted her right. Her nose, with a ring through the right nostril, looked as if it had been broken, and more than once. Two more rings pierced her lower lip. The interior of the house reeked of fried food and marijuana, though not as badly as she did.

"Good afternoon," Carter said. "Savannah Gruber?"

She stared at him as if a kangaroo had leaped onto her front porch.

"The fuck wants to know?"

Carter raised his left hand to display the envelope he held. The one he reserved for such occasions. The envelope with *Lottery* printed in large black letters on the front.

"I have a delivery for Ms. Gruber. Unfortunately, I do need her signature. Is that you?"

The woman eyed the envelope hungrily.

"Yeah. That's me."

"Excellent."

Carter raised his right hand and squirted the canister of Mace twice. Mouth, nose. Cutting each spurt short so as not to overdo it.

Savannah gasped, swore, staggered.

Gently, Carter grabbed her left hand, twisted her arm behind her back, and marched her inside, using his left heel to swing the door shut.

"*Wha the fuu—*"

"Shhh," Carter said.

He pushed the woman two steps forward, forced her to her knees, then flat onto her stomach. It wasn't difficult; she was quite high, in his estimation. Nevertheless, she tried arching her back to escape Carter's grip and almost managed it since she outweighed him by fifty pounds, easy. He bore down, grasped her wrists tighter, and said in a conversational tone of voice, "It would probably be a good idea not to struggle. Based on the condition I left Cody in."

She went still. He retrieved a remaining pair of zip ties and bound her hands and feet. Satisfied, he stood and glanced at the mess in front of him. The living room looked as if someone had dumped a McDonald's dumpster onto the floor of a parlor just straightened for Sunday guests. Piles of dirty laundry and rags covered the pieces of antiquey-looking furniture that weren't occupied by fast food bags and take-out containers. Two fishing tackle boxes sat on the mantel above the fireplace, blending into the scene as naturally as a pair of caged squirrels.

Carter recalled that this was Savannah's grandmother's house. He wondered where the grandmother was. He had a bad feeling on that front. No matter. Someone would figure that one out sooner rather than later. Carter opened the front door and signaled Nelson to step inside.

They found Fernanda in the basement locked inside a tool room next to an oil furnace. She was blindfolded with duct tape and her hands were bound behind her back with copper wire, with the wire woven into a link in a chain that circled a rusty iron pipe at least six inches in circumference. The chain was held in place with a padlock. An overturned five-gallon bucket served as Fernanda's toilet. Everything involved in her captivity available at a big-box hardware store. Family Dollar evil. But still evil.

Carter instructed Nelson to carefully remove the duct tape while he dashed outside to the Suburban for his bolt cutters.

"You're dead, mister, you know that?" Savannah said as he passed.

"No one's promised tomorrow," Carter said.

After freeing Fernanda, Carter helped Nelson walk his sister up the stairs. She was having trouble with her balance. She was shaky and couldn't stop crying. It took both of them to ease her into the passenger seat of Nelson's car.

"One sec," Carter said when they were finished. He re-entered the house, checked to see that Savannah was okay—she was, just pissed—and grabbed the tackle boxes. He opened them. As with the glove compartment find in Cody's truck, he was not surprised at the contents.

"Here," he said, handing the boxes to Nelson.

"What's this?"

"I didn't count it bill for bill but I'm guessing between the two boxes, it's in the neighborhood of fifty thousand dollars. Use it how you see fit. I wouldn't flash it around, if you know what I mean. Maybe you could . . ."

"Could what?"

Carter nodded at Fernanda. "Get her some help?"

"It's Cody's, isn't it?" Nelson said. "He's going to want it back." Nelson pushed the boxes into Carter's hands and put his hands behind his back.

"In theory, yes. In a couple of minutes, he's not going to be in a position to do anything with it. Either way, might be a good idea to lay low for a few days." Carter pushed the boxes back at Nelson. "Take a vacation or something. Visit relatives in Praia?"

For a few moments, Carter thought he'd won the day. Nelson glanced at his sister and back to Carter. Then, to Carter's surprise, Nelson took one of the boxes and placed the other at Carter's feet.

"Take one."

"I said—"

"Not for you. For the lady—the one you're trying to find. I bet she could use it as much as us. From what we saw on the video."

Carter found he could not argue with Nelson's logic.

Back in the Suburban, Carter selected two burner phones from his current supply. He used the first one to call 911. He informed the dispatcher that a large newer model gray pickup truck was parked in the last stall of a car wash next to Narragansett Get 'n Go. Inside the truck were two men. He gave general descriptions. He mentioned the gun on the dashboard. Carter explained that inside the truck's glove compartment were two vacuum-packed plastic bags of white powder it might be worth testing.

Again with the Family Dollar evil. Still evil. Also stupid, driving around with that kind of supply.

Carter hung up as the dispatcher asked his name. He used the second phone to call 911 again, reaching a different dispatcher. He gave the woman who answered Savannah's grandmother's address, and said, "I think someone's in trouble in that house. I thought I heard someone moaning. Also, I haven't seen the old lady who lives there for several days." He paused. "The front door's open."

"Who are you, sir?"

"Concerned citizen," Carter said, and disconnected. He checked the time: already past two o'clock. He started the Suburban and placed it in drive. He needed to get going. According to the link he'd found online, Shaun V. Volpe's calling hours began in less than an hour.

TEN

Randy Carmichael's phone vibrated with a text. He glanced at the number and shook his head.

Pauley.

Could this day get any shittier?

Tomorrow, Randy responded.

What time?

Asshole.

Randy checked his inbox to distract himself. The scheduler at Heritage Trails Senior Living Home had a question about weekend staffing. One of their regular nursing aides wrenched her back lifting a resident off the commode and was out of commission for a week. At least a week. *Oof,* Randy thought, thinking about the strain that would put on the perpetually understaffed long-term care facility up in Quincy. Per the protocol that Randy wrote into Second Act's contract with Heritage Trails, the scheduler had copied the nurse who would be on duty that weekend along with the facility administrator.

Randy clicked "Reply all," typed Shouldn't be a problem, and positioned his cursor over "Send." And paused.

On the one hand, he was being honest. It shouldn't be a problem. He could pull Shona from Green Gardens Retirement Home in Worcester, which was almost back on its feet, and reassign her through Monday. She wouldn't be happy about it, especially with the extra travel time, but he'd toss in an Amazon gift card to ease the blow. He'd make it for $100. He wasn't going to be a jerk about it.

On the other hand, huge problem.

Thanks to their current situation—thanks to the late, in hindsight not-so-great Chuck Gibbons—Randy had to proceed carefully. Very, very carefully. There was no downplaying the danger awaiting them if Chuck's computer fell into the wrong hands. Especially, God forbid, the hands of federal agents with expertise in forensic accounting.

All the details of what he considered his greatest grift to date were on that computer. If someone accessed its contents, opened the folders, saw the spreadsheets, read the company emails stored there, found the data, the gig was up. Over. Kaput. It would only be a matter of time before the handcuffs slapped shut on his and Monica's wrists. And on Aiden's—can't forget Aiden.

With the laptop in the wind, Randy knew the prudent thing was to shut down Second Act Staffing Solutions for a while. Lay low. Maintain the status quo.

Except.

If they shut down and hung Heritage Trails out to dry, they could lose that contract. Which was something Randy very much did not want to do.

Because Heritage Trails Senior Living Home was owned by Quadrant Horizons. And Des Moines–based Quadrant Horizons was coast-to-coast. And Randy very much wanted the reams of PHI currently sitting on Quadrant's servers. He considered the company's pretentious descriptor: *A Health Care Consortium*. Please. Health-care conspiracy, more like it. He set the thought aside and focused on the size of

Quadrant Horizons' patient and client caseload. Thousands and thousands of people, all with their own unique financial data. PHI—personal health information. A treasure trove of credit cards and bank account numbers. Data that dark web buyers were lining up to pay for, as Randy had already found out from his lower-profile efforts. But those were penny-ante compared to what was up for grabs at Quadrant Horizons.

He was looking at millions of dollars. Millions for himself, but more importantly, for Michelle, his daughter. What was left of his daughter. Millions for the taking, which Randy had been ready to do right before Chuck died.

The numbers were simple, according to the latest financial projections that Randy received from Michelle's gold-plated care home on the outskirts of Albany. Projections showing that, adjusting for inflation, the cost of Michelle's current level of care would run in the neighborhood of three hundred thousand dollars annually.

No telling his daughter's exact lifespan, but foolish not to plan for a minimum of thirty additional years. To generate that kind of annual interest, Randy would need above $10 million, maybe a lot above, when all was said and done.

"Of course, there's always Medicaid," the administrator of the facility in Albany had reminded him in a follow-up phone call four days earlier. The day before Chuck died, if you were counting. "Not the same level of service, by a long shot, but essentially free. I could recommend several more than adequate facilities we could transfer her to."

"Okay," Randy said. "And here's my recommendation. You mention transferring her again, I'll drive there, reach down your throat, grab your sphincter, pull it out through your mouth, and shove it back down again. Is that adequate enough for you?"

The clinic administrator did not immediately reply.

Monica was sympathetic enough when Randy relayed the gist of the conversation to her. She was always sympathetic on the subject of Michelle. She never questioned his ultimate goal for the money he planned to make from the Quadrant Horizons job. From Operation Michelle.

Not to his face, anyway.

Back in the office, Randy shook his head in frustration. Thought of Michelle on the hospital bed, all that equipment. All that expense. The score he planned with the Quadrant Horizons job finally providing him what he needed to make things right. A job that couldn't fail.

Except now Chuck was gone. All they had was Aiden. Aiden had his uses, for sure. A useful guy—very useful—despite his unorthodox appearance—as if one of the ZZ Top guys clothes-shopped in a dumpster and existed on nothing but Dunkin' Munchkins. He'd been a decent background complement to Chuck.

Now Aiden was it.

Randy's phone buzzed with another text. Pauley again. *Jesus, this guy.* Here Randy was, his future teetering in the balance, and he had to deal with this fuckwad, a Cosa Nostra poseur who talked like he spent twelve hours a day watching *Sopranos* reruns.

Except Pauley currently had Randy over a barrel. Which happenstance, like Chuck Gibbons's untimely death, was threatening to derail the Quadrant Horizons operation and all it meant.

Noon, Pauley's text said.

Shit.

Can't do noon. Have a thing

What kind of thing

2:30, Randy typed, and put the phone in his shirt pocket. It vibrated again but he didn't bother looking at the message.

Instead, he thought about Quadrant Horizons. About the operation he and Chuck had been ready to launch. He made his decision. He needed to proceed. For his sake, and for Michelle's. Randy clicked around on his computer until he found the scheduling document Chuck had built. The one with the malware embedded deeply inside. It was risky as hell proceeding by himself with whatever Aiden could assist with, but it had to happen. Randy couldn't afford to wait any longer.

He attached the scheduling document and clicked "Send" on the staffing email.

He immediately felt a weight lift from his chest.

Randy was smart enough to know the feeling didn't mean that he'd made the correct decision. Just that a decision had been made. Which sometimes was all you could do. It had been like that in the old days and it was still like that. Actions always trumped words.

As good as making a decision felt, it didn't resolve the other problems Randy was facing.

Starting with: Chuck's death and his missing laptop.

Moving onto: The threats from Pauley Carnevale.

Concluding with: The fact that Monica was fucking their security chief behind his back.

Which, knowing Monica, meant not that she was sex starved (well, not much), but that she and Vickers were up to something.

Something Randy needed to dig up and snuff out, pronto.

Truth be told, Terri thought, the pills were a relief.

A lot of times, Terri wouldn't even be half undressed before they kicked in. It was almost funny to watch the guys' faces change. The ones Donny and Jimmy targeted tended to be first-timers who were already nervous and not sure what to expect, beyond the obvious. Half of them wanted to talk first, anyway, starting with their dopey questions.

What kinds of stuff did she do for fun? (*Really?*) What shows did she watch? Her favorite: Had she ever been on a sailboat? Like she was some party girl warming a bar seat at Applebee's and not a trick for the night in a shitty motel room or back seat of a car. That, or going on about themselves. And on and on. Jesus, how many problems could a guy have with his wife? Sometimes, getting down to business was a welcome diversion.

Except that part didn't happen much recently. Because of the pills.

"Brazilian Viagra," Donny told the johns with a wink, explaining he was tossing it in for free.

They weren't Viagra.

For a while, Terri sincerely thought they were heavy-duty sleeping pills. Why wouldn't she, the way the men snored once they were out, the heavy, wet sound like slow-motion chain saws? While she put her shirt back on, Donny or Jimmy would pick the johns' pockets, palm their phones, empty their wallets, and they'd be outside five minutes later. Opening the johns' cars might delay them a further five, depending on what was inside. Usually junk, but they'd scored a laptop recently, which was something.

"The perfect crime," Donny boasted, and he had a point. Who was going to report it? At least half the guys were married, judging by rings on left fingers, and that's not counting the ones who took the rings off before entering the room, like that somehow made it better. It would be hard enough for them to secretly cancel and replace stolen credit cards, especially on shared accounts, let alone cover up the little matter of a police investigation. *Why exactly were you at this motel room, sir?*

Then Terri overheard Donny talking to Jimmy one day when she wasn't supposed to be listening and realized that not all the men woke up again. Some passed out permanently.

"That's murder," she protested, formulating the words with difficulty through the haze clouding her brain between the weed and the stuff Donny gave her to keep her from clawing her eyes out.

"It's not murder if they take the pill themselves," he responded, which she knew was bullshit. But she wisely kept her mouth shut and instead figured out her next move.

Fight back, that's what. Try to escape. Clock Donny in the junk with a two-liter bottle of soda and escape in a downpour.

That worked out so well, Terri thought, back in the apartment building where Donny kept her and Sheena and a couple others. Warmer and drier than her hiding spot by the river, but that was about it. A virtual prisoner, because no way was Donny taking her to another motel for a while. Which had him in an even worse mood, because it wasn't like he could risk drugging the johns here and add body disposal to his résumé if they didn't wake up.

Which didn't work out so well for Terri, either, because the johns here were awake the whole time. Every time.

A knock at her door.

Terri stiffened, tensed.

The door opened and a nervous-looking man eyed her like something in the butcher display case at Star Market.

Terri shut her eyes, thought briefly of her grandmother. Opened them, nodded at the man, reached for the drawstring on her sweatpants.

Here we go again.

ELEVEN

Naturally, there was a wreck in I-195's eastbound lanes. The resulting slowdown nearly doubled the length of Carter's trip, meaning forty minutes had passed by the time he arrived at the funeral home in Fall River for Shaun V. Volpe's calling hours.

On the way, Carter reviewed what he and his uncle had learned about Volpe.

Thirty-seven years old. Divorced. Two kids as far as they could tell. His most recent job appeared to be service writer at a Ford dealership in Attleboro.

"Service writer?" Carter asked.

"The front-facing guy in the repair department," his uncle explained. "Writes up the estimates, delivers the bad news, takes the crap so the repair guys can actually get things done. Like that."

"Got it."

It was the kind of thing his uncle would know. Years ago, he worked as a dispatcher at Rochester Express Delivery, communicating with drivers as they made deliveries up and down the East Coast. He liked to joke he'd had fewer problems coordinating a fleet of fifty semitrailers than helping direct the activities of a single freelance courier. He also made it clear he had no regrets about his career change.

As with Jason Schulte, the one thing Carter and his uncle couldn't determine about Shaun V. Volpe was a cause of death. "Died suddenly" was all the obituary said. Which in Carter's experience meant one of three things: suicide; an accident; or, more and more these days, a drug overdose.

Normally, the cause of death wouldn't matter. Except when both the deceased were tied to a single night's events at the Narragansett Get 'n Go in Pawtucket, Rhode Island. How had the woman at the bank put it when Carter finally reached her? *Mr. Schulte has tragically and unexpectedly passed away.* Dismissing this as coincidence was the equivalent of ignoring the fact you saw two black cats walk beneath two ladders on the same day. In Carter's experience.

Resthaven Memorial Funeral Home sat at the end of a wide, smooth asphalt driveway that curved through an expansive lawn sloping upward from Main Street. Mature maples in the front yard and behind the home shaded the long, single-story cream-colored brick building. The parking lot gleamed like misted charcoal. Carter backed the Suburban into a space at the far corner of the lot away from other cars. He slipped into the rear of his SUV, swapped his shorts and T-shirt for khakis and a long-sleeve blue button-down Oxford, and headed inside.

The carpeted parlor reserved for Volpe was maybe half full. Most people stood, speaking in whispers; a few great-uncle and great-aunt types slumped in chairs and couches. Most of the mourners were Black, Carter noted, and one or two stared at him a few moments before resuming their conversation. The air smelled of coffee, fresh flowers, and Febreze; the mood was heavy with disbelief and loss. At the front of the room, two men and a teenage girl formed a half circle around an open casket, the polished walnut coffin bookended by several wreaths heavy on carnations. Off to the side, a video montage of family photos played on a flat-screen TV. The faces in the room that Carter glimpsed wore the grim expressions you'd expect at services for someone who'd "died suddenly."

He waited until the trio by the casket left their post and edged to the left to view the photo montage, then strolled casually across the room. Whatever the cause of death, Volpe looked peaceful enough now. Carter had never been a fan of open caskets, dating to the calling hours after his father's murder, but he had to admit Resthaven had done an admirable job with the remains. Volpe almost looked asleep. Peaceful, whatever his demons were in life. Trimmed goatee, shiny bald pate, strong chin. Outfitted in a serviceable blue suit, white shirt, and red paisley tie.

The sound of someone stepping forward to stand beside Carter, followed by a sigh. He turned and discreetly examined the woman next to him. Maybe early forties, so relatively close to Carter's age, dyed red hair short on the side, curly up top, sleeveless purple dress that stopped an inch or two above her knees. Wide arms with just a hint of sag. Stocky but not fat. Legs bare. Gleaming red nails visible through open-toed sandals. Black, like Volpe. Carter sought in vain for a family resemblance, then returned his attention to the body. As good a time as any, he thought.

Carter cleared his throat and said, "Sad."

No response. He debated what to say next. He wasn't sure how to go about this, or why he was even there, to be honest about it, other than to further the effort to deliver a ruby-red ring to Terri Watkins. Finish that job so he could get on his way, make his original delivery to Lenny Pellegrino, the elderly gentleman in Providence who'd seen Lou Boudreau play, and then head home.

"Yeah," the woman said at last. "Real sad."

Though spoken in a voice barely above a whisper, the undercurrent of sarcasm was impossible to miss, like the *pffft* of a pop can opened at a fine wine tasting.

Carefully, Carter said, "I guess I didn't know him all that well."

This caught her attention. She turned and studied him.

"And you are?"

He looked at her, keeping his face neutral. "Mercury Carter. I wanted to pay my respects."

"Is that so? How did you know Shaun?"

"Like I said, I didn't know him all that well." He paused. "Sounds like you did, though?"

Instead of replying, she looked down the length of the parlor, settled on a face, nodded. Carter followed her gaze and watched as a big man in jeans, black T-shirt, and leather jacket approached.

"This guy says he knew Shaun. But *not that well*," the woman said, enunciating the last three words.

The man examined Carter the way a party host might study a bag of dog waste dropped beside the canapés.

"Are you him?" the man said at last.

"Who?"

"The reporter. The one who called."

"I'm not a reporter."

"You got a lot of nerve, showing up here."

"As I said, I'm not a reporter."

"Who are you, then?"

Carter readied his reply. He thought he might weather the encounter. Swing them over to his side. Then the woman said, "He gave some bullshit name. *Mercury*. Uh huh."

"Beat it, asshole," the man said.

"If I could explain."

Which turned out not to be the correct response. The next thing Carter knew, the man grabbed Carter's left arm, swung him around, and marched him roughly across the room. Several pairs of eyes gaped at the spectacle. Carter thought about struggling but decided to go with the flow. No reason to make a bigger scene. Plus, the man's grip was like an industrial-level C-clamp. Nothing you casually shrugged off.

"Get the hell out of here and don't come back," the man said, shoving Carter out the Resthaven front door.

Carter thought about obeying the man. He didn't want the kind of trouble he saw brewing in the man's exhausted, bloodshot eyes. And in the bright eyes of the woman with the red hair who materialized a moment later behind him, mouth twisted in scorn. Carter recognized when people were in pain. In agony at a loss. He would have walked away. Except for what the man said inside. *Are you him? The reporter. The one who called.* That struck Carter as potentially useful.

Carter saw only one way to do this. Not his first choice, especially after the way he was feeling from the rough stuff the night before and at the gas station earlier today. But his instinct told him that, right at the moment, rational discussion wasn't going to cut it. Sometimes you took a detour to reach your destination. Sometimes the detour wasn't scenic.

Carter faced the man. "What if I am a reporter? What are you going to do about it?"

As he feared, and expected, that got the job done. The comment lit something up inside the man. Turned the man's pain red-hot. His eyes widened and he charged Carter without a word, lumbering toward him with arms up and fists balled. Backpedaling, Carter made out forearm tattoos and thick leather bracelets. Feeling his shoes hit the lawn, he glanced behind him at the wide trunk of the biggest of the Resthaven front yard maples. He made for it, staying one step ahead of the man. Barely. His back to the tree, Carter stopped. He raised his hands defensively.

"I warned you, asshole," the man said, launching a haymaker at Carter's head.

Carter had been hit enough for one day. The man didn't have anything close to the skills of Cody, Fernanda Ramos's kidnapper, but there was weight behind the arm curving his way. Carter easily sidestepped the punch, which threw the man off-balance. Before he could recover, Carter grabbed his right hand, twisted the arm behind the man's back, and compressed the man's thumb. The way they'd been taught in Basic Inspector Training at the USPIS academy in Potomac, Maryland. Some things you didn't forget. Carter made sure of that. The man gasped in pain. Carter glimpsed the surprise in his eyes at what was happening to him. Carter maneuvered him around as if he was manhandling a dresser on a mover's dolly and pressed him face first into the maple.

"Listen up," Carter said, which was right when the redheaded woman rushed forward with a cry and pounded Carter's back with her fists. He hated to do it, but he had no choice. He looked down, calculated the distance, and brought his right boot down hard on the woman's painted toes. She shrieked and stepped back, hopping up and down.

Carter made his pitch as fast as he could to the man pinned against the tree.

"I'm not a reporter, okay? I'm looking for a missing woman. I know about Shaun because someone used his credit card at a gas station in Pawtucket last night. I can't be sure, but I'm guessing that person might be connected to what happened to him. I'll tell you everything I know. I'm not trying to make trouble. I apologize for showing up at calling hours like this. My only interest is in finding the woman. I have something for her. But if I can help with Shaun, I will."

Now came the gamble. Carter released the man's right hand, hearing him exhale as the pain dissipated, and stepped back. He stood in a way that formed the third point in a triangle between the woman, gingerly putting weight on her foot, and the man, who faced Carter with sweat brightening his freckled cheeks. Carter let his arms hang at his sides. He waited for what would come next. He'd been hit enough for one day. But maybe the day wasn't over yet.

The man stared at him, muscles tensed as if ready to pounce.

Carter braced himself.

The man said, "What gas station?"

TWELVE

They reconvened inside Resthaven, in an anteroom off the parlor with ivory walls and showroom chairs. Carter brought them Styrofoam cups of coffee from Resthaven's hospitality counter—cream for her, black for him—and grabbed a water bottle for himself since there was no tea.

When they were settled, Carter said, "Let's start over. My name's Mercury Carter." He looked at the woman. "For real. I'm sorry for your loss. And for outside. By the tree, I mean."

The pair exchanged glances. After a moment, the woman introduced herself as Rhonda Rausch.

"I'm Shaun's stepsister. Oldest stepsister. This is my husband, Braden."

Braden nodded at Carter but didn't extend a hand. "Sorry I lost my temper." Spoken in a gruff, weary voice. "This whole thing's been a fucking nightmare."

"Not a problem. I can only imagine. I'm sorry I showed up like this. Out of the blue."

Rhonda said, "You said Shaun's credit card got used at a gas station?"

"That's right." Carter reviewed the information he'd learned from Nelson Ramos, leaving out the confrontation with Cody and Tweedledum and the subsequent rescue of Nelson's sister.

"You some kind of cop?" Rhonda said.

"Not a cop, though I used to be." He gave them the standard background, once again leaving some things out. A while back, an agent with the US Postal Inspection Service, with a final posting in Rochester, New York. Maybe the lowest profile of federal law enforcement departments, but he was a sworn officer nonetheless. After deciding to switch careers, he ended up as a freelance mailman, delivering things for people that, for whatever reason, they didn't trust normal shipping companies with.

"Like drugs?" Braden said, dead-eyeing Carter. "Is that what this is about?"

"No drugs. To be honest, my top delivery last year was French bulldog puppies. You can't believe what those things are worth. What people will do to get their hands on them."

Rhonda looked skeptical, but said, "What about this woman? The one you said is missing?"

Carter went over the job he was doing for Jim and Valerie Watkins. Delivering an heirloom ruby ring to their daughter, Terri Watkins, a junkie and prostitute. Once he found her, that is.

At the mention of *prostitute*, Braden and Rhonda exchanged a quick glance.

"I don't know," Braden said at last. "It sounds like a bunch of bullshit."

"Why should we believe you?" Rhonda added.

Carter thought about it. "It's up to you whether to believe me or not. Convincing you isn't my goal. I still need to make my delivery to Terri Watkins, and I'm hoping you can help me. In return, I'm hoping what I said about the credit card could help you."

"The police didn't tell us anything about that," Rhonda said.

"Probably because they don't know about it. I only found out about it today. It's information you're free to use."

"You didn't tell them?"

"Not yet," Carter said.

The couple exchanged glances again.

"What do you want from us?" Rhonda said.

"You mentioned that a reporter called. Do you mind if I ask what he wanted?"

"He said he was doing a story on Shaun," Rhonda said. "I told him to go to hell."

"What kind of story?"

"About how he died."

"I see. If I may ask, how did he?" Carter said.

At that, Rhonda's face fell. She unsuccessfully choked back a sob. Fat tears rolled down her cheeks. Braden reached out and placed his hand on hers, nearly covering her fingers. He looked at Carter and shook his head. He said, "As far as we can tell, he got high with a hooker and overdosed."

Curled on a mattress in the fetal position, the john gone, Terri's mind floated, unmoored, like a street fair balloon slipped free from a toddler's chubby hand.

Second day of sophomore year in high school. Terri and a girl she knew only as Peewee. Vaping pot in the girls' room when they were supposed to be in civics class. Peewee got a text and scurried away, but no such luck for Terri. Busted by the day custodian. Terri begged the woman not to tell, but the bitch wasn't having it. Ten minutes later, Terri was sitting on the couch in the assistant principal's office.

"Really, Terri?" he said. "The second day?"

"Sorry," she mumbled. Not sorry.

"I have to call your parents. You know that, right?"

"I guess."

But privately Terri cringed at what this would do to her mother. After everything else Terri had put her through.

"You broke school policy," he said. Mr. Shifflet. Assistant principal, and also assistant football and basketball coach. Wavy black hair with some product in it, cringy toothbrush mustache, and a habit of sucking his belly in to hide it. A bunch of framed diplomas on the walls behind his desk interspersed with photos of him, his wife, and a couple of kids.

"Okay."

Mr. Shifflet rolled his desk chair around to face her. "That policy requires me to call your parents."

"Right. I got that part."

"And record this on your permanent record."

"Fuck that," she said, unable to help herself. "That's bullshit."

"Language. In any case, rules are rules."

"Easy for you to say."

"It's my job, unfortunately. Though I agree it seems a shame to write you up, so early in the school year. Getting off on the wrong foot like this."

Without warning, he reached out and took her left hand. Studied it as though it weren't attached to the rest of her arm. A second later, he set it atop his right knee and held it in place.

Terri suddenly couldn't breathe.

Mr. Shifflet said, "What I hear you saying is that calling your parents and putting this on your permanent record might not be ideal? Escalating things, I mean?"

She sat, frozen, staring at her hand on Mr. Shifflet's knee, the scene like it was something on Netflix and not real life.

"Terri?"

He dragged her hand up his thigh toward his waist.

"Terri?"

Her face burned. She thought about how much she hated her parents. And school. And everything.

"Terri?" he said, angling her hand toward his crotch.

"Sure," she whispered. "Not ideal."

"Terri!"

She jerked awake. Donny stood in the door, filling it like a tall chest of drawers.

"Yeah."

"I said, one more time, what did you give that lady?"

She tried to formulate a response. It wasn't easy. Her head felt fuzzy, and not only from the back-to-back slaps Donny had administered when he'd dragged her into the van after finding her hiding spot by the river. She was pretty sure he'd given her something in the water bottle he offered on the way back. Something affecting her brain and her tongue, which felt thick and swollen, as if she'd been stung by a bee. The john's awkward thrusting just now hadn't helped.

"Nothing," she managed.

"That's bullshit, and you and I both know it. You had something in your hand when you ran outside."

"I said, it was nothing."

He lifted his right hand and Terri flinched. He snickered at the movement. Despite the fear she felt at the moment, she couldn't help reminding herself of Donny's girlish laugh. Though he thought it made him sound deranged, all it did was make him sound like a playground reject. It was something she kept to herself. Something she could call her own about Donny, that no one else knew.

Instead of hitting her, he picked up a brown paper bag and set it on the chair beside him. He reached inside and removed a large coffee.

Even with her brain fog, she could smell the coffee. Her caffeine receptors lit up.

"Two creams, two sugars," Donny said. "Just how you like it." He dipped into the bag again and pulled out an apple fritter. Her mouth watered at the sight of the smeared icing. She hadn't eaten in nearly twenty-four hours.

"You must be hungry," Donny said.

She nodded, unable to help herself.

"Your favorite, right?" He gestured at the coffee and the pastry.

She nodded again.

"Mine too," Donny said, cramming half the fritter into his mouth, chewing with his mouth open in front of her. He washed it down with a swig of coffee.

"Let's try again. What did you give that woman?"

For the past few months, the only two things that Terri felt were hers and hers alone were her secret about Donny's laugh and her grandmother's ruby ring. Sometimes, the only two things that kept her going day to day. It had taken almost everything, nearly every ounce of will, to slip the ring into the envelope that night next to the banker guy's business card. The guy from the Night Owl Inn. Later, handing the ring to the woman pumping gas, knowing full well she might never see it again, Terri felt like she'd torn her heart out.

"Terri!"

"Nothing," she said, ignoring her growling stomach. "I didn't give her nothing."

Carter processed what Braden said. Thought about his conversation in Jim and Valerie's modest living room in Cranston. *We knew things had gotten bad. She was working the streets for a while.* Considered the demeanor of the man he'd seen in the casket in the other room.

Cautiously, Carter said, "Addictions can be challenging."

Wiping her eyes, Rhonda said, "That wasn't Shaun."

Carter didn't say anything.

"What I mean is, he wasn't a drug addict, as far as I know. He drank too much. I admit it. That's why Rita left—Rita, his wife. He knew he had a problem but wouldn't do anything about it. As far as the prostitute?" She looked at Braden, who nodded after a moment. "It wasn't his first time. That was the other reason Rita left."

"Where did this happen?" Carter said.

"Attleboro. Parking lot of a city park. A dog walker called it in the next morning."

"Attleboro. Did he live there?"

Rhonda shook her head. "He lived here but works at a dealership there." She rubbed her eyes. "Worked."

"You're sure it was . . . that he was with someone?"

Rhonda confirmed it. "It was kind of obvious what happened. There were, you know, condoms and stuff, according to the cops. Plus, he'd been robbed. Phone, wallet, credit cards. What a fucking mess."

"He didn't do drugs," Carter said. "Could he have been slipped something? Or made an exception? No offense, but it doesn't sound as if he was in a great headspace."

"I don't know," Rhonda said, crying again. "I wish I knew. Oh, Shaunnie."

Frowning at Carter, Braden wrapped his arms around his wife, nearly enveloping her.

Carter stayed quiet. He didn't like what he was hearing. Taken by itself, Volpe's death could be written off. A guy with a drinking problem who frequented prostitutes was rolling life's dice to begin with. Things happened. But a guy who died, after which his credit card was used at the Narragansett Get 'n Go? At the same gas station, on the same night that Terri Watkins wrote *Help* on the back of the business card of a guy who also died under mysterious circumstances? Something wasn't adding up here.

Or just the opposite: maybe it was.

"What do you think we should do?"

Rhonda, sniffling as she spoke. Carter refocused, formulated a reply.

He said, "I may be off base, and I'm sorry to put it this way. I think you should proceed on the assumption that Shaun's death wasn't an accident."

"What do you mean?" Braden said. He sat with his arm around Rhonda. His anger earlier, in the parlor, made more sense. He struck Carter as the kind of guy who would jump in front of a speeding locomotive to protect his wife. Frankly, despite the tears flooding her eyes at the moment, Rhonda looked like the kind of gal who would return the favor in a heartbeat.

Carter gave them the gist of what he knew about Jason Schulte, explained his theory that the two men's deaths seemed too much of a coincidence given the common element of the gas station.

"Was this Jason guy robbed too?" Braden said.

"I don't know." Carter explained about the awkward conversation with Schulte's bank colleague. "Given the proximity of his death to your brother-in-law's, I'll hazard a guess and say probably. It would be good to know, one way or the other."

"Can you find out?" Rhonda said.

"Me?"

"Yeah. Once a cop, always a cop sort of thing?"

Carter was about to say it wasn't like that. That he ended that life long ago and began another with no desire to go back. Then he thought about what brought him all this way to begin with, his unofficial and ongoing inquiry into the whereabouts of Earl Madden. Madden, the man who'd set his father up to die, then tried to have Carter killed to boot. How was this any different?

It was different, in that Carter had purely personal reasons for finding Madden. What exactly he'd do when he did, he wasn't sure. He hadn't allowed himself to think that far. Whereas finding out if Jason Schulte was robbed before or after he died checked a professional box. It was important only in so far as it helped Carter find Terri Watkins so he could deliver the ring to her, make his other delivery to baseball fan Lenny Pellegrino, and go home.

He'd never missed a delivery and wasn't about to start now.

Carter glanced at the wooden lamp table between them. Magazines artfully arranged in a fan. *People. Sports Illustrated. Better Homes and Gardens.* Most random of all, a copy of *The Old Farmer's Almanac.* Beneath that lay a rectangular Resthaven-branded scratch pad. Carter retrieved his wallet and pulled out a business card, the one with just his name and his number on it. In return Rhonda provided him with her and Braden's numbers.

"Give me a day to find out what I can about Jason Schulte. Then I'll circle back."

"What then, though?" Braden said, a hint of a growl back in his voice. "Where does that leave us in the meantime?"

Carter was about to respond, offer some recommendations, when his phone went off. Unfamiliar number. Normally, something he'd let to go voicemail. Maybe not today, with everything going on. He apologized to Braden and Rhonda and answered.

"Mercury Carter?"

"That's right."

"Detective Papaleonardos, Pawtucket Police Department."

THIRTEEN

"All right," Monica said. "Let's start with what we know."

They convened in The Bunker. Vickers was the one who came up with the nickname for the space, a little dramatic in her opinion, but she had decided to let it go. It was accurate, after all, and the name's implied hint of conspiracy was a useful reminder of the stakes in play.

Her, Vickers, Randy. Gathered around a table at the far end of the room—*Okay, of The* Bunker—on the first floor of the building housing Second Act Staffing Solutions. Everyone in sweaters or sweatshirts because of the AC. Uncomfortably chilly, but the servers needed the cool air. Aiden on the other end of The Bunker, studying a monitor, fingers hammering his keyboard. He knew he was on deck but not needed right away. Staring at the bag of donut holes beside Aiden, Monica tried not to think about the amount of grease on those fat fingers.

"Scott?" Monica said, glancing at Vickers. She flashed briefly to his thumbs snagging her panties a few hours earlier as he kneeled before her. Drawing them down, parting her legs, finding her with his tongue. She frowned and dismissed the thought.

"Nothing at Chuck's house, as you know," Vickers said. No sign if he was recalling the same moment as Monica. "The laptop's gone. His wife, Stacy, knew what I was talking about but said it's not there."

"You believe her?" Randy said.

Vickers nodded after a moment. "She's too broken up to lie, in my opinion. She kept talking about how they were supposed to go to Hawaii next month."

Dissatisfied, but not sure what else to do, Monica gestured for him to continue.

"After that, I talked to a guy I know who's on the job. As far as they can tell, Chuck answered a personal ad, went to the hotel, met a girl, and overdosed. Someplace in there, he was robbed. Wallet, phone, laptop."

"Security video?" Randy said.

Vickers shook his head. "Not that kind of establishment."

"It's been three days. Any sign we've been compromised?"

"So far, so good," Vickers said, glancing across the room at Aiden. "Chuck had strict orders to keep everything locked down on the laptop, starting with the passwords. You'd need federal-caliber expertise to crack it."

"Let's hope it wasn't a fed who stole it," Randy said.

"Not a lot of feds where he was."

"Sure about that?"

"Yes. What's your point?"

"My point is, you were supposed to—"

"All right, all right," Monica said. This was all she needed: a pissing match between her husband and her fuck buddy when they were all three in danger of swirling down the toilet.

Before either man could speak, Monica said, "Any chance whoever took the laptop was a bad actor?"

"What do you mean?" Randy said.

"This looks like a random robbery. But could Chuck have been set up? Was he targeted? Did someone set a honey trap, whatever?"

"I wondered the same thing," Vickers said quickly. Monica rolled her eyes, deciding she didn't care if he noticed.

Vickers looked across the room. "Aiden's doing what he can, tracing Chuck's movements beforehand. Looking at messages he has access to. Who stole the laptop is a legitimate concern. If it helps, my source says that that motel's notorious. Cops are always running hookers and pimps and junkies out of there. The computer's useless to people like that."

"If the cops know that about the motel, plenty of other people would too," Randy said. "Somebody could have lured Chuck there precisely for that reason. Covered their tracks. Lot less obvious than offing him at the Omni."

"Who, though?" Monica said.

"In this town? Take a ticket."

Her husband had a point. Infiltration had been a worry since they started Second Act. It would have been a concern anywhere, but especially in Rhode Island. A place where one set of lowlifes sniffing out illegal activity by another set and trying to piggyback onto it was a competitive sport. If there were a state with lazier criminals, Monica hadn't seen it. The fact that she and Randy were hardly lowlifes didn't make the fear any less real.

Still, there was something about the look on Randy's face. Like he might have a bad actor in mind. But who?

"We've been airtight up to this point," Randy said, as if reading her mind and wanting to allay her suspicions.

"I'll circle back to my guy in the cop shop, see if there's anything else I can find out," Vickers said. "I mean, it's not unreasonable to think in that direction. Since it's been a few days and we haven't been contacted yet, that's probably a good sign. But it's worth nailing that angle down."

Monica nodded and realized in that moment that Aiden was staring across the room at them. Ignoring him, she said, "It goes without saying that we freeze operations, at least until we figure out what's going on?"

"Makes sense," Vickers said. "Hopefully, Chuck just dipped his stick into the wrong skank."

Monica shook her head at the comment.

"What?" Vickers said. "We're all thinking the same thing. Either way, best if we recover the laptop first before moving ahead."

"Right," Monica said. "Okay. Freezing operations. Are we agreed?"

Randy looked ready to disagree but never had the chance.

"Excuse me," Aiden said, just as Vickers's phone buzzed with a text.

"Yes?"

"You might want to take a look at this."

"At what?"

Aiden approached cautiously. Monica nodded her permission. He set a laptop on the table.

Chuck Gibbons, with his matching fitness wear, $300 kicks, shaved head, and sunglasses, had represented one side of the dark web hacking culture. "Black Sea Cyber Punk," Vickers had called him behind his back. For his part, Aiden stuck with the stereotype. Sagging sweatpants; stained gray hoodie that rode high, providing unwanted glimpses of pale white tummy; long, unkempt beard.

"At this," he said, a hint of a wheeze at the back of his throat. Monica couldn't read the expression on his face for a moment until she realized it was embarrassment.

"Well, fuck," she said, looking at the screen.

"That's one way of putting it," Randy said drily.

Monica had broken into enough homes at certain points in her career, brought enough laptop screens to life in darkened dens, to know porn when she saw it. And the image on the screen was a lot to see.

"It's not the only site," Aiden said, a note of apology in his voice.

"Meaning?" Randy barked.

"Not the only site that, well, Chuck visited."

"How many?" Monica said.

"Dozens? It's going to take me a while to decrypt his search history. That's the first one I came to."

"That's just great." Monica turned to Randy. "You said Chuck came highly recommended."

"He did," Randy said. "And it's not like he hasn't delivered. Look at how it's been going. He's got the goods, no question." Paused. "*Had* the goods. Whatever this is"—he gestured at the laptop, assiduously averting his eyes from Aiden's computer—"it didn't affect his performance."

"Unless it's what got him killed in a motel room with his laptop, which is now in the wind," Monica said.

Aiden wheezed again. Monica permitted a glance in his direction. He stared at her briefly, then turned away.

Embarrassment?

Or something more?

Monica realized there was a lot she didn't know about this mountain of a man who suddenly held their fate in his grubby hands.

Randy cleared his throat. "So what now?"

Monica studied her husband's face. She knew he was upset. Freezing operations was more than a business decision. For Randy, the planned Quadrant Horizons infiltration was personal. It promised a windfall guaranteeing Randy a better future for his daughter. A future that, unfortunately, Monica was going to spoil. Regrettable, but shit happened. And it wasn't the end of the world. *There was a reason they invented Medicaid, right?* The look on Randy's face had her thinking it might be time to act sooner rather than later. As soon as they wrapped up this laptop fiasco.

She thought about pushing it, probing Randy. She never got the chance.

"Okay," Vickers said, looking up from his phone.

"Okay, what?" Monica said.

"Time for a road trip. My source has a possible bead on a guy running girls out of the motel where Chuck died."

"That's progress. Where are you going?"

"Attleboro," Vickers said.

FOURTEEN

Carter excused himself without identifying the caller to Rhonda and Braden, walked out, and took the call from the Pawtucket police detective in the parking lot. Gus Papaleonardos.

"Gus," Carter said. "Short for Kostas?"

A pause. "That's right. How do you know that?"

"Went to high school with a kid named Kostas. Everybody called him Gus."

"Here?"

"Rochester, New York."

"Never been. You left a message. Something about a ring?"

Right to business. Fine by Carter.

He provided an outline of the past day, including the discovery of the ring, Jason Schulte's business card, the word *Help* scrawled on the back of the card, and Carter's meeting with Jim and Valerie Watkins.

He continued on: the couple's decision to hire him to deliver the ring to Terri—which, by default, meant finding her first—and finally, Carter's determination that someone, presumably the man who confronted Linda Stauch and then pursued her through the rain, used the credit card of a deceased man named Shaun V. Volpe to buy gas.

He left out several other details.

Papaleonardos didn't say anything for several seconds.

"You there?" Carter said.

"I don't know where to start."

"It's complicated. I'll give you that."

"Handing over evidence connected to a crime isn't complicated," the detective said. "In fact, not doing so is itself a crime."

"I only discovered the ring this morning. I called as soon as I could." *Technically true.*

"You didn't come to the station, though, like you told dispatch."

Carter decided not to quibble over the fact he said he *might* swing by.

Papaleonardos said, "Where's the ring now?"

"I have it. I'm trying to find Terri Watkins so I can deliver it."

"You can't deliver evidence."

"Maybe consider it a transfer? I find Terri Watkins, you'll be the first to know after her parents."

"Nice try. What about the business card? There could be fingerprints."

Carter thought about the soggy card he pulled from the wet envelope that spent the night in his soaked utility vest.

"It's in pretty bad shape."

"That's my call, not yours."

Carter looked at his watch. Already pushing five. "Okay. I could drop it off now."

"Them. The ring and the card. Where are you?"

Carter told him.

"What's in Fall River?"

"I took a wrong turn."

"Right. Be here in an hour," Papaleonardos said, and disconnected.

"He has a point," Carter's uncle said a minute later, after Carter called him. "It is evidence, of a sort."

"I also have a contract with Terri's parents."

"I think a police investigation overrides that?"

"Overrides a delivery?"

"Mercury." A pause. "Wait a second. Is this about Tomeka?"

Carter looked out the Suburban window. At the far end of the parking lot, by the Resthaven entrance, Rhonda and Braden emerged arm in arm. They walked around the corner, separated, and both hunched over. A moment later they straightened, lighted cigarettes in their hands. As he watched, Braden put his arm around Rhonda and she leaned into him.

"No," Carter said. "Maybe."

In the past few months, Tomeka had been stopped twice by white suburban cops on the way to her accounting house calls, despite the fact she drove a new RAV4. Or maybe because of it. The incidents angered and ashamed Carter.

"You have every reason to be upset," his uncle said. "But the guy does have a point about evidence. Plus, he's there, not a Rochester 'burb."

"You're right."

"Okay," his uncle continued. "Finding Terri would fulfill the contract, right?"

"Without delivering the ring? Not really."

His uncle sighed. "Maybe you could do it backwards? Find her, get the ring back from the police, deliver it."

"It's unorthodox. And unlikely. They're not going to release evidence like that."

"Your entire job is unorthodox."

Neither of them spoke for a moment.

"Back to Jason Schulte for a second?" his uncle said.

"Yes."

"That's a big coincidence, between him and Volpe. You think Terri Watkins could have had something to do with their deaths?"

"I'm not sure. It's possible she's the one Shaun met at the park the night he died, but we can't know that for certain. I'm more interested in the guy using Shaun's credit card at the gas station. The one who came after me when I tried to help Linda Stauch. If he has Terri under his thumb, he could have been the one calling the shots. Closer we get to him, closer we get to Terri."

"Agreed. It would help if we knew how Schulte died. Right now we're making assumptions."

"Still nothing on the news?"

His uncle confirmed it. "No obituary either. It's only been a day. Maybe this detective could help us out?"

"Maybe."

"Why not? He owes you, you think about it. Who knows if the thing with the credit card would have been found without you?"

"You're right," Carter said reluctantly.

After they disconnected, Carter drove to the Resthaven entrance, apologized to Rhonda and Braden for the interruption, and explained he'd be in touch about Jason Schulte.

"Thanks," Rhonda said wearily.

Braden nodded but didn't reply.

Carter plugged the Pawtucket police department into Google Maps and pulled out of the funeral home parking lot. He found a late-season Red Sox game on SiriusFM to distract himself. As he headed for the highway, Carter thought about what it would have been like to see Lou Boudreau play. An amateur shortstop like himself admiring a professional, one of the best to ever play the game. It would have been pretty cool, he decided.

Fifteen minutes into the drive, Carter's phone vibrated. Carefully, he peered at the message. From Jim Watkins.

How's it going?

Carter was accustomed to such messages. On the surface, they were naïve at best, unfair at worst. He'd hadn't even had the contract to deliver the ring to Terri a full day, despite everything that had happened. Barely enough time to write out a to-do list. But for Jim and Valerie Watkins, like many of Carter's customers, time was irrelevant. Carter's efforts on their behalf were a lifeline, a handhold for a swimmer who thought he was drowning but now could be saved.

Debating how to respond, Carter reviewed the video footage that Nelson Ramos showed him, a terrified but determined Terri clubbing Pats Jersey with a two-liter bottle of Diet Dr Pepper, forcing her captor to drop his Monster Energy can as she ran into the rain for help.

Carter couldn't stop thinking about the look on Terri's face. Determination laced with fear.

Also: The fact that he had never missed a delivery.

And wasn't in the mood to start.

He pulled over and typed a response.

Nothing yet

Carter didn't pull back into traffic right away. Instead, he thought about Tomeka's face when she told him about the second time she was stopped by a cop. Then he considered his uncle's argument that Detective Gus Papaleonardos had a point about the evidence. Carter weighed his options, made a decision. He had one other thing to do before handing over the ring to Papaleonardos. He needed to know how Jason Schulte died. Short of any official explanation, there was only one option for finding out.

A variation of how he'd learned the truth behind Shaun V. Volpe's death.

He'd just ask Schulte's family.

What's the worst that could happen?

He found out quickly enough after parking on Schulte's street thirty minutes later and undertaking his usual reconnaissance.

Carter was not the only one watching Jason Schulte's house.

Darkness came early around here; Carter had forgotten that about the East Coast. The curtains were drawn on the front windows of the green split-level in the cookie-cutter subdivision in Rumford. But as far as Carter could tell, every light inside was on, illumination leaking from cracks and crevices like an alien arrival movie scene. Three cars crowded the driveway and the street was lined with more on either side. Twice in the past fifteen minutes, couples had walked to the door, shoulders hunched, rung the bell, and entered a few moments later, arms extended for embraces.

Despite the activity, Carter spotted the van almost immediately. Parked three spaces behind him, but thanks to the positioning of a maple tree in the next-door neighbor's yard, with a marginally better sight line of Schulte's house than Carter had. The van wasn't hard to miss; it was the same vehicle that pulled up behind Carter two nights earlier in the pouring rain in Pawtucket after he stopped to check on Linda Stauch.

Not the same driver, though. In place of Pats Jersey, a skinny white guy sat behind the wheel studying his phone and pretending not to watch the comings-and-goings as carefully as Carter was. Chosen disguise: sunglasses and Red Sox cap. This neck of the woods, the van didn't exactly blend, thanks to some rust and dents and dings. But in the era of practically 24/7 home delivery, it was anyone's guess what he was doing there. Which fact Carter assumed the guy was counting on.

Either way, he was cramping Carter's style. Carter couldn't very well leave his post and walk up to Jason Schulte's door with this guy keeping watch. Because this was a development. A big one. Same van, different guy implied a team. A gang, maybe. Others besides Pats Jersey had a vested interest in whatever connection Jason Schulte had to Terri Watkins. A connection complicated by Pats Jersey's confrontation with Carter in the rain. This development—someone else watching Schulte's house—threw a wrench into Carter's efforts to find Terri. But it also, he realized after a second, offered an opportunity. He just had to figure out how to take advantage of it.

Asking Schulte's family about Jason's death was off the table for now. He wasn't sure if the man in the van would figure out who he was if he spied Carter, but he couldn't risk the chance that Pats Jersey had spread Carter's description around.

He also couldn't risk the van driving away while Carter was inside Schulte's house. Under different circumstances he could sneak a GPS tagger under the van's bumper and stay on top of him that way. That could be tough in the current situation.

Meanwhile, he had Papaleonardos to think about. The detective had been understandably unhappy with Carter's text that he was running a little late.

A little late—perhaps an understatement.

In short, Carter was stuck.

And exhausted. The pain from the blows he'd taken in the rainstorm last night and from Cody at the gas station this morning was running neck and neck with the relief provided by the ibuprofen he'd been shotgunning since leaving Cody's grandmother's house. Pain versus pain relief: He had a feeling how that contest would shake out. Plus, though Carter wasn't much of a drinker, his preferred beverage for taking the edge off—ten-year-aged sake—wasn't jumping off a lot of local liquor store shelves. A hot shower someplace might have to suffice. Not for a while, though.

Carter was resigning himself to a long stakeout when he went back to the 24/7 delivery thing for a second. He appreciated the concept. He'd never gone that route professionally, but he understood the attraction. The ability to set your own hours, work when you wanted.

Yes, he thought. *This just might work.*

FIFTEEN

Carter pulled out his phone and launched the DoorDash, Grubhub, and Instacart apps. He found his location on the Maps app, formulated a description of the van, and went to work.

Twenty-two minutes later, Carter watched in his rearview mirror as a small black Ford Focus sedan pulled up alongside the van. The driver emerged, brown McDonald's bag in hand, and tapped on the van's passenger window. As Carter had instructed when placing the order.

Carter was still trying to make out the ensuing conversation—"Get lost" the only clear phrase drifting down the street—when a second car, what looked like a Honda CR-V, stopped behind the Focus. The driver honked and emerged, Burger King bag in her hand, and approached the van. Now both food delivery persons were talking to Sox Cap. Soon enough, another car drove up, stopped, and discharged a third person, another lady holding a paper bag, who also beelined for the van.

Carter correctly counted on a two-part dilemma. The first, Sox Cap's paranoia at a convention of food delivery persons materializing at his van. Secondly, the ire of other drivers trying to go down the street. Sure enough, one arrived like clockwork, slowing and stopping, unable to continue. The driver laid on his horn long and loud, because: New England. Yet Carter couldn't blame him. It was a busy residential street even in the early evening; this kind of blockage wasn't going to cut it.

A few seconds later, Carter heard the van's engine start and watched in his rearview mirror as its lights flicked on. Apparently, Sox Cap had

had enough. Carter kept his head down as the van passed him in a hurry, put the Suburban in drive, and pulled out in pursuit.

It was time to see who else was so interested in Jason Schulte.

Monica was in the kitchen, plugging the address for the Chamber of Commerce into her phone for tomorrow's event, when the text message popped up.

Can you talk?

Vickers.

One second

She peeked into the living room. Randy was on the couch, oblivious, scrolling on his phone, half watching one of the John Wicks. Monica slipped outside.

"What's up?" she whispered, standing on the deck, Valentino cashmere cardigan on against the cool evening air.

"I'm at this apartment."

"What apartment?"

"In Attleboro. More of an apartment building. Three units, side by side."

She looked inside the house through the sliding glass door. "What about it?"

"My guy who told me about someone running girls from that motel? This is the address he gave me."

Monica furrowed her brow. "You think that's where the laptop is?"

"I'm not saying that. Right now, it's as good a guess as any. Plus, some sketchy guy just walked out behind this skank girl."

She didn't respond. That word again. *Skank.*

"Not exactly probable cause."

"Disagree. I think I'm onto something."

Monica sighed. She recognized the tone in Vickers's voice, the fishing for a compliment. Suggesting he'd gone above and beyond once again when all he was doing was fixing a mess he made. The arrogance of the guy. Something the men in her life had in common. The cops and the cons. Sometimes hard to distinguish.

Deciding to go with the flow for now, she said, "What's your play?"

"I need to get inside. Look around."

"Alone?"

"Not sure there's another option right now."

This is a bad idea.

"Are you carrying?" Monica said.

"Of course."

"The Glock?"

He confirmed it.

She heard a sound. Turned and saw Randy in the kitchen, freshly opened Sam Adams in his hand, looking out at her. She raised her hand with her forefinger extended—*one minute*—and returned to the call.

She said, "I don't think we're there yet."

"Where?"

"I don't think we're at a place where we can afford the kind of attention you could draw starting a firefight inside a brothel in Attleboro, Massachusetts. You catch my drift?"

"That wouldn't happen." Petulant, like a twelve-year-old boy negotiating with his mom for a ride to the mall.

Monica said, "In that case, what would happen? Inside this brothel, I mean?"

"Really?"

"Just looking at the big picture here."

Vickers's voice dropped to a whisper. "You know, you're not the only one with a lot to lose if we don't get that laptop back. I'm up to my eyes, too. *Both of us are.*"

She thought of the look on his face that morning as she drew him inside her, like Christmas and his birthday came early with extra cake. She weighed that expression against his implied threat. She wondered once again who was using whom, exactly.

Nevertheless, Monica knew he had a point, as reluctant as she was to admit it. There was a lot riding on their post-Randy planning.

A whole lot.

"I'm aware of the stakes," she said evenly. "I just think we need to go slow. You've done good work, finding that place. Really good. No surprise, obviously," she added, piling it on a bit. "It's what you do, right?"

"Thank you."

"Go ahead and sit on it for a while. See what you see. Let me talk to Randy, figure out the best way to proceed. You have bandwidth to hang for a while?"

"Duh."

"Let's do that then. Listen, gotta go. But Scott?"

"Yes?"

"Speaking of getting inside, this kind of hard work deserves a reward." She whispered herself now, threading in some scorch. "*Capisce?*"

"Nice," he said. But she could tell she'd touched the right nerve. So to speak.

"Later," she said, and went to disconnect.

"Shit. Wait."

"What?" Monica said impatiently, meeting Randy's eyes through the patio door.

"Something's going on."

"Like what?"

"Like some guy in a blue van just pulled up."

SIXTEEN

Carter drove past the three-unit red brick apartment building, noting one of the unit numbers—607—as he went around the blue van, hoping the Suburban wouldn't attract the man's attention. Carter looked in his rearview mirror. So far, so good. Carter reached the end of the street and turned right. He drove for two blocks, parked, and texted the address to his uncle.

On it, he replied.

Carter pulled out, circled the block, and reparked opposite the apartment with a clear view of the front doors of the first two units. The parked blue van, the one he'd followed from Jason Schulte's house in Rumford, shielded the view of the third unit. Now the van appeared empty. Carter had to assume the driver—Sox Cap—had exited and gone inside while Carter was around the corner texting his uncle. He unconsciously tapped his Beretta holstered beneath his utility vest—*not making that mistake again*—and considered how to proceed.

First consideration: Pats Jersey was inside—sans Terri Watkins, who was still on the run—and under the right kind of questioning might provide insights into how Carter might locate her. Complication: Sox Cap was also inside and probably in a bad mood because of the food delivery trick.

Second consideration: Terri Watkins was inside, but not Pats Jersey, which fact could enhance Carter's chances of making good on his promise to Terri's parents, delivering the ruby ring, righting things with

Papaleonardos, and getting on his way. Of course, same complication applied as with the first consideration.

Third consideration: Both Terri Watkins and Pats Jersey were inside, which would compound complications all around.

Fourth consideration: In addition to Pats Jersey and Sox Cap, a baker's dozen of other guys favoring New England sports team accessories were holed up as well, considerably diminishing Carter's chances of making it past the front door. After the day Carter had had, he wasn't in the mood for engaging anyone at the moment, let alone a posse.

Fifth—

Hang on.

What's this?

As Carter watched, the middle of the three doors opened. A woman peered out uncertainly. *Terri Watkins.* She stepped across the threshold and a moment later was joined by a large, unshaven man. He was wearing an oversized red flannel shirt tonight and moving stiffly, the cadence of a man twenty years his senior, but there was no mistaking him. Especially with the bandage on the left side of his face.

Pats Jersey.

All right then, Carter thought, unbuckling. Maybe he'd have Terri back to her parents by day's end after all.

He had just opened the Suburban's driver's side door when he heard another car door open two spaces down from him and a man's voice shout, "Hey!"

At the sound of the man's voice, both Terri Watkins and Pats Jersey looked up. Already, the man who had called out was entering Carter's peripheral vision, now halfway across the street, walking fast as he closed the distance to the front of the apartment. Carter took note of the speed with which the black-clad man moved, an agility that spoke of operational training; law enforcement or maybe military. But Carter's attention was more focused on the handgun the man draped loosely alongside his right thigh.

Carter wasn't the only one who noticed this; seconds later Pats Jersey grabbed Terri, pulled her inside, and slammed the door shut. The guy with the gun flew up the steps and without hesitation shouldered the door, once, twice, three times. It flung open. Carter heard shouting and, a second later, a gunshot.

Crap, he thought, and sprinted for the apartment door.

"Scott," Monica said, not bothering to keep her voice down now. Screw the neighbors. "Stay put. It's not the time. Do you hear me?"

"I need to see what this guy is up to. Hang on—he's going inside."

"Let him. We talked about this. We can't afford trouble right now."

"I'm not going to make trouble."

"What's going on?"

Randy, stepping onto the deck.

"It's Scott. He's in Attleboro. He thinks he might have a lead on the laptop."

"Really?"

She turned back to the phone. "Scott—are you there? What's happening?"

"Nothing. The guy just went inside. It's all quiet."

"Good. Keep it that way."

A minute passed, then two, Scott's breathing just audible over the phone. Randy placed both hands on the deck railing as he looked across the lawn at the line of trees ringing the pond behind them. A plop as something slipped into the water from the muddy bank. Crickets sawed at the night. Overhead, a bat snapped at a mosquito. They'd chosen Seekonk for the tranquility. So why did Monica feel like she was standing in a war zone?

"Scott? Are you there?"

Nothing.

"Scott?"

Silence.

"Scott?"

"*Hey*," she heard him say, and the phone went dead.

Carter eased his way inside the apartment, Beretta raised. He was in a narrow, unlighted foyer crowded with junk. Ad fliers ripped from the front door and flung to the floorunopened; mismatched sneakers; disconcertingly, what looked like a pile of empty .380 cartridge boxes. The house where Cody kept Fernanda Ramos prisoner was a staged model home by contrast. Carter took two more steps and peered into a darkened living room that smelled of mildew and rotten bananas. A pale figure slumped on a couch in shorts and a T-shirt; a woman, on closer inspection, age indeterminate, asleep or unconscious, chest slowly rising and falling, light snores like someone ripping strips of cardboard off an Amazon box.

Carter stepped farther down the hall. Where was everyone?

He got his answer a minute later in the form of a man shouting upstairs.

"I need that fucking laptop!"

The shout followed by a crash, a woman's scream, and two men yelling over each other. He jogged to the end of the hall, looked into a kitchen filled with empty pizza boxes and Chinese take-out containers in lieu of cookware. Carter's attention was drifting to a half-opened duffel bag in the corner, his eyes processing what he was pretty sure were its contents, when he turned at the sound of thunder on the stairway to his left.

Stumbling more than walking, groaning softly, white face drawn in fear, Terri Watkins pitched into sight, right hand gripping the banister as she tripped down, left hand curled into a fist as if she was in pain or her fingers were going numb.

Right behind her was Pats Jersey, meaty left hand around her neck. He stopped for a second, eyes widening.

"The fuck?" he said, recognizing Carter.

"We meet again. Drop the gun."

The man responded by producing a gun in his right hand, firing at Carter, and rushing Terri ahead of him into the kitchen.

"Stop," Carter said, ears ringing from the errant shot. He sighted the Beretta between Pats Jersey's shoulder blades.

"Help!" Terri yelled.

Carter pursued them as they headed for a back door in the kitchen. He had to make a decision. He wouldn't shed any tears over Pats Jersey, but he knew instinctively that further gunplay wasn't going to improve the situation and might endanger Terri. He had a strict policy against wounding clients taking delivery of items. He slapped the Beretta into his left hand and reached for the pepper spray instead.

"Stop," Carter repeated, readying himself to jump onto the man's back and hope for the best. Terri yelled again as she was shoved hard through the back door.

"I said—" Carter said, but didn't get a chance to finish. He felt himself flung forward as someone with the body mass of a battering ram collided with him from behind. He went down, seeing stars as he clipped his head on an edge of the counter. Dots swarming before his eyes, he raised his head in time to see the man who'd lit the fuse outside by yelling “Hey” stumble past him, gun in his right hand, massaging his head with his left.

“For the love of Mike,” Carter mumbled, using his last bit of energy to reach out, grab the man’s right calf, and hang on tight. The man swore, lost his balance, and went down himself, lying half in and half out the back door threshold.

“Gotcha,” Carter said, which was the last thing he remembered as the dots before his eyes bloomed into an impenetrable black curtain.

SEVENTEEN

"Where are we going?" Terri said.

"Shut up," Donny said.

"What's going on?"

"I said, shut up."

Terri shut up. And tried to process what just happened as she sat in the back of the van, shoulders hunched in exhaustion, while the vehicle raced through the night.

One second, Donny was pushing her out the door to another motel job, apparently satisfied he could lengthen her leash a tad. The next, he was dragging her back inside as some guy who looked like a cop broke into the house shouting all kinds of crazy things—starting with: "I need that fucking laptop!" Before she knew it, the guy chased them upstairs after shooting a gun into the ceiling. Terri figured the blow to the head Donny landed on the guy on the second-floor landing would settle things, but damned if the guy didn't bounce up after half a minute and chase them downstairs.

By the time they reached the kitchen, Terri didn't give their chances two cents considering the way the guy moved in comparison to the giant, lumbering Donny.

Until, out of the blue, another guy not much bigger than Terri herself saved the day. Slowed down the looks-like-a-cop guy long enough for Donny to hustle Terri out the back and into the van.

Though not long enough to give Donny time to grab the duffel bag of drugs. The "Brazilian Viagra." A lapse, he reminded Terri every ten seconds, that was a "big goddamn deal," implying it was her fault he left them behind.

Anyway, who the hell were any of these guys?

Donny wasn't saying. He also wouldn't tell her where they were going. Or if Sheena or any of the other girls were coming too. All Terri knew was she was supposed to keep quiet and to let him drive.

She let Donny drive.

What else was she supposed to do?

"Anything?" Randy asked wearily.

"Not yet," Monica snapped.

"This is all we fucking need."

"Tell me something I don't already know."

They glared at each other like boxers in opposing corners of a ring.

Back inside their condo, in the living room, sitting on each end of the Italian leather sofa that arrived two weeks ago. Randy had argued against its purchase. "We've got more important things to spend money on," he said.

"There's more than enough to go around," Monica replied, adding: "Even with Michelle."

"Really?"

It was the "Even with Michelle" that got him. Like Michelle was an extra car payment and not his only daughter, sentenced to a life of long-term care. Randy knew in his heart that Monica was paying lip service to his plans to secure Michelle's future, but did she have to be so blatant about it? His suspicions about what she and Vickers were up to had only deepened. Putting their clumsily disguised affair to the side—he had the pictures to prove it squirreled away, just in case—Randy had to assume that Monica and Vickers had their own grift in the works.

Which Randy guessed might mean they had different thoughts on what to do with the Quadrant Horizons windfall. Which meant, as much as he didn't like to think about it, the time might be ripe for both Monica and Vickers to—

"Hello?"

He looked up. Monica had her phone to her ear. She gave Randy a thumbs-up.

"Slow down," Monica said, placing the call on speaker. "Start at the beginning."

The call lasted ten minutes. Randy shaking his head at Vickers's stupidity-laced brazenness as Monica periodically interrupted with questions or expletives. Maybe she was faking it, but to Randy's mind she sounded legitimately pissed at Vickers.

Because it turned out that Vickers had done exactly what Monica asked him not to. Namely, chased someone—a guy and a girl, probably a hooker—inside the Attleboro apartment building by himself. Making matters worse, he fired off a shot while he was at it.

"Shooting was necessary why?" Randy said.

"Things got complicated."

"Complicated how?"

"Fog of war stuff."

Randy rolled his eyes. He could tell Vickers was leaving out a Mount Everest–sized chunk of information, including the fact said guy probably got the drop on him and Vickers didn't want to admit it.

Randy was about to press Vickers for the truth when his phone buzzed.

Where?

Pauley Carnevale, again. *Jesus. Did he ever stop*?

"Hang on," Randy said.

He felt his stress levels rocketing, as if they weren't already sky-high. He'd already been dreading tomorrow, and that was before the disaster with the laptop. The Chamber of Commerce thing wouldn't wrap up until one thirty at the earliest, and how was he supposed to—

It came to him. The Chamber thing might just give him the cover he needed. This could work. Might work. Had to.

He texted a reply to Pauley.

Providence Place. Food court. Back table

Nothing. Then, Pauley's reply:

You're buying

Asshole.

Randy came back to the moment.

"Any cops?" he asked Vickers.

"No," Vickers said, sounding offended.

"You're sure?"

A moment's hesitation.

"Yes."

Randy and Monica looked at each other.

"Okay, then," Randy said. "Just so I have this straight. You Rambo-ed your way inside after Monica expressly told you not to. Then you went bull in a china shop on the guy who has the laptop, which is basically you shouting at the top of your lungs that the computer's valuable enough it required someone with a gun to come looking for it. Now that guy is who the hell knows where, figuring he's got something important, and also knowing what you look like. Which means our chances of getting the laptop back are shrinking faster than a pecker in a blizzard. How'm I doing so far?"

Out of the corner of his eye, Randy saw Monica smirk in spite of herself.

"You left one thing out," Vickers said over the phone.

"What's that?" Randy said, taken aback by Vickers's confident tone.

"The pills."

"What pills?" Randy glanced at the muted TV, where a black-clad John Wick was throwing a man through a plate-glass window.

"I grabbed a duffel bag of pills they left behind. I'm thinking high street value."

"We're not in the pill business," Randy said. That was all they needed.

"We aren't," Vickers said, his voice like a Texas Hold'em player revealing a straight flush. "But looks like the people who have Chuck's laptop are. And I'm thinking they're going to want them back."

"So?"

"So that's our leverage. Their pills for our computer."

Silence settled over the table. Randy looked at Monica, who shrugged.

Shit, Randy thought.

That's actually a good idea.

EIGHTEEN

Carter blinked, groaned, raised his head. And rested it back on the floor.

As he lay there, assessing aches and pains like he was at the end of a run and not a late-night brawl, he listened. For what, he wasn't entirely sure. Someone else with a spare foot or fist to throw his way? Not as far as he could tell. Sirens? All quiet on that front. Probably a good thing, though you could never be sure. Gunshots? Fortunately not. Two were enough for the night.

Satisfied he was safe for the moment, Carter adjusted his glasses and rose onto his hands and knees, sighing with the effort. Glanced around, stood. No sign of Pats Jersey or, more importantly, Terri Watkins. No sign of the man chasing those two, the guy whose ankle Carter grabbed and sent flying. The operative type. Who was that, and why was he after the pair? The evening's events slowly came back to him. The stakeout in Rumford, the food delivery trick, following the blue van here. The whole reason he was in this building, on this floor, in the first place.

The van's driver. Sox Cap. Where was that guy?

Carter checked his phone. His uncle had called twice, as had Gus Papaleonardos. There was also another text from Jim Watkins asking again about his progress. Carter texted his uncle to let him know he was all right, pocketed his phone, and set off to explore the house.

Upstairs, he found two beds, just mattresses on bed springs, each room with a large flat-screen on the wall and little else in the way of furniture. The rooms smelled of mildew, pot, body odor, and sex. Neither was occupied. Nothing in either one indicating who Pats Jersey was or where he might have taken Terri Watkins. Carter decided he'd seen enough and descended downstairs.

Back in the living room, the same woman was still slumped on the couch, snoring softly. Carter checked her pulse without her stirring. Fifty-four. Low, but not "Call 911" low. He used his handkerchief to wipe spittle off her chin. Looking around, he spied a red afghan on the couch that, despite fraying yarn ends, was basically in one piece. He draped it over the woman. Satisfied, he searched the rest of the room and the dining room as well but found only greasy take-out bags, syringes, and empty cans of Monster Energy.

Back in the kitchen, Carter pulled a plastic trash can out from under the sink. He retrieved a pair of latex gloves from his utility vest, snapped them on, and sorted through the garbage. He'd performed the thankless task more than once in his USPIS days, with a fifty-fifty success rate finding bankable information. On some days those were better odds than he got interviewing suspects.

Halfway down, Carter found the only thing that wasn't food related. An empty envelope from the Attleboro Water Department, shiny with grease stains. Carter almost ignored it, turned it over at the last second. On the back, someone had scrawled ten digits. A phone number? Gingerly, Carter folded the envelope in half, then in quarters, being sure not to smudge the numbers, and placed it in a lower right-hand pocket of his utility vest. A clue? Maybe—

Behind Carter, a floorboard creaked. Carter went still but didn't turn around.

"Don't move."

"Not moving," Carter said.

"Turn around and show me your hands."

"Yup. Just hang on." He didn't move, weighing his options. They were slim, he decided.

"I've got a gun. I'm not messing around."

"I believe you," Carter said. "Thing is, though, my hands are disgusting. You really want to see them?"

"Now, asshole."

Carter lowered both hands to his sides and turned around.

The driver of the van. Sox Cap.

Squeezed-in eyes as if he were perpetually squinting into the sun, matted tufts of black hair jutting from beneath his hat's brim, stubble shading a sharp chin. In his right hand, a gun nearly as big as the one Pats Jersey had leveled at Carter as he approached Linda Stauch's car in the pouring rain last night.

"Who are you? Where the hell is Donny?"

Carter blinked, taking in the question. "Is Donny the big guy who's with Terri Watkins?"

The question seemed to perplex the man. "Why do you care? Who are you, anyway?"

Carter said, "I'm a guy who doesn't hide at the first sound of trouble."

The man flinched, as if Carter had flicked his middle finger against his cheek.

"Fuck you. Answer the question."

Carter considered his situation. The way he was positioned, garbage bin slightly to his right, a decent chance existed he could kick the can and loft it and its contents at the guy. Hit him more or less dead center and hope he had an aversion to grease and half-eaten chicken wings.

But it wasn't surefire, and Carter was guessing the guy would get a shot or two off first, and where would that leave Carter?

Slowly, he said, "My name's Mercury Carter. I don't know where Donny is. I don't care, either. I'm interested in Terri. Any idea where *she* is?"

The man adjusted his Sox cap, looked not at Carter but at a point over Carter's shoulder, as if he expected someone else to be there. "What are you talking about?"

Carter repeated his explanation.

"Are you a cop?" Raising the gun slightly as he did.

"I'm not a cop."

"Which is what you'd say if you were."

"I'm not sure I follow. In any case, I'm not a cop."

"Why are you looking for Terri?"

"I have something for her."

"What?"

Carter hesitated. "A ring."

The man squinched his eyebrows as if reacting to an exorbitant bar tab. "What kind of ring?"

"One that's important to Terri. One that has nothing to do with Donny," Carter added, hoping that were true.

"Show me."

"No can do."

"Are you fucking kidding me? Show me the ring. Now." The gun in the man's hand was even with Carter's throat.

"The thing is, it's a rules and regs situation. I'm a type of mailman. Freelance. I'm on assignment here, with this ring. I have a strict policy when it comes to safeguarding deliveries. I've already bent the rules by telling you it's a ring. It's not advisable to do anything beyond that."

"Five seconds, you stupid fuck." The gun extended further, the man's hands steady on the grip.

It was an awkward move, and skirted with the letter of the law on the divulging of deliveries front. But it was all Carter had. Pretend to reach for the ring, grab the Beretta instead, roll left, hope for the best . . .

"Now!"

"Okay, okay," Carter said. "It's just inside my—"

"Jimmy? What's going on?"

Raspy, feminine voice. Carter watched as the woman who'd been passed out in the living room, the one he covered with an afghan, appeared in the shadows behind Sox Cap—behind Jimmy. Carter was processing how much older she looked awake when Jimmy, startled by the sound, reflexively turned around. Good enough. Carter lofted the garbage can with a well-placed kick and launched himself behind it. The bin no sooner struck Jimmy, smearing him with grease and coffee grounds and some things Carter didn't want to think about, than the pair collided. Jimmy, taken by surprise and off-balance, went down hard, landing with a grunt on his stomach. The woman gasped, took a step back.

First priority, Jimmy's gun. Carter grabbed Jimmy's wrist and bent it forward, registering Jimmy's cry of pain at the exact moment the gun slipped from his grasp. Carter reached for it, pulled it in an arc around and to the side. He wanted it away from the woman; no telling whose side she was on. Next, he retrieved the Beretta from the holster under his utility vest and rested it gently against the back of Jimmy's neck.

"Jimmy. That's your name?"

The man swore. Carter applied extra pressure to his neck, the barrel of the Beretta puckering a pale ring in Jimmy's white skin.

"Jimmy?"

The man nodded.

"I was telling the truth earlier. I don't know where Donny is. I'd like to, though, assuming Terri's with him, so I can find her and give her the ring I mentioned. Since I'm asking the questions now, back to you: Do you know where either of them are?"

"Fuck you."

Carter sighed. He kept the gun in place and looked at the woman standing in the doorway.

"What's your name?"

"Me?"

"Yes."

"Sheena."

"All right, Sheena. Do you know where Donny and Terri might have gone?"

"Terri's gone?"

"That's correct. Any idea where?"

"Me?"

Patiently, Carter said, "Yes, you."

"I don't know what's going on," the woman said. Carter waited for her to say more, then watched as she braced herself against the doorframe, slid to the floor like a sheet fluttering free from a clothesline, and closed her eyes.

"Okay," Carter said, turning to Jimmy. "Back to you."

For a second he thought he was in luck. Rather than curse him out, or shake his head, or try to wiggle free, Jimmy licked his lips. The way you do when you're on the cusp of saying something important. It might be an important truth or it might be an important lie, but it felt like progress. The moment never came. A voice, loud and insistent, interrupted them.

"Attleboro police. Anyone here?"

Shoot.

"Police. Everything all right?"

Down the hall, at the door to the apartment. The one the operative type smashed open and which Carter hadn't bothered to close. Someone heard something after all, either the gunshots or one of the ensuing struggles.

"Hello?"

Carter had maybe thirty seconds. Door clearly forced open, shots fired, sketchy address, all added up to exigent circumstances. Not a warrant situation. No cop worth his or her salt would back off now when someone might be in trouble.

"Don't move," Carter said, and pulled himself off Jimmy. He switched the Beretta to his left hand, leaned over, and picked up Jimmy's gun. Quickly ejected the magazine and unchambered the live round, and quietly set the whole kit and caboodle into the kitchen sink.

"Attleboro police. Show yourself."

Carter took once last look around, shook his head, and darted out the kitchen door and down the steps. He jogged across the yard, looked left, right, and made his decision. He grabbed the top of the wooden fence at the back, planted a foot on the remains of a rusted grill, and vaulted up and over.

Fifteen minutes later, back in his Suburban, he eased his way up the street, permitting himself a glance in his rearview mirror at the circus of blue-and-white flashing lights outside the apartment building. Only a glance. He pointed the SUV in the direction of a

Motel 8 he found online, checked in paying cash ten minutes later, brushed his teeth, and stripped to his shorts. He was about to drop into bed when he remembered something. He reached into the rear pocket of his cargo shorts, retrieved the envelope he'd found in the trash bin from his vest, placed it on the TV cabinet to dry, went to the bed and pulled back the covers, and was asleep within two minutes.

NINETEEN

Carter slept until almost nine thirty. Giving himself a minute to wake up, he breathed deeply as he compiled a new list of aches and pains. It took a while. A lot more than he had after a run around the Cobbs Hill Reservoir or three rounds with the boxing bag in the basement. He was also nursing a headache, whether a remnant of the gunshot-induced TBI almost always triggered by stress or from hitting his head on the apartment's kitchen counter the night before. Or both. It had been a strenuous couple of days.

Out of bed at last, Carter made himself a lukewarm cup of tea from the in-room machine and carried it into the shower, where he stood until the hot water ran out. After toweling off, he stretched on the floor for fifteen minutes, grateful for the yoga classes he'd started doing with Tomeka at the Y—she'd practiced for years. He made a second cup of tea using an English Breakfast bag from the supply he carried with him.

Finally awake, headache dulling, Carter reviewed the events of the previous day. Meeting the Watkinses. Quizzing Linda Stauch's sister in the hospital waiting room. The run-in with Cody Washburn at the gas station. The subsequent rescue of Fernanda Ramos and Carter's acquisition of a tackle box full of cash that was currently locked up in the Suburban's metal utility box. Carter's conversation with Shaun Volpe's stepsister and her husband. His failure—no other way to put it—to make good on his promise to Detective Gus Papaleonardos. Trekking to Rumford in hopes of learning the truth about Jason Schulte's death, only to end up following Sox Cap—Jimmy—to a scuzzy apartment building in Attleboro where all hell broke loose.

Grimacing as he recalled digging through the trash, Carter remembered something. The greasy envelope with the ten digits—a phone number?—written on the back that he'd removed from the bin. He took it from the TV cabinet, flattened it, and dialed the number. One ring. Two. Three—

"You've reached Sherm's. Leave a message and I'll call you back."

Sherm's. Carter Googled the number and the name Sherm. The result popped up two seconds later. Sherm's Pawnshop, with an Attleboro address.

Carter searched for the shop and found a Facebook page:

ABSOLUTE TOP DOLLAR FOR YOUR COLLECTIBLES, VEHICLES, APPLIANCES, JEWELRY, FIREARMS, ELECTRONICS, COMPUTERS, AND MORE.

Computers.

I need that fucking laptop.

Okay, Carter thought. *Time to move.*

Monica could think of a lot of places she'd rather be "at the moment" than the annual Small Business Service Awards at the Rhode Island Chamber of Commerce. Starting with trapped inside a full porta-potty on a hot day with no food or water and moving up from there. Which, she admitted, was ironic given that it was her fault they were sitting here. Nevertheless, the timing couldn't have been worse, from the crap going on with Chuck and the missing laptop to the corner they'd been backed into, namely: trading a duffel bag filled with illegal narcotics for said laptop. All thanks to Vickers. What an idiot, barreling inside that apartment in Attleboro after she specifically warned him not to. Served him right, whatever happened to him inside—

"And of course, Providence's own Randy and Monica Carmichael!"

Monica froze, brought herself back to the moment, manufactured an ear-to-ear grin, half rose out of her chair along with Randy, acknowledging the applause.

Shit. Shit. Shit.

When lunch was served, she forced herself to eat to keep up appearances. And figure out what the hell they were going to do.

"Any word from Vickers?" Randy growled, spearing a bite of chicken breast.

"Nothing new."

"You sure?"

"Of course I'm sure. Why wouldn't I be?"

"Dunno. You tell me."

Monica frowned, staring at her husband, not liking where this was going. Instead, she repeated, "I'm sure," keeping her voice neutral, and turned to small talk with a boutique coffee shop owner from Woonsocket on her left. The servers had just removed the lunch plates and replaced them with slices of cheesecake when she heard the Chamber's marketing director say their names again. Monica looked up, confused.

". . . and now it's my sincere pleasure to present them today with this year's Rhode Island Chamber of Commerce Small Business Saints Award in recognition of all they've done for the community!"

Shit. They'd won. *You've got to be fucking kidding me.*

Smiles plastered on their faces, Monica and Randy rose and made their way to the podium.

I guess this day could get worse, Monica thought.

Of course, she only had herself to blame.

It had been her idea to join the Chamber. Drape their operation in a blanket of respectability. "We hide in plain sight," she said. "Oldest trick in the book."

"The oldest trick in the book is the first prostitute's first job," Randy replied with a growl. He hadn't been a fan. Didn't like the extra scrutiny it could mean. He'd gone along, reluctantly, after she persuaded him it could enhance their chances of small-business loans if and when another pandemic hit. The fact she knew how many thousands of dollars in fraudulent business loans Randy had pulled down beginning in April 2020 didn't hurt her cause.

Now, positioning themselves on a raised platform beside the Chamber marketing director, Monica realized with a sinking stomach what a mistake this had been. Randy was right. She should have trusted him. With Chuck dead and the laptop gone, this kind of attention was the last thing they needed. More to the point, the last thing she and Scott needed. How was it going to look when Randy, cowinner of a prestigious business award, suddenly and inexplicably went missing? If, you know, that's what ended up happening—

Her thoughts were interrupted by the marketing director reviewing the history of Second Act Staffing Solutions, including Randy and Monica's unorthodox prison love story that resulted in Randy's inspirational rehabilitation. How the two of them went on to found Second Act, a temporary employment agency. The company pairing nonviolent ex-felons who'd earned janitorial and health aide certifications with nursing homes, assisted-living facilities, and hospitals squeezed by a crushing post-COVID worker shortage.

"In just three short years, Second Act has placed more than fifty former offenders"—the marketing director pausing slightly at the word, as if someone had blown cigarette smoke into her face—"in stable, good-paying jobs, many of which have led to full-time employment and a new life for some of society's most . . . tragically disadvantaged individuals."

Cue applause. Monica and Randy, wearing their practiced sheepish smiles, waved in acknowledgment once more. The marketing director paired her nuclear-wattage smile with the kind of doe-eyed appreciation normally reserved for panda cubs or centenarians. She shook both their hands and handed them their trophy.

"Thank you," Randy said, drowned out by applause. He raised a placating hand with a grin. Slowly, the room quieted. Monica's heart pounded. *Was he up to this?*

"Well, what an honor. And a surprise."

Understatement of the year.

Randy stood quietly for a moment, as if at a loss for words. Monica felt a full-blown panic attack coming on. Then, to her amazement, Randy cleared his throat and spoke with the confidence of a minister addressing a flock hungry for salvation.

"The thing is, we didn't start Second Act for recognition or awards, and definitely not to make money"—good-natured laughter—"but receiving this kind of acknowledgment from our business community peers is truly meaningful. As someone who's received more than his fair share of forgiveness"—three-second glance at Monica, which she managed to return just in time with a dewy smile, earning more applause—"I can honestly tell you we don't just change people's paychecks, we change their lives."

Monica looked at the audience in disbelief. They were hanging on his every word.

Thank you, Jesus.

"In conclusion, we're so appreciative to the chamber for helping support our dream. As we like to say, 'Second Act Staffing: Because There's Always a First Time for Second Chances.'"

The last line killed. Monica waited for the applause to die down, then shifted to the microphone. She kept it short.

"Thank you for all your support, and especially for giving us a platform to remind the world that wishes really can come true."

As they made their way back to their seats, the audience on its feet now, Monica linked her left arm in Randy's right and leaned in.

"Now what?" she whispered.

"Now we get the fuck out of this banquet hall and pretend like the world isn't ending."

TWENTY

It had been a gamble, suggesting they take two cars to the Chamber luncheon. Randy wasn't sure what he'd have done if Monica didn't buy his story of needing to stop by the office to check on Aiden and the Quadrant Horizons situation. To his surprise, she went along with the idea easily. Which probably meant something to do with Vickers. Something Randy should really be monitoring. Which he would, as soon as he figured out how to deal with Pauley Carnevale.

Randy made a circuit of downtown in his car, assured himself he wasn't being followed, reparked, and walked as casually as possible into Providence Place. Inside, he shook his head at the trendy stores, the crowded concourses, the gleaming escalators. He had to give credit to someone. When he was a kid, downtown Providence was a retail desert inhabited by bums, polluted by empty city buses, inadvisable to set foot in once the sun set. Then some genius remembered there was an actual river running below all that asphalt, opened it up, created a crazy-ass tourist trap called "WaterFire" that was inexplicably popular, and, oh yeah, built a luxury mall.

Now there was a grift Randy wished he'd been around for.

Talk about water under a bridge.

Randy spied Pauley as soon as he turned the corner. Slouched at a table between a Starbucks and a soft-serve ice cream place. How could you miss him? Bright red hooded sweatshirt with matching cargo sweatpants, red-and-white Air Jordans the size of tugboats, wraparound mirrored sunglasses, and—Jesus wept—a black do-rag. He couldn't have stood out more had he hauled himself buck naked to the top of his food court table and recited the Pledge of Allegiance.

"Amazing," Randy said, standing over him. "You look like Elmo and Lady Gaga hooked up and had a kid, only ten times uglier."

"Funny guy." Pauley extended his right fist for a bump. Randy kept his hands by his sides, willing himself not to spit on Pauley's fist. Grinning, Pauley withdrew his hand and gestured for Randy to sit. Randy sat, eyeing Pauley's drink. A concoction that appeared to be four parts milk, five parts sugar, and enough chocolate drizzle to jump-start diabetes.

"What's up, my dude?" Pauley said.

"I don't have long," Randy said, ignoring the question. "What do you want?"

"Down to business. I appreciate that." Pauley took a generous gulp of his drink, wiping off the accumulated mess from his mouth when he was done. He missed a bit on his chin that Randy didn't mention.

Pauley should have been handsome. Like other male members of the Carnevale crime family, he had his grandfather's dark eyes, hawklike nose, and olive skin. But whereas the combo had given the old man movie star charisma, Pauley always came off looking like a guy who spent too long in the sun drinking bottomless margaritas.

"So," Pauley said. He waited for Randy to respond.

Randy didn't say anything.

"All right then." Another gulp of his drink. More schmutz on his chin. "I'm a reasonable guy. I think you know that. I've given this a lot of consideration, even though we haven't exactly seen eye to eye on things. I think forty percent is a fair number."

"Forty percent."

"That would be correct. What do you think?"

"I think you're out of your fucking mind."

"Well, now, my dude, that would be where you're wrong. I don't see it like that. I see myself as very much on top of things. A businessman, like yourself." He reached his right hand into his sweatpants pocket. Randy flinched, not sure what was about to happen, only to gape as Pauley pulled out a roll of bills the size of a baseball.

"A businessman who likes his Benjamins," Pauley said with a grin.

Jesus. This guy.

"You use that to rub your chub or what?" Randy said.

"Sticks and stones, my friend," Pauley said, replacing the wad.

"A businessman who likes his Benjamins," Pauley repeated, "and who's also expended some capital to get us where we are today and, in return, would like something for his efforts. Something fair." Pauley lifted his cup but didn't drink, instead leaning back in his chair, exposing the dark line of the grip of the semiautomatic tucked into his waistband. A move as blatant as if he'd scrawled *I have a weapon!* in Magic Marker on a napkin and tucked it under his chin.

"Nice pop gun."

"Glad you like it. So, you in or not?"

"Let's go back to the part about you expending capital, as you call it."

"Exactly." Pauley eased forward, returning all four legs of the chair to the mall's tile floor like a kid who sees the teacher coming but isn't all that concerned. "Sweat equity, so to speak."

Randy thought about ending things right there. A fist to Pauley's jaw, popping his head back, lights out.

He resisted. Probably not a good look for this year's winner of the Rhode Island Chamber of Commerce Small Business Saints Award.

Still.

Sweat equity, my ass.

If that's what you called Pauley being on the right Federal Hill barstool at the right time one night when a girl—Maya—rebounding from a bad breakup talked trash about her ex.

An ex who'd cheated on her with a girl named Kristy. As it happened, Kristy had gotten out of the joint recently. She'd then gotten a job cleaning bedpans at a nursing home through a company called Second Act Staffing Solutions.

Kristy, bless her, had hooked up a couple of times with the nursing home's business manager in exchange for an off-the-books raise. On her knees in his office one evening, blinds drawn, Kristy happened to look up and see an email on the business manager's computer screen that said something about a potential data breach at the nursing home.

All of which information had rolled downhill, like shit does, first to Maya's ex, then to Maya, then to Pauley, whose roll of Benjamins tended to keep his barfly pickups both talking and fucking, at least until they couldn't take Pauley anymore.

Either way, the chain of information led the weasel to Randy and the truth behind Second Act. What Randy and Monica were really up to. Secretly mining personal health information like the gold mine it was.

And for that—for nodding sympathetically at a girl on a Federal Hill barstool in exchange for some free tail and gossip—Pauley wanted forty percent of their take?

"You listen to me."

"Listening," Pauley said, the look on his face like a man condescending to hear his wife's idea for new bathroom towels.

Problem was, Randy had nothing to tell him. Pauley had him by the short hairs and knew it. One phone call and Randy and Monica and Second Act Staffing were toast.

Not to say that Chuck and Aiden hadn't put out fires before. The breach that Pauley found out about thanks to Kristy was actually one of two in the past eight months. The cybersecurity at a lot of these medical facilities was an absolute joke—the equivalent of wooden stockades against Abrams tanks. It was the reason Randy targeted them to begin with. They could be inside for months without detection. But the enterprise wasn't fullproof, which was one of the reasons they were keeping things small in preparation for Quadrant Horizons. For the mother of all personal health information jackpots.

On those occasions when they were detected, they were prepared. Randy fell on his sword once alerted to the problem. *Someone must have attacked you through us. I promise you full transparency as we figure all this out.* Chuck and Aiden went to work. Crisis averted.

Except for Pauley. At least for the moment.

It had probably been a mistake not telling Monica about Pauley. Randy intended to. He and she were in this together, right? Then he figured out Monica was jumping Vickers's bones, which he knew instinctively meant she was up to something beyond the sex since she still got plenty of that at home. Until he worked out Monica's plan, Randy decided to deal with Pauley himself. Especially as an idea was beginning to form.

He turned to Pauley, doing his best to hide his bemusement at the ridiculous figure the man cut. "First off, you're dreaming in regards to forty percent," Randy said.

"Oh, really?"

"Secondly, even if the world was about to end and I agreed to that, what assurances do I have that you wouldn't fuck me over anyway, or come back in two months with your hand out again?"

"Assurances?" Pauley said, smiling like a sated hyena. "I'm offended. You have my word."

Finally. An opening.

Randy leaned across the table.

"Your word? Your grandfather's word was gold. You could take it the bank, every time, from here to New York. You? Your word's not worth a bucket of shit on a diarrhea farm."

As Randy expected, the mention of Pauley's grandfather—legendary head of a Providence crime family—hit home. After Pauley's release from juvie and his "internship" in Palermo (he'd hosed out stalls at a racetrack), Pauley had gone to great lengths to claim he was his own man. A hard worker who'd earned the right to trade on his family name fair and square. Regardless, the only people he was fooling were two-bit thugs even lower on the food chain than him. Them, and girls rebounding from bad breakups by sitting on Federal Hill barstools and trolling for the biggest money clips walking through the door.

And Pauley knew it, judging by the way his smile stayed flash-frozen on his face a moment too long before drooping downward like the onset of a stroke. For the first time since he sat down opposite the punk, Randy felt as if he was looking at the real Pauley.

"You think I'm bluffing," Pauley said at last, lowering his sunglasses and narrowing his eyes in a manner meant to project violent death. An effect somewhat undercut by the schmutz on his chin.

"I think you're an asshole," Randy said. "But I guess I don't have a choice here, do I?"

If Randy's remark about Pauley's grandfather took the wind out of his sails, Randy's capitulation buoyed up the wannabe gangster. At least to judge by the smile dawning on his pimply face.

“That’s what I’m talking about,” Pauley said. “An accord. A compact. A conformity between friends with mutual interests.”

“A conformity.”

“How’s Monday work? For the first deliverable? Same time, same place?”

Randy gritted his teeth so hard he felt sure his jaw had locked.

“Monday. It is.”

Three days.

Everything on the line.

Now what the fuck was he supposed to do?

TWENTY-ONE

Sherm's Pawnshop sat on a side street a few blocks from downtown Attleboro sandwiched between a long-vacant video store and a Subway. Traffic was moderate, mostly cars and vans with an occasional box truck rumbling past.

The shop wasn't big; two picture windows extended on either side of the door displaying guitars, hand tools, and kitchenware. On the far left perched what appeared to be an early 2000s computer monitor, big and bulky as an anchor. Five or six bicycles blocked most of the sidewalk outside the entrance.

Carter checked his watch. Already past eleven. He decided to give it a few minutes before taking his chances and strolling inside, seeing if he could determine if the laptop was still there. Maybe weasel information out of Sherm about Donny. A phone number, maybe. It wasn't much, but it was all Carter had.

As he settled in, he thought about what he knew so far.

A young woman from Cranston, Rhode Island, named Terri Watkins, a drug addict and prostitute, disappeared and was presumed dead by her distraught parents. End of story. Except suddenly, it turned out she was very much alive to judge by her effort two nights ago to escape her handler-slash-pimp, a big guy named Donny, by fleeing from a gas station in a downpour. As Terri ran, she thrust an envelope holding her grandmother's ring and a businessman's card with her parents' number written on it into the hands of an innocent bystander.

So far, so good. Except it turned out that the businessman, a banker named Jason Schulte, was dead. *Tragically and unexpectedly passed away.* Cause of death unknown, but Carter had his suspicions. Suspicions based on the death of a second man, Shaun V. Volpe, who according to his stepsister was declared dead of an overdose after meeting a prostitute in his car and subsequently being robbed. The prostitute not a surprise but the drugs out of character. Volpe was possibly connected to Terri because Donny used Volpe's stolen credit card to buy gas at Narragansett Get 'n Go the night of Terri's escape.

Enter Carter, who randomly happened upon a woman named Linda Stauch trapped in her wrecked car in the rain after fleeing the gas station and Donny. Carter made Donny's already bad night worse by refusing to leave the scene. A day later Carter came *this close* to meeting up with Terri after following an underling named Jimmy from Jason Schulte's house to the Attleboro apartment.

Now came the confusing part. More confusing.

A new player was on the scene. The guy who breached the door at the Attleboro apartment building and went in gun blazing. A professional, in Carter's judgment. An agility that spoke of operational training. Maybe a cop, but based on his rogue movements either on the take or more likely off the force. More important than who he was, was the question of why he was at the apartment to begin with. Besides the obvious: *I need that fucking laptop*. Why? What was so important about that computer that the guy, the operative, would opt for a gonzo entry like that? Did he know the people inside, who turned out to include Donny and—in a tantalizingly close encounter—Terri Watkins? Was he a john who, unlike Jason Schulte and Shaun Volpe, had escaped their fate and was seeking revenge?

Carter retrieved his phone and texted Rhonda Rausch, Volpe's stepsister, on the pretense of checking in. He added a question about whether Shaun was missing a computer. It was a longshot, but nothing about the past few days was normal. No immediate response. Oh well.

Carter returned his thoughts to the new player in Attleboro. He dismissed the idea that he was a john. The guy, with his Steven Seagal black-ops duds and CrossFit physique, had the look of a man on a mission. A mission involving a laptop that the new player wanted, and badly.

So now here Carter was, parked outside a pawnshop where he could only assume Donny had taken the stolen laptop. Taken it before he realized it had more importance than just some hardware worth a few bucks? If that was the case, hopefully Donny would be back wanting to know what was really on it.

Carter leaned against the headrest as he mulled everything. As often happened, what was supposed to be a simple delivery had gotten complicated. The job for Lenny Pellegrino was on hold. On hold while Carter tried to find Terri Watkins to make a second delivery—the ring—so he could get back to his first job, wrap up his business out East, and drive home to Rochester and Tomeka.

Despite his best efforts, Carter's eyes were winking as exhaustion from the past couple of days kicked in. He couldn't afford to fall asleep now, staking out the pawnshop, but he was so tired. Fortunately, his phone buzzed with a call.

He recognized the number.

Pawtucket police Detective Gus Papaleonardos.

Wherever they were, Terri's new digs weren't much better than the shithole in Attleboro. She thought maybe the south side of Providence, but couldn't be sure. At least she wasn't working—for now—so there was that.

Of course, there was the whole prisoner thing to deal with.

Donny had crimped a straight steel brace around Terri's right ankle tightly enough to draw blood if she wiggled her foot too much. He'd hooked one end of a heavy-duty padlock through a hole at the end of the brace and slipped a chain link onto the lock. He'd clicked the lock shut and used another lock to secure the other end of the chain to a bedroom radiator. Then he acted like the Pope because he left enough play for Terri to reach the bathroom. Sometime that morning, while she was still asleep on the room's thin mattress, he placed a bottle of water and a pile of microwaved burritos in a bowl next to her like she was no better than a dog.

Which maybe she wasn't. He needn't have worried, though Terri didn't tell him as much. His threat to put her back on the streets if she complained was enough to keep her quiet.

Staring dully at the room's flaking wallpaper printed with red roses, Terri thought about Sheena and hoped she was okay. She wondered about her parents and her grandmother's ring. She considered with a sinking heart whether she'd thrown the keepsake away for nothing. What an idiot she was, believing she could save herself by relying on a stranger, a startled woman pumping gas in a downpour who probably saw Terri as the total loser she was and tossed the ring as soon as she spied Donny charging out of the gas station. Terri wiped away a tear at the thought of it lying crushed in an oily puddle in the station parking lot or worse, gone forever down a storm sewer grate.

Overwhelmed by despair, Terri examined her prison. A small bedroom with one window, its tattered shade drawn over the interior security bars. No furniture other than the mattress and a file cabinet in the corner. Casting around, her eyes settled on the room's empty closet.

Slowly, legs as heavy as if she were trudging through deep snow, Terri rose and approached the little room. Her chain clinked like in that cartoon about a Christmas ghost. She made no effort to disguise the noise. Whatever happened, happened.

She peered inside the closet. A hook on the left, like you'd hang a dress on, or a blouse, or a going-out jacket if you had money and a life and weren't a tricked-out junkie chained to a radiator God knows where. Somebody with value. You could hang other things there too, she thought. Slowly, Terri lifted a strand of the chain that Saint Donny had shackled her with. She raised it to eye level like she'd seen a priest do with the chalice at mass long ago. Then, almost without thinking about it, she looped the chain around her neck. Once, twice. A third time. Hand sweaty, fingers trembling, she lifted a length of the chain—two feet, no more—and slipped a link over the hook. She tugged on it. It held. The hook was screwed to the wall as solidly as a branch jutting from an oak trunk.

You saw stuff in movies, on TV. Read about things on the internet. She was pretty sure you kind of leaned forward. Let your weight do the rest. She didn't know how long it would take. How much it would hurt. Right now none of that mattered. Why should it? Someone like her, who did the things she did and then threw away the only thing she owned that mattered, didn't deserve much in the way of pity.

Terri squatted, testing the hook. No give at all. Slowly, she dropped her right knee to the closet floor, feeling the chain dig into her neck. The discomfort was immediate but also a relief of sorts. All she had to do was drop her left knee, fall into position, let her weight do the rest. Why not? At this point, after everything that had happened, maybe it was for the best.

TWENTY-TWO

"Where the hell are you?" Papaleonardos said. "What happened to you dropping off that evidence—the ring and the business card?"

Eyes on the pawnshop door, Carter hesitated a moment, weighing the pros and cons of showing his hand. Mostly cons, he decided. Thought briefly of Tomeka's anger over those traffic stops. Plunged ahead anyway.

"I'm in Attleboro."

"I thought your delivery was in Providence."

"It is. As I explained, first I'm trying to find Terri Watkins. I'm sorry about yesterday. Something came up."

"In Attleboro?"

"Sort of. I happened upon a possible lead here."

"'Happened upon?' What's that supposed to mean? What kind of lead?"

He hedged a bit. "Information on the guy who's controlling Terri." Carter paused. "The guy I got into it with the night Mrs. Stauch had her wreck."

"What kind of information?"

Carter instinctively reached back in time and put his cop hat on. "In the course of my investigation, I developed a lead that suggested he was here."

"Lose the jargon. This guy—got a name?"

Carter hesitated again, but only for a second. "First name Donny. Don't have a last name."

"Donny?"

"That's right."

"That's one step above nothing. Wanna guess how many Donny LNUs New England has?"

"Point taken. Nothing off his gun, I assume?"

"Not that it's any of your business, but no usable prints. All the rain that night didn't help."

"Sorry to hear that. Unfortunately, that's all I've got right now. How's Linda Stauch doing, by the way?" he added before Papaleonardos could reply.

"Out of the woods, but still in the hospital. I talked to her and her sister again this morning."

Carter thought briefly. "Her sister. Abigail? Abigail Shipley?"

"That's right. You should have mentioned you were there the other day. Abigail told me you asked her some questions."

"That's true."

Carter heard a sigh on the other end, as if someone had saddled Papaleonardos with a month of weekend shifts.

Reluctance in his voice, Papaleonardos said, "They're grateful to you for your assistance. Linda doesn't remember anything after she hit the pole, but the incident at the gas station is coming back to her. The guy—Donny—terrified her. She thought he was going to kill her. How about you?"

"How about me what?"

"Do you think he would have killed her?"

Weird question, Carter thought, *but this whole week was turning out weird.*

"Objectively speaking, I would say he was extremely angry in the moment. I think he was more interested in what Terri gave Linda than in harming Linda herself. But that could be a distinction without a difference."

"What she gave Linda?"

"The card and the ring."

"All the more reason I need them ASAP."

"Understood. And I promise—"

"Linda said he was a big guy," Papaleonardos said, interrupting. "Six four at least. Heavyset, but quick."

"That's right."

"I made Abigail describe you. She said you're the opposite of a big guy. She remembers thinking she was surprised you fended him off—Donny. How'd that happen? You were unarmed at first, right? According to your statement?"

Carter unexpectedly felt his temper flare, as if Papaleonardos had suggested the Toronto Blue Jays didn't count as real baseball.

"I'm five ten, as it happens. I'm guessing you know my background. USPIS agents get the same training as all the other feds. Maybe more. The feebees chase crooked accountants. I went after guys who pistol-whipped mail carriers."

Carter felt himself winding up. He took a breath. Papaleonardos had touched a nerve, but further explanation was pointless. Plus, despite a lingering chip on his shoulder, Carter wasn't USPIS anymore.

"I wasn't implying—"

"Hang on."

A familiar blue van turned onto the street and parked two doors up from the pawnshop. *Well, well.* After a moment, Donny emerged, the look on his face like a man dead set on claiming his lottery ticket payout, and shouldered his way through the store's front door.

"Carter?"

"I'm here," Carter said, shifting in his seat. Mind turning over, recalling last night's events. Donny LNU holed up in a crappy apartment possibly doubling as a brothel. Donny maybe hoping to make a few bucks off a laptop he previously delivered to a pawnshop, when out of the blue an unannounced visitor suggests the computer might have intrinsically higher value than Sherm could offer for it.

"Carter?"

"Listen," Carter said, eyes pinned on the pawnshop door. "Something else has come up. There's a good chance I can get you the ring and the card—what's left of it—by the end of the day. It isn't going to happen right now or the next couple of hours."

"Are you kidding me?"

"Unfortunately not. I understand your position. I also made a promise to Terri Watkins's parents. You can check with them if you want."

A long pause.

"Detective?"

"As it happens, I spoke to them earlier today."

"And?"

"They confirmed your story. About contacting them. And them hiring you to find Terri." Papaleonardos' begrudging tone that of a man acknowledging that UFOs might be real.

"Good to hear. They say anything else?"

Another pause. "They're appreciative that you're willing to look for their daughter."

"Just appreciative?"

A sigh. "Deeply appreciative."

"Also good to hear."

"Mrs. Watkins wasn't pleased when I told her we might have to charge you with obstruction of justice unless you handed over the ring."

"She's gone through a lot." Carter recalled the grief paralyzing the quiet woman's face as they gathered in the Watkinses' living room, the spaniel resting its head on her lap. Grief followed by the glint of hope, like the twinkle of quartz in a wall of slate, when she saw the ring and processed what Carter was telling them about Terri. He flashed to the story Jim Watkins told him outside, away from Valerie, of his bereft wife giving up cooking.

Papaleonardos said, "Be that as it may, I still need to find this Donny whoever, which includes factoring that ring and the business card into the mix."

"I understand. But—"

Carter stopped. Donny had reemerged from the pawnshop, a slim gray laptop in his hands, a look of fierce determination on his face.

Carter said, "What if I find him for you?"

"This is a police matter, Carter. You should know that better than anyone. Injecting yourself into an active investigation isn't advisable."

"Give me twenty-four hours. If I don't have anything after that, I'll be in your office with the ring and the card within the hour. Promise."

"It doesn't work that way."

Donny got into the van, started the engine. Carter positioned his right finger in front of the Suburban's engine-start push button. He didn't like putting Papaleonardos off because he knew the detective was right. Carter also knew he had a delivery to make, and he valued his priorities, as unorthodox as they might seem.

The van pulled away from the curb. An idea came to Carter. He brought the Suburban's engine to life.

"Got a pen handy?"

"What?" Papaleonardos said.

"I'm going to give you a couple of names you might want to add to the mix."

"What names? What's this have to do with anything?"

"Here they are. Jason Schulte and Shaun V. Volpe."

Papaleonardos made Carter repeat them. He said, "Who are they?"

"I've got to go," Carter said, pulling into traffic.

"Answer the question. Who are these guys?"

"They're dead," Carter said, and cut the call.

TWENTY-THREE

"Terri?"

Doorknob rattling like a window shaking during a storm.

She didn't answer. No need. She'd thrown the dead bolt herself.

"Terri, open the door."

She crawled farther under the blankets.

"Terri, open the goddamn door." The rattling even louder; her grandmother seriously pissed.

"Go away."

"I'm not going away."

Silence for maybe five minutes. Terri thought she was in the clear. She poked her head out of the blankets, fighting through the haze of her high long enough to take in her surroundings. Her grandmother's upstairs spare bedroom, a cave of polished wood furniture, most of it buried beneath her grandma's crocheted blankets. White bookshelves lined with photo albums, beach shells, and paperbacks with covers of bare-chested guys with serious six-packs reaching for scantily clad girls with boobs the size of softballs. You go, Grandma Dottie. *In the corner, a TV smaller than most microwaves that got exactly two crap stations. A room that had started out as a respite from the latest screaming match with her father but was turning into one more place where she'd tried to hide but couldn't.*

The silence continued. Another minute passed. Then a sound, loud, from outside, like a board slapping the side of the house. A pause, followed by a series of metallic creaks. Something or someone was out there. *Terry sat up in bed and stared. A moment later, to Terri's astonishment, her grandmother's head appeared in the window.* What the fuck?

"Grandma?"

"Stand back."

As Terri watched in disbelief, her grandmother reared back and stabbed at the window screen with a kitchen knife. Three stabs later, a long gash split open the screen mesh. Slowly, like something in a dream, Terri's grandmother pushed herself through the opening, balanced for a moment on the windowsill, half in, half out, then tumbled to the floor like a seal sliding off a rock outcropping.

Jesus Christ. *Terri didn't know such a thing was possible, let alone that her petite grandmother, five one in stocking feet, could accomplish the task.*

"What the hell is going on with you, anyway?" her grandmother said, standing and brushing herself off.

"Go away," Terri mumbled.

"Fat chance of that, Cupcake." Her grandmother sat on the bed and took Terri into her arms.

"Don't call me that."

"Call you what? Cupcake?"

"Stop it."

"Stop what, Cupcake?"

"Jesus, Grandma—"

"Cupcake. Cupcake. Cupcake."

Terri swore and tried to wriggle free, but her grandmother held her all the more tightly.

"Oh, Terri," she said. "Oh, Cupcake . . ."

Terri jerked her eyes open, gasping for breath. It took all her remaining strength, but she lifted her right leg enough to raise her knee an inch or two. Planting her foot on the closet floor, she pushed up, feeling the pressure lessen on her neck as the loop of chain biting into her throat lost its grip. She took a deep, shuddering breath, grabbed the chain above her, and slowly pulled herself into a standing position.

She paused a few moments, immobile, legs trembling as if she'd run up three flights of stairs from a cold start. She looked around, taking in the bare room, the peeling wallpaper, the stained mattress, the radiator that the long chain binding Terri was locked to. Her latest prison cell.

Also an empty cell, other than her.

So who said her grandmother's pet name for her—*Cupcake*—loudly enough that it jolted her out of the fatal unconsciousness she'd been slipping into just seconds before, chain looped around her neck, despair numbing her veins like the sweetest, deepest, longest hit she'd ever taken?

What the hell just happened?

Slowly, massaging her throat, Terri limped across the room, dragging the chain behind her, and stepped into the bathroom. She didn't bother shutting the flimsy door while she peed. Finished, she returned to the mattress, sat down heavily, took a swig of water, and bit off half a burrito. It tasted like a mass of cold, wet cardboard but she choked the mouthful down anyway. When she was done, she tugged half-heartedly at the chain, but the lock securing it to the radiator was solid and the bolts securing the radiator to the wall didn't budge.

The sound of the chain made Terri think again of that show about the Christmas ghost. After the voice she heard in the closet, the ghost thing had her wondering. *Cupcake.* So loud and distinct, the speaker might have been standing beside her as Terri gave up and let her dead weight take over. The possibility froze her bowels, as if the radiator itself had spoken. Up until this minute, Terri wouldn't have said she believed in ghosts. She still wasn't sure she did. But she knew her grandmother's voice, despite her being gone since—she thought, forcing herself to remember—a year at least. Could that have really have been her, come back from the grave to keep Terri from joining her there?

Eyes wet, she recalled the bizarre day her grandmother banged a ladder against the side of her house, climbed it, and tore up a screen window with a kitchen knife rather than let Terri stew inside alone. By then, Terri had already seen some weird shit, and some bad shit—really bad—but that kind of thinking had never occurred to her.

"You're crazy, Grandma," she whispered that afternoon after giving up the battle to resist her grandmother's embrace.

"As a spinster banshee," she replied, repeating one of her stock phrases that Terri never understood.

"The fucking window," Terri said.

"You got it, Cupcake. And watch your fucking mouth."

Terri laughed in spite of herself. In spite of the high she was still coming down from that day. Rage burning her up inside. Despair darkening her vision like a wool cap forced over her head and held in place no matter how she struggled.

"The window," Terri whispered.

"There's always windows, Cupcake," her grandmother said, holding her even tighter. "Never, ever forget that."

Terri shook her head, forced herself to focus. Outside, down the street, someone shouting. Farther off, the sound of a car horn. Incongruously—like a violin at a baseball game—a gull's cry in the near distance.

She took another bite of burrito. She rattled the chain. She thought about wrapping it around Donny's neck and grinned. The first time in a while.

Fucking window.

"That's a lot of pills," Monica said.

"A fair amount," Vickers replied.

She stared at the dozens of small, blue ovals packed into clear, shrink-wrapped plastic bags inside the duffel bag currently sitting on her and Randy's kitchen island.

"These are Oxycodone pills?" she asked.

"Fake oxycodone," Vickers corrected. "These are fentanyl, or fentanyl laced. They're generic looking-enough to pass for anything from Ambien to Viagra, but they're deadly."

"How do you know that?"

Annoyance flitted across Vickers's face, like the shadow of a raptor gliding over a country road. "It's the kind of thing you pay me to know."

That's not what we pay you for, Monica thought. But what she said was, "You just took them?"

"More or less. After I went inside, I saw the bag by the kitchen door. It seemed like an opportune moment. I figured, why not?"

"No one tried to stop you?"

Vickers's eyes danced back and forth for a second. The motion barely perceptible. But Monica knew that look. The one that meant he was lying.

"Nope."

"No one else was there?"

Back. Forth.

He shook his head.

A sound in the hallway. They both looked up. Randy appeared, back from the visit to the office after the chamber luncheon. Assuming that's where he actually went. She'd deal with that later.

"Well, well," Randy said, entering the kitchen and crossing his arms as he eyed the duffel bag.

"Told you," Vickers said, unable to disguise his excitement.

"Okay," Monica said, still bothered by Vickers's response to her question of whether anyone tried to stop him. "So, how much?"

"Not sure. Few hundred, easy."

"She means, how much are they *worth*?"

Trust Randy, pulling up a chair beside her at the thick end-grain butcher block island that cost twice Monica's first car, to get to the crux of the matter.

Vickers hesitated a moment before replying. "Three hundred thousand? Maybe three twenty-five, three thirty."

If Randy was impressed by the figure, he didn't show it. He said, "These guys are dealers?"

"Looks like," Vickers said. "But nothing to write home about. Street level at best."

"Any idea their source?" Randy said.

"Hard to say. New England's swimming in this shit. Whole East Coast is. Probably Mexican. Possibly Chinese."

"Okay. What's the play?" Randy said.

"Like I said before, it's bait, pure and simple. They're going to want this back. We agree to return them in exchange for Chuck's laptop."

"Assuming they still have it and it's not in some teenager's bedroom after they pawned it."

"Assuming that, yes," Vickers said, annoyance back on his face. "If that's the case, we trade for the information instead. Force them to prove to us the thing's out of commission permanently."

Now it was Monica's turn. "Is that how Chuck died?"

"What do you mean?"

"He took one of these?" She gestured at the package on top of the pile. "Was he a drug addict on top of the porn and sex thing?"

"I think it's safe to say that one of these pills is what killed him," Vickers said. "Whether he knew what he was taking is beside the point. Guys do drugs with whores all the time. He probably wasn't stopping to ask what she was giving him. What matters is they had the pills and now we do. And they're going to want them back."

"Specifically, how do we work it?" Randy said with a familiar growl. Vickers looked at his watch, a weighty chunk of multiple dials and digits that seemed better suited to a safari in Botswana than a townhouse in Seekonk.

"I'm guessing by now they know they've been ripped off. Just to be sure, we give them another hour or so, then we make contact and cut the deal."

"How?" Randy said. "It's not like we've got their phone number."

"True. But they've got something even better."

"Which is?"

"I've seen the police report, remember? Chuck's laptop wasn't the only thing missing. Whoever these guys are, they took everything. Including his phone. We call that."

"Unless they pawned that too."

"Well, yes," Vickers said. "Hopefully they hung onto it."

Randy didn't hide his dissatisfaction. But from Monica's perspective, she had to admit it was an elegant solution, if a little messy around the edges. She'd give Vickers that. There were times when she had second, and third, thoughts about their plan to go into business together. Once Randy . . . well, once he wasn't around anymore.

Then came the times when Vickers served up a ballsy plan like this, something she never would have considered, and she thought, *You know? This could actually work, the two of us.*

Monica looked at Randy for confirmation that he agreed. The look he returned was not what she expected. He looked relieved, to be sure. Relief tinged with natural frustration at their predicament. There was something else there, something she hadn't seen in his eyes in recent weeks.

It was the look he flashed when he initially showed up at the RIDOC medical clinic. And flashed again when, four days later, he took her for the first time, from behind, in the clinic bathroom as she gasped at his thrusting, urging him on.

It was the same look as when he broached the concept of Second Act Staffing Solutions—the real concept, not the shiny façade part. A look, like a flag snapping in a different direction as the wind changes course, that meant going on high alert to prepare for whatever was coming next.

It was a look Monica knew well.

A look of opportunity.

And right at the moment, with so much on the line, it was making her damn nervous.

TWENTY-FOUR

Carter stayed two, then three car lengths back from Donny. He couldn't afford to be seen, but he couldn't afford to lose him, either. Not if he wanted to find Terri once and for all.

Ahead of him, Donny blew past the turn that would have taken him back to the Attleboro apartment building Carter tracked him to the night before.

Interesting.

Following Donny's progress, Carter realized he had two objectives. The first, obviously, was to find Terri. As far as he could tell, no simpler way of doing that than keeping Donny in the crosshairs. Whatever Donny was up to with the laptop, Carter felt certain he would circle back to Terri eventually. In this scenario, Carter was the cat following the rat to the cheese.

The laptop, though, created a complication that led to Carter's second objective.

The complication came in the form of an unknown operative so hell-bent on retrieving the computer that he rushed into the Attleboro apartment building willing to face whatever he found alone.

That was a guy whose single-mindedness Carter could respect, if not his intentions. The kind of guy who would stop at nothing to achieve his goal. Again, something Carter, who had never missed a delivery, might admire. The fact that the operative seemed not much better than a mugger in a dark alley notwithstanding.

All of which meant Carter had one extra thing to do besides finding Donny and then Terri.

He had to get to her before that guy did.

Randy eyed Monica out of the corner of his eye. He knew the look on her face. He recognized it the first day he saw her in the RIDOC medical facility, an expression he found almost as enticing as her curves, grin, and attitude. Absent that look, he likely would have carried on with their affair regardless, as long as he was serving out his time anyway. With the physical spark between them, he'd have been a fool not to.

He readily agreed to continue things on the outside, however, because of that look. The look that confirmed he'd found a kindred spirit. The look of a born grifter, like himself.

A look of opportunity.

And right now, with everything on the line with Michelle, it was making Randy nervous as hell.

First and foremost, Randy blamed himself for what happened to his daughter. How could he not, since the accident occurred when he was inside?

At a basic level he knew that wasn't realistic, not that he gave a shit. Things were long over between him and Bethanie at that point. She'd moved on literally and figuratively and taken Michelle with her. Her winning full custody had been a slam dunk given Randy's record. Albany might as well have been the moon considering everything he had going on in Providence and environs, even before he went back to prison, although he did what he could. Which amounted to two visits in three years. Which was where the blaming himself part kicked in like a shotgun blast to the gut.

Next, he blamed Bethanie for hooking up with Howie, a certified loser if Randy ever saw one.

Randy supposed he couldn't fault her, at least at first. The nest egg that Howie came with was undoubtedly attractive, since a lot of Randy's early schemes didn't pan out all that great. What Randy didn't get was why she kept Howie on after he drank and smoked most of the money away. Kept him around when Howie couldn't replicate his supposed prowess at the poker tables, either online or in person, which was where the nest egg came from in the first place. Allegedly. Somehow those "construction jobs" Howie took to fill in the gaps between down times never produced actual paychecks. And soon it was Bethanie, working as both a Walmart picker and a part-time call center customer rep, who carried them on her back.

Last but not least, Randy blamed Howie. Because it was his idea to take Michelle swimming at his buddy's apartment complex pool. Ostensibly to give Bethanie a break on a rare Sunday off. Really to provide cover for the afternoon of partying with his buddy that Howie had planned. Partying that started in his buddy's apartment with grain alcohol–laced Red Bulls and blunts the size of a middle finger and continued poolside with a cooler crammed with Heinekens and Coronas. The two of them plus Michelle, alone after a brief rainstorm cleared the pool an hour earlier. Not a real surprise when Howie's buddy stumbled off to take a leak. Or that Howie, sprawled on a pool recliner, passed out as Michelle splashed dully in the shallow end.

How was he supposed to know she couldn't really swim, Howie said later. Hadn't he told her to stay away from the deep end?

In his darkest hours, Randy cursed himself for thinking that it might have been better if the woman who made out Michelle's still form on the bottom of the pool had arrived two minutes later.

Because, as a doctor tried to explain to a hysterical Bethanie that night, two minutes more and Michelle would have been past help. Miraculously—the doctor said—the estimated three and a half minutes Michelle was under was short enough to give them hope.

Of course, that was before the doctors knew the full impact of the brain damage Michelle suffered during those three and a half minutes.

A diagnosis that Randy learned about three days later, when Bethanie finally got around to notifying him via a JPay message.

He bided his time and did what he could. Working his connections, he diverted five thousand dollars from a state emergency housing fund with help from a stolen Social Security number and sent the money on to Bethanie to help with expenses. He started a side business hustling cell phones into the prison, all profits of which went to Michelle.

Once he was out, Randy went to work in earnest. He couldn't believe the money that was available for the taking by sending a few texts and emails. By promising certain returns on investments that never quite materialized. Laughable compared to the pittance his one and only bank robbery netted him, and with none of the risk of physical harm. People, especially old people, seemed to be looking for any excuse to open their wallets to a stranger. Mention abused animals, wounded veterans, or children with birth defects, and the money flowed like cold beer on a hot day.

Yet somehow it was never enough, given the cost of Michelle's care. That expense, and then—in a twist that even coldhearted Randy regretted—Bethanie's breast cancer diagnosis. That's why Randy thought he struck gold when a friend of a friend offered to sell him stolen Google Drive usernames and passwords in exchange for a cut of any proceeds.

That feeling only intensified when, on the third day of trolling accounts, Randy found pictures of a smiling, sandy-haired, hail-fellow-well-met sort on a yacht. Doing things below deck with girls who definitely weren't out of high school. A couple of emails and phone calls later, Randy was staring at sums he thought might solve his—and more importantly, Michelle's—problems permanently. In hindsight, he realized he went too far in desperation, especially after Bethanie entered hospice. Apparently, even pillars of Newport society had their limits, teens' loose bikini bottoms be damned.

Back inside Randy went, with his daughter well cared for, for the time being, but with monster bills coming down the road. Which was right around the time Randy persuaded a CO to take him to the RIDOC medical clinic for a sore arm. An arm hurt when Randy rattled the teeth of a fellow inmate who objected to Randy's request for overdue payment on a cell phone delivery. An ache Randy passed off as a workout injury.

Once at the clinic, prepared to dish his usual bullshit, he instead found himself staring at a no-nonsense, full-figured, bleach-blond nurse named Monica who took one look at him, said, "Sore arm from push-ups, my ass," and that was that.

Finally, he'd found someone with ambitions to match his. Which was why, in an odd way, he regretted telling Monica about Michelle.

It's not like he had much of a choice: his marriage to Bethanie was public record and Michelle's accident had been in the news. Regardless, he knew Monica resented the expense. Fair enough: he resented it, too. Like him, Monica operated first and foremost on a "Look Out for Number One" philosophy. Which was one of the reasons he appreciated her so much. That look of opportunity. And also why he kept an eye on her.

The problem was, because Monica knew about Michelle, she also knew about Howie. More to the point, what happened to Howie. His disappearance. Which was messy. And protracted.

Because Randy had first wanted to make sure that Howie understood—that he fully appreciated—the role he played in Michelle's accident. Understood, before Randy finally heeded Howie's pleas for mercy and put him out of his misery.

Randy's misery, he meant.

Monica knew all that. And Randy knew she wouldn't hesitate to use it against him if the tides shifted. For example, if she decided she could cut a better deal with Vickers.

Which was why he'd been thinking Monica might have to go.

A simple enough solution, if regrettable.

Then this shit show with Chuck went down.

Fuckwad Chuck, piling onto Randy's other problem. Namely, the squeeze that that two-bit, rat-faced, small-time operator Pauley Carnevale was putting on Randy. A squeeze that had Randy ready to launch the Quadrant Horizons operation despite the plan not being fully developed. Because without the windfall from Quadrant Horizons—and they were talking so much money, *so many* patient records ripe for the picking—Michelle would . . .

Randy didn't allow himself to finish the thought.

Instead, Randy went back to the newest hitch in his plans. Vickers's cockamamie scheme to trade a stolen duffel bag full of drugs for a stolen laptop. Yeah, what could go wrong there?

Except, as had just occurred to Randy, the cockamamie scheme had a possible flip side. A silver lining. A kill-two-birds-with-one-stone vibe. If Randy could make this work, and it was a big if, he could deal permanently with Pauley and stay on track with Michelle.

Make that, kill *three* birds with one stone.

It was a real opportunity.

Randy stepped away from the kitchen island on the pretense of hitting the head. Door closed, he retrieved his phone, found Pauley's number, and sent a text.

We need to talk

TWENTY-FIVE

Sure enough, Carter saw, they were back in Attleboro again, but nowhere near the apartment building from last night. That made sense, he thought, recalling the police pounding on the door. Whatever that place was to Donny—a brothel way station, a hidey-hole, a fencing joint—it was officially compromised.

Donny's van came to a stop on a narrow residential street lined with two-story houses in competition for the most dented siding, peeling paint, or sagging roofs. The houses, most so close that a woman with a decent wingspan could stand between a pair and touch windows on each side, sat below a forested hill—a park of some sort. Cars lined both sides of the street.

Seeing too late how crowded and congested the block was, Carter caught a break—halfway up the street an alley cut to the right. He turned into it just before it would have been almost impossible to turn around and risk exposing himself to Donny. Carter turned right onto the next street, thought about how to proceed, side-eyed the woods behind the houses, and drove up the hill. Hopefully a bird's eye perspective would get him the answers he needed.

"Backup," Monica said to Vickers.

"Just a couple guys."

"A couple."

"Maybe three," Vickers said.

Heads bowed together at the kitchen island, Randy in the bathroom. The two of them whispering. Why, she wasn't sure. Close enough that she smelled Vickers's sandalwood cologne. Not that long ago, she'd smelled that scent as he'd taken her on this very island—Randy away for the afternoon—giving her a newfound appreciation for the smoothness of a properly cared for butcher block surface. That felt like a long time ago, though it had been only a few weeks. A lot had happened since then, including Vickers's unsanctioned breach of an apartment in Attleboro he supposedly was visiting for reconnaissance purposes, nothing more. Despite Vickers's proximity at the island today, the only stirring Monica felt at the moment was impatience.

"Why three guys?"

"It's a belt-and-suspenders thing. You can't be too careful with drug dealers. In my experience."

"Which experience is that?"

"Duh."

He meant his experience on the job in Providence. Or rather, that was the impression he was trying to give. More and more, Monica was wondering exactly what kind of experience Vickers had on the job.

In any case, she knew the backup he was talking about. The same guys she'd nixed the night before—high and tight buzzes, washboard abs, pecs the size of small moons. For just a moment Monica second-guessed herself. Maybe if she'd gone along with that plan, they'd have the laptop back and wouldn't be screwing around with pissed-off drug dealers with connections to God knows who.

"Plus, it's kind of a test run," Vickers said.

"A test run?"

"Like a tryout."

Monica didn't reply. As much as she hated to admit it, Vickers had a point. His second good idea in the past twenty-four hours, if you included the drugs-for-laptop scheme.

Although the opportunity that she and Vickers privately dubbed The Plan was solid, in her opinion, it also hadn't been means-tested. The Plan she and Vickers had cooked up sans Randy. On paper, it looked doable. Start with Second Act's business model as developed by Randy—the infiltration of health-care facilities under the cover of temp employment. The business model plus the seed money that Chuck had been helping them squirrel away without Randy's knowledge. Add Vickers's vision: a private security company specializing in protecting high-value properties.

Under the cover of providing that security, gather information about the occupants of the houses—the mansions—and their guests. Plant cameras left and right. Document everything. Compile the information into portfolios. When the moment was right, present the owners or their guests, or both, with the information and suggest extra fees might be in order.

It had almost worked for Randy, hadn't it? With the guy on the yacht and the teenage girls? Randy always maintained, at least privately, that his biggest mistake was greed. Making too big an ask.

Monica disagreed. Randy's mistake hadn't been greed. It was threatening to expose the mark and stopping there.

Therein lay the brilliance of The Plan. She and Vickers weren't going to use the portfolios to threaten people undertaking illegal actions with exposure.

They'd use them to suggest improvements to the illegal actions. Along with a request to be cut into the deal.

It was a viable scheme. But with expensive start-up costs. Costs that the expected revenue from the Quadrant Horizons breach would cover.

Except much of that money was earmarked for Randy's handicapped daughter's long-term care. Money Randy refused to give any ground on. It's not as if Monica was heartless. But wouldn't Medicaid provide nearly as good care?

Randy hadn't taken kindly to that suggestion.

Which was why she'd decided to move ahead with The Plan without him. Because she'd been thinking that Randy might have to go.

Down the hall, the sound of a flushing toilet.

"Two," Monica said to Vickers.

"Two of us against an unknown number of perps? Not smart."

"*Perps.* Really?"

Vickers rolled his eyes. "*Baddies.* Whatever."

"What I meant was, two *more.* You and two of your buds makes three. That's it. Anything else and it's like a battalion or something. We're trying to avoid trouble here, not publicize it."

"Three more would be better. And safer."

"Just do what I'm asking for once, how about it? If three of you guys can't wrap this up, I'm not exactly sure what we're doing here."

Monica could tell by the look in Vickers's eyes that the "we're" struck a nerve. Implicit in their affair all along had been the understanding that, at some point, they'd execute The Plan. Themselves, without Randy, whatever that looked like. Just as soon as Quadrant Horizons came off.

All that was implicit in Vickers's understanding, anyway. Beyond launching The Plan, Monica couldn't make any promises. She hadn't gotten this far by divulging her secrets to whichever man she was currently using.

"Listen," Vickers hissed.

"Shhh," Monica said.

Randy emerged from the bathroom at that moment. He stared at Monica and Vickers. Pretending to study her nails, Monica splayed two fingers on the edge of the table.

"What?" Randy said.

"Nothing," Vickers and Monica said at the same time. She cursed under her breath. Randy couldn't have looked less convinced had he caught them in flagrante delicto.

But what he said was, "Let's get this party started then, why don't we?" His normal bass even deeper, like a foghorn at the bottom of a well. "We don't have all fucking day."

Terri dozed off and on, lying on the thin mattress, waking up occasionally to sip water or eat more of the now sodden, stone-cold burritos. She called out a couple of times but either her voice was too weak to carry or Donny and them were ignoring her. The latter, she figured.

She scraped the chain binding the crimped metal brace to her foot against the radiator to see if it would break. All she did was cramp her hand and cut her forefinger. The five minutes of work left barely a scratch on the chain link. Maybe if she had a week uninterrupted. *Right.* Otherwise, she was stuck. No, not stuck. Trapped.

Ghost or not, the memory of her grandmother's wacky window maneuver had Terri thinking about a plan. Mainly, that she needed one. But what? It's not like she had the physical strength to do anything. Donny could swat her down like a one-winged fly if she tried to take him. Escape seemed unlikely, either from this room or Donny's clutches. He'd lost her once, at the gas station. She could be damn sure he wouldn't make that mistake again.

She shook her head. She needed something else. Something . . . clever. Clever like Grandma Dottie. The problem was, Terri had no idea what. Her mind didn't work that way, even when it wasn't addled by the shit Donny had her on. Frustrated, she hugged herself. She scratched her belly, praying against hope the mattress in the shithole Donny had stuck her in wasn't full of bed bugs. She jammed her hands into the pockets of her sweats.

And felt it, in her right pocket.

She pulled it out. Brushed off the lint. Stared at it. She had no recollection of why she had it. How Donny lost track of it. But there it was. Small, oval, blue as a baby's blanket.

She permitted herself a small smile, then remembered her confidence by the river right before Donny found her. She zipped her mouth shut. Frowned for good measure. And tucked her find back into her pocket. It wasn't much. It might not work. But it was something.

Terri had found a window.

TWENTY-SIX

Up above, at the top of the hill in Attleboro, Carter came almost immediately to a service road leading into a light industrial park that abutted the woods. He took his first left, pulling into the half-empty parking lot of Overton Jewelry, a wide, single-level brick building with an official-looking, glass double-door entrance. Carter parked the Suburban in a space in the business's last row, beside the thin strip of lawn separating the parking lot from the service road. Overton had a tired feel to it, with a weed or two poking through the mulch lining the front walkway and cracks spiderwebbing portions of the parking lot. Tired or not, a jewelry manufacturer meant Carter was probably on camera, which time-limited his mission. Which was fine. Because this was hit or miss regardless.

Grabbing a pair of binoculars from his utility vest, Carter walked across the parking lot, crossed the road, and entered the woods with the stride of a man on a mission. A few yards in, he glanced back at the road and the Overton parking lot. All quiet. Satisfied, he followed a narrow animal path through the trees until he reached the far side. He looked down, found Donny's van on the street below.

A minute passed. Carter glanced behind him again, but he'd come far enough that the trees blocked his view of his Suburban in the Overton parking lot. He couldn't stay parked there for long, but hopefully he had a little time.

Five minutes.

Seven minutes.

Eight.

At nine minutes, a pickup truck with two heads visible inside turned onto the street and pulled even with Donny. Windows were lowered, words were exchanged. Carter was too far to make anything out. A moment later, the truck advanced and pulled into a spot one car ahead of Donny, the last free spot on the street. After another minute, the pickup's doors opened and two men stepped out.

One, Carter didn't recognize—Black, built, gray hoodie, face as blank as something chiseled from obsidian—but the other he made immediately: Jimmy, from the night before.

Okay. That was a development.

The last time Carter saw the man, he was laid out on the kitchen floor of the Attleboro apartment with the cops thirty seconds from entry. With an almost-had-to-be trafficking victim named Sheena babbling in the haze of her high behind him.

The fact that Jimmy wasn't pacing inside an Attleboro jail cell but instead was free and easy in a down-market neighborhood meant the cops hadn't had enough to hold him. Which triggered something in Carter's memory. Something he'd forgotten until now.

Just before Terri staggered downstairs, Donny's gun to her back, Carter had noticed a duffel bag in the corner of the apartment's kitchen. Half opened, but the shrink-wrapped plastic bags of blue pills inside were unmistakable.

When Carter awoke after his brief tussle with the operative, the duffel bag was gone.

Donny and Terri, hightailing it out the door, hadn't taken it. He was sure of that.

It wasn't there after Carter awoke and rooted through the garbage for clues, just before Jimmy got the jump on him.

Which left only one person.

The operative, the ex-cop-looking guy, swam into Carter's vision. The guy hell-bent on finding a laptop.

Movement below caught Carter's attention. Donny emerged from the van, laptop under his arm. He and Hoodie, trailed by Jimmy, mounted the chipped concrete stairs of a house just up from Donny's van, stepped past a mud-green couch bowed in the middle, kicked a pair of empty beer cans out of their way, and approached the door. Hoodie knocked, hard. In almost no time at all, the door opened and all three—Donny, Hoodie, and Jimmy—disappeared inside.

Carter glanced behind him again. Close to fifteen minutes had passed. He couldn't have much longer before his Suburban drew unwanted attention from the jewelry company.

Just when he was ready to give up, return to his car, and gamble he could drive back downhill and figure out a way to keep an eye on Donny unseen, the three men reemerged from the house.

Without the laptop.

By mutual agreement, Monica and Randy let Vickers test the theory that the people who had Chuck's Second Act Staffing laptop also had his phone.

Misplace something? Vickers texted the number, along with a photo of the duffel bag.

Too flip for Randy's tastes, but he let it go.

Vickers waited an additional five minutes before dialing Chuck's phone. He placed the phone on the table and set it on speaker. It rang unanswered.

Minutes passed. Vickers tried again. Nothing.

"What do I do?"

"Once more," Randy said. "After that, we assume they don't have it."

One ring. Two. Three . . .

"Yeah?"

Itching to move, Carter forced himself to stay on the hill and observe a moment or two longer. The three made it to the street and were about to return to their respective vehicles when something happened. Jimmy stopped, reached into his pocket, pulled out a phone, and answered. A few seconds later, his look of boredom was replaced by shock as he lowered his phone and studied it as if it might go off in his hand.

What was happening here?

Carter set aside his concerns about his Suburban and the jewelry company parking lot and continued his vigil.

Vickers said, "See the text I just sent?"

Silence. Then the voice again, scratchy and high-pitched. "Who the fuck is this?"

"Someone who wants to make a trade."

Silence. Almost a full minute passed. Then, a new voice.

"Whoever this is, you're screwed beyond belief."

The new voice was deep and guttural, summoning the image of a two-pack-a-day smoker who yelled a lot during NFL games.

Vickers replied too fast, but Randy couldn't hold his hand forever.

"Maybe. Or maybe it's someone with an offer you might want to listen to."

A long pause, followed by a sound—the clearing of a throat—like a downshifting tractor trailer.

"Offer of what?"

This time, Vickers took his time replying. The strategy made Randy think that Vickers believed he had the upper hand. That he was going to enjoy the encounter at every turn.

"A trade," Vickers said. "You get that bag back." Emphasis on *back*, Vickers underlining he'd pulled a fast one by taking something from the caller. "In return, we get the laptop belonging to the man whose phone you're talking on."

Now it was the man with Chuck's phone's turn to pause.

"Why would I trade for something you stole? Maybe I'll just take it."

Vickers laughed. "Good luck with that."

Another pause. "Not sure luck's got anything to do with it. How about I drive down to Maynard Street, kill everyone I find there, take what's rightfully mine, then burn Second Act Staffing to the ground?"

Vickers froze, the man's threat hanging in the air over them. Sensing disaster looming, Randy reached out and muted the phone.

"What the fuck," Monica said.

"Shit," Vickers said. "The company name must have been on the laptop."

Rage ballooned inside Randy's head. It was all he could do to keep from grabbing the phone and smashing it into Vickers's face. Right between his eyes. Smashing until the screen cracked and slivers of glass needled Vicker's pupils. This was his *job*. Managing shit like this. Making sure that Chuck's liabilities as a human being—and they were legion—didn't affect the deployment of his mad computer skills. Which Randy had needed more than ever in the past couple of weeks, what with Quadrant Horizons coming up. With the financial killing he needed to make on Michelle's behalf.

Thinking of Michelle brought Randy back to earth. Reduced his blood from boiling to a low simmer. Reason returned.

Eyes on the phone's timer ticking away the length of the call, Randy waited for a count of five, took a deep breath, and said, "Use your head. Our name wasn't on that laptop. Even money says Chuck had his wallet with him and they found a business card or business receipt or something. It's not like Second Act isn't a real company." He thought bitterly of the Chamber of Commerce award. "The guy's just trying to scare us." Staring at Vickers, Randy said, "Set the meet so we can get this over with."

"But listen," Vickers said. "What if we . . ."

"What if we what?"

"Couldn't Aiden trace this guy? The fact he knows about us changes everything."

"Knows about us thanks to you."

"Fuck you. It's not my fault Chuck had a thing for porn and skanks."

Randy saw Monica flinch.

"I'll be the judge of that," Randy said. "Anyway, we don't have time for that. Plus, Aiden has more important things to do."

"Like what?"

"Like Quadrant Horizons?"

No one said anything. On the other end, the sound of the man's heavy breathing.

"This is not my fault," Vickers said at last.

"Finish the job," Randy said by way of reply. "Now."

Frowning, unsuccessfully hiding the flick of his eyes in Monica's direction, Vickers unmuted the phone, and said, "Congrats. You know the name of the company. Along with half of Rhode Island. You come after us, we're shooting first, take my word for it. We don't want that. We want to make a simple trade."

"Not so simple," the man said.

Randy tensed.

"Meaning what?" Vickers said.

"Meaning you seemed pretty desperate last night when you tried to shoot us up. You and that other guy. Which has me thinking this laptop's worth something. You want to make a trade, it's gonna cost you."

Monica and Randy shared a glance.

Other guy?

What other guy?

TWENTY-SEVEN

Confused, Carter studied the scene below him. Jimmy, looking pissed, had handed the phone to Donny after a few moments. That much was clear. Carter could also tell that whoever was on the line with Donny, he or she wasn't calling with good news. The anger in Donny's eyes was visible even this high up. As Carter watched Donny's face grow darker and darker, he scrambled to put things together.

How was any of this related to the mess at the apartment building the night before? Could it be connected to the duffel bag of drugs that Carter suspected the operative type had grabbed on his way out? How did Terri Watkins fit into this scenario?

Most importantly: How much longer until Carter could deliver the ring to Terri and get back to Rochester?

Below, Donny glanced at Jimmy, directed his attention to the phone, and drew his forefinger across his throat.

Randy paused a second, considering what the man on the other end of the phone had just said. *You want to make a trade, it's gonna cost you.* He nodded at Vickers.

"Cost me what?" Vickers said.

"Fifty thousand. Plus the bag."

"Are you fucking kidding me?" Vickers shouted. Randy reached out and muted the phone again.

"Scott."

Vickers snapped to attention as if Randy had slapped him.

"What?"

"What 'other guy' is he talking about?"

Vickers eyed Monica. To her credit, Randy thought, she ceded nothing, offered no port in a storm. Her blue eyes were lakes of ice keeping a drowning man in winter from reaching air.

"Scott," Randy said again.

"No one. I don't know. Some guy who was there last night. I don't know who he was."

"A john?"

A moment's hesitation. "I don't think so."

"A cop?"

Vickers shook his head, but not convincingly.

Monica said, "Why the hell didn't you mention him before?"

Vickers looked from one to the other. A squirrel trapped by two dogs. "I didn't . . . I don't know. It didn't seem important."

"Another witness to your screwup didn't seem important?" Monica said. "Didn't seem worth mentioning?"

"Things got chaotic. I wasn't sure it mattered."

Randy couldn't help himself. "*Fog of war*?"

Suns of anger flared behind Monica's icy eyes. Randy met Monica's gaze. A glance they didn't try to disguise. He saw in her expression the same contempt he was feeling toward Vickers. It might not repair the damage over her betrayal, but it was something. He calmed down slightly. He rolled a couple things around in his head. Thought about the whispered conversation in the bathroom he had with Pauley after Vickers first proposed the drugs-for-laptop trade.

"I might have a new opportunity for you."

"Like what?" Pauley said, bored.

"Like an introduction to the big time."

"I've already got that, my man. It's called Second Act Staffing."

"Don't be a dipshit, Pauley. That's penny-ante crap compared to what I'm talking about."

"Who's the dipshit now? I know what you're up to. How much that personal health information shit goes for."

"Whatever you think that amount is, triple it. For starters."

Silence.

"What the fuck are you talking about, Randy?"

Randy counted to five.

"Ever heard of fentanyl?"

Back in the moment, Randy looked at Vickers, said, "Hold that thought," and unmuted the phone.

"Hey, dirtbag," he growled.

No reply. Then: "That you, Randy?"

Perfect. The guy had been to Second Act's website. Figured out who he was. Randy supposed it would be wrong to gouge out Vickers's eyes while this call was underway.

"You got him," Randy said.

"So?" the gravel voice asked.

"So what?"

"The deal. Yes or no?"

Randy waited a beat, and said, "No."

"No?"

Vickers stared at Randy, shocked.

"You heard me," Randy said.

"I heard you kiss your laptop goodbye."

"What you heard is someone slicing off your balls if word gets out."

"What are you talking about? Gets out about what?"

"How easy it was to lift product from you. Like taking candy from a baby, except at least a baby would flex its fat fucking fingers and hang on tight."

The line was quiet.

Randy said, "Glad I've got your attention. To be more specific, here's what I'm going to do. I'm going to spread the word down every rathole from here to Maine that you lost some valuable shit. Shit I assume you owe someone for. Someone who wants to balance his books one way or the other. Once word gets around, you'll be lucky to score an ounce of horse. Assuming there's anything left of you to find."

Randy stopped. He had more to say. But less was more at this point.

"In your dreams," the man said, but not convincingly.

Randy held his breath and didn't say anything.

Several long seconds passed. "Midnight," the man said at last, and added: "I'll text you the address."

"You'll text me shit. Here's where we're meeting." Randy gave the address that he'd come up with. That he and Pauley had come up with. "We'll have the pills. Don't be late."

Before the man could reply, Randy cut the call.

Vickers couldn't have looked more dumbfounded at the outcome had Randy kissed him full on the lips and added a crotch tug for good measure.

"What the fuck," he managed.

Randy sat back. "The fuck is, it's time to get to work."

Carter watched as Donny cut the call, pocketed the phone, and limped furiously toward his van. He looked like a man ready to tear apart the first person who crossed him with his bare hands.

Which was Carter's cue to move. He lowered the binoculars, turned, and sprinted through the woods back to Overton Jewelry and his Suburban.

TWENTY-EIGHT

Carter figured he had maybe a minute to roll downhill and renew his tail. He picked up the pace, only to emerge from the woods and spy a woman in black trousers and white long-sleeved shirt sporting a wide utility belt standing next to the Suburban. A plastic badge on the right side of her shirt identified her as an Overton security guard. The gun on her belt looked real, as did the Taser and cuffs.

"Afternoon," she said as Carter approached.

"Hi there."

"You can't park here. This is a private business." Black hair pulled into a tight ponytail. Brown eyes that never left Carter's face. Light brown hands brushing the utility belt.

"I apologize," Carter said. "I was just on my way."

"What were you doing over there? In the woods?"

Carter feigned a need to catch his breath, to give himself time to think. Now that he considered it, the Overton Jewelry parking lot was probably covered by five different security cameras. He should have counted on that.

"Sir?"

It came to him. "To tell you the truth, I was bird-watching."

"Bird-watching."

Carter raised the binoculars with his right hand and gestured across the road. Stomach churning, thinking about Donny and Jimmy and the other guy piling into their cars, starting their engines, headed for who knew where. Making their escape. What if this was Carter's last chance to learn where they had Terri?

"What kind of bird?"

"Bird?"

"The one you were watching."

"Right. Uh, coastal tanager," Carter said. "Very rare. There's been some sightings in Attleboro recently. I thought I'd try my luck. I apologize for leaving my car. I thought about parking on the side of the road but that seemed maybe dangerous." He fished his keys out of his pocket.

"Do you have ID on you, sir?"

"Of course." Slowly, Carter reached for his wallet and handed her his license. She squinted at it.

"Rochester? Long way to come to see a bird."

"Not any bird," Carter said. "The coastal tanager. Not endangered, but getting close. I could show you some pictures?" He raised his phone. "Other birds, too. I have a lot of pictures. I was in Ohio last year to see a nesting pair of roseate terns. I must have taken two hundred photos." He made to open his camera app.

"Thanks anyway," the guard said, handing the license back. "I have to ask you to leave. Like I said, private property."

"Not a problem," Carter said. "Sorry for the inconvenience."

He played it cool as he climbed into the SUV and slowly pulled out of the Overton lot, even as he cursed under his breath. Just as he feared, there was no sign of Donny's van or the other men's pickup truck as he pulled onto the street below. He must have missed them by a few seconds thanks to the guard. He briefly considered knocking on the door of the house they'd entered, quizzing the occupant, seeing what he could find out. The scene had the vibe of Donny taking the newly valuable laptop to a hacker for hire, but Carter couldn't be sure. Or be sure if he cared.

He decided to gamble, continuing down the street and turning right, the only way he could go.

He tapped his brakes almost immediately. A hundred yards ahead of him, Donny's van moved into the intersection through a green light. The pickup was gone, which probably meant that Donny, trailing, caught a red. Carter did the math in his head. If the security guard hadn't yanked his chain like that, made him produce ID, there was a better-than-even chance that Carter would have pulled up directly behind Donny at the light. Meaning a better-than-even chance that Donny, already on high alert from everything going on, not to mention that mysterious phone call he just took, might have made him.

Luck again? Carter would take it.

He drove through the intersection, paused on the other side to let a car pull in front of him out of a Shell station, and continued on, always keeping Donny in view.

The trip lasted twenty minutes. Five minutes in, Donny caught up with the pickup. They stayed on city streets, passing a highway entrance ramp. A local operation, then. Carter shadowed them as they headed into downtown Providence, then up a hill toward what looked like a university district. As he drove, Carter considered what he'd witnessed back on the Attleboro street. What was the phone call that Donny took on the street after dropping the laptop off? The one that twisted Donny's face like a man who grabbed the wrong end of a mousetrap? What was that all about? Who was calling him?

They turned onto Hope Street, headed north. They drove several blocks. Slowly, triple-deckers chopped into apartments gave way to single-family homes. Moms pushing strollers replaced students shouldering backpacks. Two men walking a pug chatted with two women walking an Irish wolfhound. With Carter's concentration broken as he glanced at the dogs, he almost missed the right turn the pickup and the van took onto a wide, leafy side street. McGandy Avenue. After the afternoon he'd had, Carter wasn't in the mood to lose Donny. He slowed, pulled over, counted out fifteen seconds, and turned right himself. A block up, he saw the two vehicles parked in front of a Colonial brick pile, set off from its neighbors by bookending lines of fir trees. He pulled over as far back as was practical, left the Suburban running, retrieved his binoculars, and waited.

Nothing happened. Donny and his companions stayed put. A cat left the yard to Carter's right, strolled along the sidewalk, ducked into a hedge.

A minute passed. Two. Carter thought he might have it wrong. Maybe this was another wild goose chase. At best, a random stop to touch base with someone higher up on the food chain, or a chance to get their bearings before the real excitement started. Hard to believe they had Terri stashed in a neighborhood this upscale. Maybe Carter's best option was to return to Attleboro after all, lean on whoever was inside the house the laptop disappeared into, and hope the info led back to Donny.

Just then, a third vehicle arrived on the scene. New-looking black Ford F-150. Gleaming like it had just been washed and waxed. The driver rolled past Carter, hit the brakes a second later, parked on the opposite side of the street from Donny's van. Right in front of the Colonial. The window lowered and someone spoke to Donny. Donny replied, pointed at the house.

Carter raised his binoculars, made the Colonial's address, 1983 McGandy, and texted it to his uncle.

On it, his uncle replied.

Another minute passed. Donny and the man in the Ford continued to speak through their opened windows. A soccer decal on the back of the F-150 read *Club Tijuana*. Nothing about this felt ordinary, but Carter also couldn't fathom what was happening. Why were Donny and Jimmy and Hoodie and whoever was in the black pickup truck here? Who was in that house? What did any of this have to do with a missing laptop or Terri Watkins?

At that moment, to Carter's surprise, Donny started his van and pulled away.

Carter placed the Suburban in drive. He wasn't sure what was going on here, but Donny was his focus. Not Jimmy, or the other guy from the street in Attleboro, or this new guy, Club Tijuana. Carter had Terri Watkins to think about, and the laptop, and the duffel bag of drugs, and how all three might fit together. He was about to move in pursuit when his phone buzzed. A text back from his uncle. He stopped long enough to read the message.

That address comes back to someone named Charles Gibbons

Thanks, Carter replied.

Carter thought about leaving it at that. Curiosity overtook him. Foot on the brake, he plugged the name into his phone. The result popped up almost simultaneously with his uncle texting him the same information.

OVERDOSE SUSPECTED IN PROVIDENCE MAN'S DEATH.

Carter put the Suburban in park and turned off the engine. As he did, Jimmy, Hoodie, and the man in the Ford opened their vehicle doors, climbed out, and headed for the house.

TWENTY-NINE

Eyes on the Colonial, Carter once again considered his options. Once again, they weren't great; someplace between a 3–2 count and an infield pop fly. He didn't have much time to execute them, either way.

He watched from the Suburban as Jimmy pressed the bell on the house's front door. A minute passed and the door opened a crack, no more. That was enough—Jimmy forced his way inside, followed quickly by Hoodie and Club Tijuana.

This couldn't be good. The fact that Donny's crew strong-armed its way into a house owned by another person who died of an overdose—like Shaun Volpe, and presumably Jason Schulte—could hardly be a coincidence. They weren't there to borrow a cup of sugar. Who was Charles Gibbons? Could he be the owner of the laptop so valuable to so many people? With Gibbons dead, who was inside the house that Donny's crew needed to talk to so urgently? A spouse? Another player in whatever scheme Carter had stumbled upon?

Carter patted his Beretta, feeling it bump against the blackjack nestled in a pocket. He climbed into the Suburban's backseat, unlocked his metal storage container, rifled through it, brushed the top of the tackle box full of cash, thought about a flash-bang, changed his mind—too loud for residential operations—made his selection, and stuck the winner in his left pants pocket. He grabbed his standard-issue clipboard, the one holding an official-looking document that was actually a 2024 Rochester Amerks schedule, left the Suburban, and headed for the house.

Carter skipped the front door and instead strolled casually down the driveway toward the rear of the Colonial, an imposing line of dark firs on his left. Just another official-type guy checking stuff out. Ahead of him sat a two-car garage, door down. Passing a house window, Carter heard a man's voice, low and angry, followed by a woman's voice, equally angry but with a hint of desperation beneath it, like a car engine giving off a suspicious whine.

Then he heard her scream.

Carter shifted the clipboard to his left hand, slowed as he reached the back of the house, and cautiously stepped around the corner. A medium-sized yard revealed itself, tastefully maintained and landscaped. Paving stones encircled beds of mums and asters. Someone had a green thumb. Carter turned his attention to the two-level redwood deck jutting away from the back door. Grill on the lower level, patio setup above. He eyed the door. He was counting on rear entry, but there was always the problem of the door being locked. He caught his first break. The screen door was closed, but behind it the house door swung open against a hallway wall. The news wasn't all good. A shadow loomed in the hallway. A lookout. Made sense.

Carter heard a second scream, muffled now. Briefly, before the sound ended like a song on a radio abruptly turned off. A neighbor would be forgiven for mistaking it for something on TV. Carter moved fast, mounting the steps, pulling the screen door open. Hoodie, planted in the hallway, stared at him, no less surprised than if a bird—a coastal tanager, say—had flown inside.

"Sorry to interrupt," Carter said, raising the clipboard in his right hand like a man half-heartedly flagging a cab.

"The fuck—"

Carter forestalled further conversation by jabbing the bottom of the clipboard into the man's throat, hard and fast, just below the man's Adam's apple. The man made a sound between a gulp and a gasp as he sought air. His eyes widened in fear and his hands rose to his throat. One of them didn't get there. Carter dropped the clipboard, thrust his right arm out, a striking adder, and grabbed the man's right hand. He yanked the man's arm down and across his torso, spinning him off balance. As the man *glug-glugged* in panic and tried to regain his posture, Carter kneed him, paused, grabbed both shoulders, and rushed him through the door and out, the man rocking like a bar patron seven drinks in. Outside, the man stumbled forward and went down, striking the top step face-first with a wet smack. Carter waited. The man didn't move. Carter reached for his Beretta, paused, realized the man was still. He knelt, ran his hands around Hoodie's waist, found his gun, stuck it in his own waistband. He thought about binding the man's feet, studied the slow rise and fall of his chest, considered what was happening behind him in Gibbons's house. Best to leave him where he was and address whatever was happening inside. He pushed the door shut quietly, turned the lock, retrieved the clipboard, and headed deeper inside.

Carter had gambled on there being a smoke alarm. It was a risk. Some people didn't want them in the kitchen for obvious reasons. Cook a steak and have your eardrums pierced. No thanks—he got it. He had a couple directions he could go in but caught another break. The alarm was affixed to the kitchen ceiling close to an open door leading to what looked like a basement. Footstool height to reach, but that was okay. He was prepared. Carter set the clipboard on the counter, reached into his vest, retrieved the flea bomb he'd removed from the Suburban's metal locker. Holding it his left hand, he depressed the top, turned his face to the side, and raised it toward the smoke alarm as the fog poured out. It took longer than he hoped. At least a count of ten. The alarm was plenty loud when it did go off.

Carter heard the change in mood in the next room even over the alarm's high-pitched screech. Voices fell silent. A chair shifted as someone stood. Time slowed. Only for a second.

Club Tijuana was first through the kitchen door, wearing an expression of bored annoyance unique to men who've been interrupted while bullying a woman. In Carter's experience. That look changed as he spied Carter and his hand dropped toward his waist with practiced speed. Carter lowered his arm and directed the fogger at the man's face no more than two inches away. The man choked, coughed, made a sound like a curse, and raised both hands defensively. Carter pulled his gun and raked it across Club Tijuana's face, spinning him into the stove. Carter grabbed the collar of his black T-shirt and yanked him up in time to collide with Jimmy as he charged through the kitchen door from the living room. Carter stepped back and the pair crashed onto the kitchen floor with a thud, like halves of beef falling from freezer-room hooks.

A second later, Carter went down as Jimmy grabbed his left ankle and pulled him off balance. A painful kaleidoscope of colors exploded before Carter's eyes when Jimmy's sharp elbow connected with his jaw. Reeling from the blow, Carter felt himself go slack and lose his bearings. He was dimly aware of Jimmy raising himself up to strike him again. At the same time, Carter sensed Club Tijuana recovering and turning toward him with a raised fist. He sought in vain for his Beretta, realized through the veil of pain that he'd dropped it as he fell. Jimmy was on his knees now, leaning over Carter, inadvertently blocking Club Tijuana. Carter raised his left hand and directed the fogger at Jimmy. A second passed, Jimmy knelt in an odd, frozen repose, and then began coughing violently. Carter slowly lifted himself up and then drove his left knee up hard into the other man's face. Both Carter and Jimmy hit the floor again. Carter took a breath, reached his hand left, and right, and found the Beretta. He was struggling to get on his knees, leveling the barrel in the direction of Jimmy and the second man, when he heard a sound.

Carter looked up and found himself staring at a woman in a red blouse and jeans, her face pale and eyes wide, as she pointed her own gun at the trio of men in her kitchen.

Carter's mind raced. "Friend of Charles," he gasped. "Here to help."

The woman hesitated. That was enough. Carter used the last of his energy to fall more than leap toward her, pushing her gun arm away from the chaotic pile. He rapped her hand against the doorjamb and heard her cry out as the gun dropped from her hand and clattered to the floor.

"You son of a bitch," she gasped.

"Hold that thought," Carter said.

"Like hell," she said, turned, and ran.

She was faster than Carter expected. Plus, after the business in the kitchen—not to mention the last forty-eight hours—he wasn't in any condition to win a footrace. By the time he made it out the front door and down the steps, she was halfway up the block.

"Hey," he yelled, aiming for the sweet spot between sounding like a concerned friend and coming off as a deranged relative. "Like I said, friend of Charles. Hang on."

This time *Charles* caught her up, but only for a second. Carter started to jog, remembering at the same time that he was still holding the

Beretta. He holstered it, glancing around to be sure the gun hadn't been seen, and picked up the pace. Ahead of him, the woman crossed the street. She paused at the opposite side, grasping a stop sign for a moment as if to recover her balance, and continued on. Carter realized for the first time that she was limping.

"Hey," he said again.

She turned and rewarded him with her middle finger. Carter saw the fear in her face. She was assuming he was with the three men who'd barged into her house, despite his efforts to thwart them. Made sense. He'd have done the same.

A moment later, the woman angled toward a woody boulevard thick with joggers and dog walkers. He'd lose any chance of safely making his case there, without question, and invite unwanted attention while he was at it. Carter broke into a run, closed the gap between them. His mind raced, figuring out how to break through her fear. A thought came to him.

"Charles didn't OD," he said to her back. "He was murdered. I need your help figuring out what happened."

The woman stopped, leaned against a utility pole. She placed her left hand over a *Lost Dog* flier stapled to the pole, covering a photo of a sad-eyed Lab. The Lab answered to *Buddy*. The woman turned warily toward Carter, and for the first time he saw a bruise forming on her left cheek.

"What did you say?"

Carter repeated his statement.

The woman took a deep breath, looked up at the sky, looked back down.

"Tell me something I don't know, why don't you?"

THIRTY

Carter gambled and escorted the woman across the street to the boulevard and the path running down the middle. On the one hand, the fear on the woman's face would likely elicit wary glances at Carter, who might be reasonably suspected of putting her in that mood. On the other, the path and its late afternoon parade of exercisers provided decent cover in case Jimmy and crew were out looking for her. On balance, worth the risk.

Carter decided to level with her. Often the best policy. As odd as the truth usually sounded. Mercury Carter. Freelance mailman. The car accident he came across in the rain two nights ago, followed by Donny's attempted assault. Jim and Valerie Watkins's request that he look for their daughter, Terri. His subsequent discovery of the deaths of Jason Schulte and Shaun V. Volpe and their similarity to what he knew of what happened to Charles Gibbons. He rushed his words, realizing he probably had one shot before she or someone else dialed 911.

Leaving a few details out, Carter also reviewed his pursuit of Donny, as well as his—Carter's—curiosity at the importance of a laptop that Donny had and that other individuals seemed to want. He wrapped up with the late-afternoon tail from Attleboro that led him to the woman's house. The woman whose name he still didn't know.

When he was finished, they walked in silence for a few steps. At last, she said, "That's quite a story."

"I guess it is. I'll understand if you don't believe me. But it's the truth."

She limped along for a few more steps.

Carter said, "Sorry to ask this, but you're . . . ?"

"What?"

"You're related to Charles? Is that right?"

"Chuck. Yeah."

Carter didn't say anything.

"I'm his wife." She paused. "Was his wife."

"I'm sorry."

"Me too."

Carter let a few more seconds of silence pass.

"I thought I was a goner," she said.

"What's that?"

"At my house. When those guys came inside. I knew Chuck was up to something, in over his head, but not like this. Drugs? I thought he was smarter than that. Shows how much I knew."

"Drugs?"

"What those guys kept saying. 'Tell us where the fucking drugs are.' Like I had any idea." She paused, throat catching as if she'd taken a drink of water too fast. Carter considered her words, thought back to the missing duffel bag of pills from the Attleboro apartment. He told the woman what he was thinking.

"I don't know about that," she said. "One of them said something about Chuck's boss, that either he had the drugs or I did. Like I know anything about that."

As she spoke a pair of joggers approached from the opposite direction, man and woman, both sporting a pair of white earbuds, which always made Carter think of mini marshmallows, each lost in their individual workout mix. Carter reached out, touched the woman's elbow to keep her from shifting her direction, and forced the couple to jog around them. A moment later, he realized Chuck's widow was staring at him.

"What?"

"Are you a cop?"

Carter shook his head. "Used to be, but not now. Like I said, these days I deliver stuff for a living."

She appeared to ponder this. Carter put her in her late thirties and observed in that moment how she was turning a few heads on the path, even after her roughing up and despite her casual clothes. Thick black hair piled atop her head in a messy bun, wide mascaraed eyes dark as ripe olives, plumped lips that probably had had some work, as had her chest, which filled her T-shirt in the same way her hips filled her jeans, but Carter wasn't there to judge. A woman of the sort his uncle, twice divorced, might call a "looker." Which had Carter momentarily thinking less about the woman and more about her late husband.

She said, "Deliver stuff like what?"

"Depends on the client. Look, I need to ask you a couple quick—"

"No offense, mister, but you're not exactly Hulk Hogan. If you're even telling the truth, how'd a 'mailman'"—her hands went up in air quotes—"how'd *you* manage all that back there? I could see one, maybe two tops. But all three?"

Carter bristled for a moment, as he had when Papaleonardos asked him the same question about Donny. He forced himself to relax.

"Beginner's luck. And I am telling the truth."

She laughed, a hollow falsetto filled with skepticism. And fear, Carter realized a moment later, seeing that she was trembling.

"How do I know you aren't with them? That this isn't a setup to get me to talk? Like bad-guy, good bad-guy shit."

Carter grinned in spite of himself. "That's a decent idea, actually. I'm gonna try that next time I'm playing a good bad guy. Short of that, you can't. You'll have to take my word for it. Or just walk away. I won't stop you. Promise."

That caught her up. She turned and glanced down the path, looked left and right, and ahead.

"For real?"

"For real," Carter said, hiding his disappointment.

The woman stopped, stepped off the path, turned her back to Carter, and hugged herself. Carter stood uncertainly, ignored the buzzing of his phone. He was reaching for a business card to hand the woman before figuring out how to circle back and retrieve his Suburban, when she sagged against a tree.

"Fuck me."

"You okay?"

She shook her head.

Carter didn't say anything.

After another moment, she righted herself and wiped her eyes, smearing a bit of mascara.

"I can't go back," she said. "I can't go anywhere." Another pause. "Fucking Chuck."

They walked three blocks to a bar called O'Malley's with wooden booths the shade of newly lacquered dinghies, each dimly lit by a hanging stained-glass lamp. Patriots and Bruins posters and pennants plastered the walls. TVs on opposite sides of the bar showed the same late-season Red Sox–Guardians game. Carter forced himself not to check the score.

They settled in a booth in the back corner. She ordered a rum and Coke with extra rum. Carter asked for a black tea, listened patiently while the server explained they didn't have tea, and asked for club soda with lime wedge instead.

"Not a drinker?"

"Not really. Except for sake."

She shook her head at that. "Whatever."

"So," Carter said when their drinks came.

She put half her drink away and looked down the aisle for the server. "Tell me again how you found me?"

"For sure. As soon as . . . Sorry, would you mind telling me your name?"

She looked surprised, as if she assumed he already knew. She introduced herself. Stacy Gibbons. Chuck's wife. Now widow. She wiped away more tears, further smearing her mascara. Carter gave her a moment, then explained once more how he ended up at her house.

When he was finished, she said. "Shit. It sounds worse than I thought."

"Meaning?"

She shook her head. "Chuck always had these big ideas. Crazy dreams. 'The next big thing,' you know?"

Carter nodded. He knew about guys like Chuck Gibbons.

"He was good with numbers and computers and stuff, I'll give him that. Like, we went to Vegas a few years ago. I don't know how he did it, and I'm not sure I want to know, especially now, but we came home with the mortgage for that house."

Carter couldn't help himself. He glanced at the bar. Four–two, Guardians. With his father and uncle being from Toronto, the Blue Jays would always be his team. But he had a soft spot for Cleveland.

He returned his attention to Stacy. "Is that what he did? Work with numbers?"

"I guess."

"You guess?"

"He did IT for this company. Second Act Staffing. It's a kind of temp agency, with a do-gooder side."

"Meaning?"

She finished her drink and looked at Carter. He nodded, found the server at the bar, pointed at Stacy's drink.

"His boss, Randy something, is an ex-con. Got out, saw the light, turned himself around. That kind of thing. Randy and his wife hire other ex-cons, nonviolent offenders, and get them placements in hospitals, doctors' offices, like that. Low-level jobs, mind you. They also help them with training."

"Second Act Staffing," Carter said, calling up the website on his phone and skimming the homepage.

> *Our mission is simple. Company founder Randy Carmichael received a second chance in life and believes others should too.* Second Act Staffing Solutions *seeks to provide not charity, but rather a helping hand for those who made a mistake, or had mistakes thrust upon them because of socioeconomic, prejudicial, and environmental factors beyond their control.* Second Act Staffing *is first and foremost a business, but a business that places profit side by side with pride, purpose, and the development of lifelong employment skills.*
>
> *Second Act Staffing. Because There's Always a First Time for Second Chances.*

Carter sipped his club soda, examined the photo of Randy Carmichael and his wife, Monica. Eyed the scar above Randy's right eye and the door-not-quite-shut tilt of a never properly set broken nose. Blond and buxom, Monica had the wide eyes and big smile of one of his uncle's lookers.

"This is who Chuck did IT for?"

Stacy confirmed it. "He started there maybe two, two and a half years ago. The money's good, I'll give him that. He took me to Hawaii every year."

"IT's a big umbrella. Any idea specifically what he did?"

"Not really. He always made a joke of it. 'I keep the goddamn lights on babe.' Beyond that, I'm not sure. I'm not that great with computers, tell you the truth."

"What do you do?"

"Work at a lighting store, down in Warwick. Or I did. I haven't been back since Chuck . . . That's why I was home today, when those guys barged in."

Carter looked at the TV on the right. Red Sox at bat, bottom of the seventh, two outs, two men on base. The server broke his concentration as she arrived with Stacy's drink and a fresh club soda for him. He nodded his thanks. He rolled some things around in his head. Running a temp agency might have its challenges. Especially when it came to placing ex-cons in medical settings. But how much IT was involved at a company like that, especially since it was a small business? Payroll, some scheduling, the website? Did a job like that pay enough for annual Hawaii trips? Unless the IT involved something else. Like the reason the three men told Stacy they were at her house.

Tell us where the fucking drugs are.

Another thought.

I need that fucking laptop.

Carter said, "Sorry to ask this. The news item I saw said Chuck died of an overdose. You said those guys were asking about drugs. You think there's a connection?"

Stacy flinched as if he'd snapped his fingers in front of her face.

"It's bullshit, is what it is."

Carter sipped his club soda. "Why do you say that?"

"Chuck wasn't into that stuff, okay? I mean, he was a trash husband, if I'm being honest about it. He cheated on me, and more than once. Plus, he had—"

Anger twisted her face. Carter waited.

"He was into porn. He saw things online and then wanted me . . . Anyway, he told me he'd stopped, the porn and the affairs, but I'm not an idiot. I can guess what he was doing in that motel room. Who he was doing it with. But he didn't go there for drugs, if that's what you're asking, and he didn't sell them. I'm sure about that."

Carter recalled Rhonda Rausch's verdict about her stepbrother, Shaun Volpe.

He wasn't a drug addict, as far as I know. He drank too much. I admit it.

"I told the guy that, too," Stacy said, taking a slug from her drink as if it were the last rum and Coke in Rhode Island. "From Second Act. He was a piece of work, tell you what."

"Who?" Carter said, distracted once more by the game on TV.

"Scott something. Here I'm dealing with the fact that my husband's dead, God knows what I'm going to do, and all he wants to know is where Chuck's laptop is. Over and over. 'You sure it's not here in the house? Mind if I look?'"

Stacy had Carter's attention now.

"His laptop?"

She nodded.

"When was this?"

She took another drink and thought about it. "Yesterday, I guess. Feels like a long time ago, though."

Carter thought about the chaotic minutes in the Attleboro apartment the previous night that started when a new player, an operative type, ex-cop or ex-military, barged inside. He described the man he'd seen to Stacy.

"Sounds like him. You know him?"

"We haven't been formally introduced. He was hot on finding a laptop the last time I saw him. You're sure he was with Second Act?"

"That's what he said. I still made him show me some ID."

"Do you remember his name?"

She thought for a moment. "Vickers. Scott Vickers."

"Okay," Carter said, pausing to text the name to his uncle.

"He seemed legit," Stacy continued. "He knew all about Randy and his wife, Molly . . . no, Monica, I think. Said how sorry they were about Chuck. Not sorry enough to call me personally, I guess. Either way, it all came down to the laptop." She paused, something occurring to her. "Same as those guys back there."

"Sorry?"

"When they first came in, they wanted to know what was on the laptop as well. When I told them I had no idea, that's when they started in on the drugs." She caught Carter studying her. "Sorry. I was so rattled I forgot that part."

"It's all right, believe me." He gave her a second, then said, "Any idea what's so important about it? The laptop?"

She took another drink and shook her head. "All I know is Chuck brought it home every night and stuck it in the back of his closet. He had another computer, a personal one, that he used in the house. I showed that one to this guy, Vickers, but he said it wasn't the one he was interested in. Other than that, I have no idea. Work stuff, maybe? Chuck was protective about it, whatever was on there. He took it with us to Hawaii last year, which I thought was a little weird since he left his personal one at home."

Carter considered this point. It seemed clear the computer contained more than proprietary HR information, payroll, and a list of Second Act clients, at least according to what Stacy was telling him, and also from his own experience. Experience from his USPIS days and more recently making some unorthodox deliveries. But what? Drug supplier and customer info? Delivery info? A new thought: Was Second Act a laundering front?

Drugs would explain the home invasion that Stacy had suffered, as well as Jimmy and crew's demands. Stacy would hardly be the first woman to learn the hard way that her husband had a side hustle involving illegal substances. In that scenario, it was possible Second Act was a cover for a drug operation, which might make sense given all the medical settings that its employees were placed in. In fact, the more Carter thought about it, the more that seemed like a decent business plan for an ex-con who, reformed or not, probably kept his Rolodex from the old days.

"Hey, you in there?"

He looked up. "Sorry." He told Stacy his theory.

"I don't know. Like stealing drugs from hospitals, you mean?"

"Maybe?" Hearing it aloud made him rethink the idea. Carter knew perfectly well that protocols put in place during since the start of the opioid epidemic made it much harder for prescription drugs to go missing these days without alarm bells going off.

"I suppose," Stacy said. "I don't know what to think anymore." Her eyes brimmed with tears. "A week ago, my biggest concern was figuring out what hotel to book on Maui this November. Now Chuck's dead and I can't even go home. What the fuck am I supposed to do?"

As much as Carter wanted to stand up in that moment, walk out of the bar, track down Second Act Staffing Solutions and an ex-con named Randy Carmichael, and shake him for information about Terri Watkins, Carter knew he first had to help the woman sitting across the booth from him. He was about to press Stacy on whether she had anyone to shelter with—mom, sibling, friend—when his phone buzzed once more. Speak of the devil. Rhonda Rausch, responding to Carter's question about whether a laptop was among the items found missing after Shaun, her stepbrother, died.

No laptop. Everything else though. Wallet, phone, watch. Even his wedding ring

Carter mulled the depravity of someone—Donny?—stooping so low as to pull the wedding ring off a man going into respiratory distress from a drug overdose. Across from him, Stacy raised her glass to drain the last dregs of liquid. Carter caught the wink of her engagement ring beside her own gold band. He glanced back at Rhonda's message, then at Stacy's tired, haggard eyes. An idea came to him. It was a long shot. But what kind was left at this point?

THIRTY-ONE

Rhonda Rausch sounded more confused than skeptical when Carter reached her.

"This lady is who, again?" she asked.

Carter stood on the sidewalk just outside O'Malley's. He paused before responding, his voice drowned out by the hydraulic squeak of a RIPTA bus carriage sinking to street level to take on a man in a wheelchair. Stacy inside the bar at their booth nursing a Coke—sans rum at Carter's suggestion. The bus operation over, Carter repeated the request. Stacy Gibbons. Widow of Chuck. A connection between Chuck and Shaun in the form of their deaths. Both overdosed, sex with a prostitute involved, a robbery afterward. Someone—possibly the same team responsible for what happened to Chuck, Shaun, and Jason Schulte—was after Stacy now.

"Jesus," Rhonda said. "This gets worse and worse."

"It's not ideal," Carter said. "I'm sorry to ask, but I didn't know who else to call."

"How long would she be staying?" A brusqueness to her tone, like Carter was asking for money.

"Couple days? I'm not entirely sure, to be honest. I think I'm getting close, though."

"Close to what? Finding that lady? To give the ring to?"

"That's right."

"You're a determined dude, I'll give you that. Lot of aggravation for someone you don't even know. Ever think about just returning the ring and calling it a day? Make it somebody else's problem?"

"No," Carter said.

"Suit yourself, I guess."

Silence filled the air, Rhonda waiting for him to reply. He didn't. He didn't have anything left to say. He began formulating a Plan B—stashing Stacy in a hotel, letting her ride shotgun for a while. Then, to his surprise, Rhonda said, "Yeah, sure."

"Sorry?"

"We'll take her. Maybe we can get some of our own answers. What time can you bring her by?"

"Thank you. But, apologies, I wasn't clear. I need you to pick her up. I don't have my car and I can't leave her alone to go get it. Too risky."

"Risky why?"

Carter hesitated. "Risky because the men after her are determined. Well, were determined."

"Were?"

"I delivered a message that pursuing her was a bad idea. I don't know how good they are at listening."

"You got a funny way of asking for a favor, Mr. Mercury Carter."

"I've been told that."

"Why am I not surprised? Anyway, it's okay. We'll pick her up. This lady."

"You will?"

"What I said."

"Appreciate it. Oh, and Rhonda?"

"Yeah?"

"Be careful. Make sure you're not followed here."

To his surprise, she laughed.

"What's so funny?"

"See you soon," Rhonda said, and cut the call.

When half an hour and then forty-five minutes passed with no sign of Rhonda, Carter went ahead and ordered burgers and fries. Going hungry wasn't going to help anyone. The time was pushing seven o'clock. He was worried about Stacy. The reality of her situation was sinking in. She sat with head bowed and shoulders slumped as if someone was physically holding her in place. Tough to blame her: husband dead, temporarily homeless, on the run, possibly for her life. While they waited, he punched out a text to Detective Gus Papaleonardos with Chuck Gibbons's name and address.

Could be related to Jason Schulte and Shaun Volpe.

No reply.

"How much longer?" Stacy said after the food arrived, absentmindedly dipping a fry in the ketchup she'd squirted beside her burger.

"Hopefully soon," Carter said, raising his hamburger to his mouth, which was when he heard the rumble of an engine outside. He returned the sandwich to the plate and moved his hand instinctively to his chest, tapping the Beretta holstered beneath his utility vest.

"Stay here."

He walked past the bar to the back of the restaurant, found the kitchen, apologized to the two surprised-looking Latino men at the grill, squeezed past them, and carefully opened the rear door. He looked up and down the alley outside, taking in more engine rumbling. He considered unholstering the gun, thought better of it, and walked down the alley and around the corner, holding his hands loosely by his sides.

He stopped a few feet from the O'Malley's green awning, staring at the scene before him.

Rhonda Rausch was emerging from an older-model Toyota Sienna parked at the curb. Behind her, two men sat atop a pair of gleaming Harley-Davidsons. Carter squinted and recognized one of the black leather–clad men seated on the hog closest to Carter as Braden, Rhonda's husband. He looked blankly at Carter, then nodded almost imperceptibly. The other man, who looked like Braden's bigger and more muscular twin brother, tapped his helmet by way of a greeting.

Rhonda walked around the front of the van, stood before Carter, and crossed her arms over her chest.

"At your service," she said. "Where is she?"

Ten minutes later, night falling, Carter was retracing his steps toward Stacy's brick Colonial. Stacy hadn't been thrilled when she eyed the caravan idling outside O'Malley's. It also didn't take a sociology degree to figure out she was surprised her rescuers were Black. If that was a concern, it melted away the moment Rhonda walked up to Stacy and enveloped her in a hug. An embrace Rhonda continued even as Stacy burst into tears. Helping Stacy into the van, Rhonda told Carter not to worry. He lied and said he wouldn't. He walked back inside, paid his and Stacy's tab in cash, and stood outside until the minivan and its two escorts pulled away and disappeared down the street.

Carter called his uncle as he walked, filling him in on everything since the encounter at Stacy's house.

"Second Act Staffing Solutions?" his uncle said. "Yeah, I got it. I'll see what I can find out. Also, on this guy Scott Vickers? Looks like he was a Providence cop at some point, but I'll get you the details."

"Doesn't surprise me. He carried himself like a cop. The way guys do who used to be cops and think they still are. On Second Act, owners are Randy Carmichael and his wife—Monica, I believe."

"You think they're connected to Terri Watkins?"

"Maybe not directly? Holding pieces of the same puzzle, possibly."

His uncle sounded skeptical, but promised to dig into the research immediately. Carter thanked him and finished the walk to Stacy's neighborhood. He took a look around; no sign of the trio. Leaned over, checked the Suburban for tracking devices—none—and headed out.

Twenty minutes later, Carter pulled in front of a two-story brown brick building with a small sign—*Second Act Staffing Solutions*—beside the glass front door. Past seven thirty, making the turn toward eight o'clock. He stifled a yawn as he left the Suburban. The day, especially the events in Stacy's kitchen, was catching up to him. Not to mention the stuff from yesterday. Carter grabbed a remaining clipboard, selecting one with the pen attached by a ball chain, and walked to the entrance.

Not surprisingly, the front door was locked. Carter tried the intercom on the right but his buzz went unanswered. Also not surprising. Nevertheless, he assumed he was either being watched or was on a camera whose footage would be reviewed. Despite the hour, he played it nonchalant. A deliveryman working overtime; no biggie.

Satisfied no one was coming, Carter strolled around to the back, lowering his head to study the clipboard as if its manifest—a Nick Tahou menu from back home—held clues to what to do next. The parking lot behind the building, seven spaces plus a designated handicapped spot, was empty except for a Subaru Forester at the far end. A placard indicated the lot was reserved for Second Act—*Towing Enforced!*—so Carter took the presence of the Subaru as a good sign.

No intercom. Carter knocked on the door. And knocked again. Glanced at the fisheye lens above the door and knocked a third time. Feeling fatigue sink into his bones, he was about to call it a day when he heard footsteps. A second later the door opened to reveal a man the approximate size and shape of a small hill staring down at Carter.

"Can I, um, help you?" Raspy voice with a hint of wheeze pitched higher than Carter would have expected.

"Hopefully," Carter said, straightening his posture as he touched the side of his ball cap. "I know it's late, but I was wondering if"—he made a show of studying his clipboard—"Randy Carmichael was here?"

Panic crossed the man's face, as if Carter had announced himself as a city zoning inspector with an emergency evacuation order.

"They're not here," the man said after a moment, and added: "They're not usually here this late."

They're. Okay.

"I see. Possible to get a message to them?"

Now the man looked confused. His pale complexion, wizard-y beard, and soft stomach left Carter with the impression of someone who didn't get outside much, or didn't care to.

"Um, maybe." The man took a ragged breath. "Who are you?"

"Mercury Carter. I'm trying to make a delivery. I'm having a little trouble. I was hoping Mr. Carmichael might be able to assist me."

The man looked over Carter's shoulder and said, "A delivery here?"

"Not exactly. That I know of. It's probably better that I speak to Mr. Carmichael in person." Carter let that sink in and then showed his cards. "If it helps, it's connected to Chuck Gibbons and his missing laptop."

The man's eyes widened as if Carter had turned over his clipboard to reveal a top hat with a snow-white rabbit inside.

"This has something to do with Chuck?" the man stammered.

"Tangentially. I'm happy to go into more detail with Mr. Carmichael."

"I suppose I could get a message to him."

"That would be great."

The man looked at Carter expectantly. Carter stared back politely. Finally, the man said, "Do you have a card or something?"

"A card?"

"Like a business card. Or a number where he could reach you?"

"I do," Carter said, reaching for his wallet and handing over his card. "But maybe you could get that message to him now? Since I'm here? Happy to wait."

The man looked as if there were several things he'd rather do in the moment than message Randy Carmichael, starting with inserting hot needles under his fingernails. At last, with Carter keeping his gaze respectfully but inexorably trained on him, the man said, "Hang on," wheezing like someone on the brink of a whooping cough jag, walked inside, and shut the door.

Ten minutes, Carter thought. Ten minutes, and he'd decide whether to unholster the Beretta.

Based on the look in the man's eyes as he headed inside, Carter wasn't optimistic.

THIRTY-TWO

"Shit," Scott said, studying the feed from the security camera monitoring Second Act Staffing's front door. "I think that's him."

"You think, or you know?" Monica said.

"It's him, yeah."

"Him," Monica said. "Meaning the other guy from last night that you didn't think to mention to us until today."

"I told you, things were chaotic."

"Chaos you created."

Scott looked as if he might respond, but then thought better of it.

Still gathered around Randy and Monica's kitchen island. Scott increasingly feeling to Monica like a party guest who'd overstayed his welcome.

Monica held out hope that Scott's plan to retrieve the laptop would work. The information on Chuck's laptop—the actual purpose of employees' assignments to those random medical facilities, whether those employees knew it or not—was worth holding her breath for. What other option was there? If things went south, the end of her and Scott's post-Randy venture—The Plan—was the least of her concerns. This was fifteen-to-life stuff.

Still, Monica couldn't get past how the gravel-voiced player in possession of Chuck's phone had almost turned the tables on them. That he knew not just who they were, but where they were. Scott, the fool, had missed that angle completely in his rush to channel his inner badass and flex some muscles. Missed the possibility that Chuck's demise would lead a bad actor to Second Act. Thank God Randy pulled them back from the brink.

Randy. A second, disturbing thought occurred to Monica. Shouldn't Randy have caught the same fly in the ointment? It seemed odd that Randy hadn't anticipated the move. Instead, he'd rushed in at the last moment, the hero, to right the sinking ship and salvage the operation with that well-timed threat to expose the drug dealers' sloppiness in handling such precious cargo.

Was she missing something here? Had Randy set Scott up to fail? Could Randy know about Scott and Monica and was taking this opportunity—now, of all times—to punish her? Turn the screw on her somehow?

Further panic. If Randy knew about her and Vickers, could he know about The Plan?

No time to dwell on that now. Things had gone to shit once more thanks to Aiden's alarming call three minutes earlier.

Monica usually wrinkled her nose at the man-child's unkempt appearance, slovenly eating habits—so many donut bags; so many liters of Mountain Dew—and stereotypically undisciplined hacker's hours. All in contrast to Chuck's buttoned-down, fast-lane, ironic touch-of-Eurotrash vibe. Christ. Talk about judging books by covers. Thank God Aiden, for all his flaws, had still been working tonight.

Come to think of it, Monica thought, glancing at Randy. Why was Aiden working there so late?

Carefully, Monica lowered her phone to her lap and tapped out a message to Scott, sitting two feet to her right.

I'm worried about Aiden. If he's up to something with Randy.

Scott glanced at the text as it arrived but didn't respond.

"Who's that?" Randy demanded.

"One of my guys," Scott said. "Wondering what's up."

"What's up is—ah, this is just great," Randy said, setting his phone down.

"What?" Monica said.

"This Carter guy. He used to be a fed." He angled the results of a Google search so Monica could see. But not Scott.

Which was fine. With Randy's attention turned away, Scott responded to Monica's text with a thumbs-up emoji and a skull and crossbones.

Refocusing, Monica skimmed the results of Randy's Google search. "United States Postal Inspection Service? Never heard of it. Anyway, these links are old. What did he tell Aiden? He's making a delivery?"

"Maybe he's undercover," Scott said. "That's why I thought he was one of them last night."

Monica rolled her eyes. Lost beachcomber was more like it, what with the guy's cargo shorts, utility vest over a gray T-shirt, and baseball cap. Were the Rochester Red Wings even a real team? Carter looked like an ocean breeze might topple him over. It was obvious that Scott was spouting crap to cover his ass, to minimize leaving yet one more loose end in the wake of his rogue behavior last night. It was just as obvious that there was nothing to do about it now. The time for that would come later.

"Either way," Monica said carefully, "we can't let him screw anything up. We need to cut this deal and move on."

"Agreed," Randy said.

"What do we do about him?" Scott said.

Randy stared as if Scott had asked him the time in a roomful of clocks. "We're not doing anything. You are."

Carter retreated around the corner to his Suburban as soon as ten minutes was up. Ten minutes after the large, wheezy, hairy man at Second Act's rear door took his business card, said "Hang on," and disappeared inside the building. Given the urgency of the situation surrounding the laptop, Carter assumed he didn't have long before the welcome wagon showed up. Welcome being a figure of speech. Despite his size, the man who took Carter's message had the air of frightened flunky about him, not coconspirator. Probably all he did was pass along the message. But even small flames lit big fires.

True to form, two black SUVs pulled into the Second Act parking lot just over twenty minutes later. Carter, parked a block away, used his binoculars to examine the trio that piled out of the cars and quickly took point. The men gauging their bearings like they were reconnoitering a Fallujah alley and not a side street in Providence, Rhode Island.

Carter recognized one of them right away. Scott Vickers. The guy who'd harassed an already traumatized Stacy Gibbons about Chuck's work laptop. He was also the guy from the apartment building in Attleboro last night who demanded said laptop. The one Carter took down before passing out. The one who was gone when Carter woke up, along with a duffel bag full of drugs. Drugs Carter guessed the trio that broke into Stacy's house wanted back, badly.

Carter didn't recognize the other two. He stayed put. This wasn't like Cody at the Narragansett Get 'N Go and his tubby lieutenant, or even Jimmy, Club Tijuana, and Hoodie at Stacy Gibbons's brick Colonial.

These guys—trim, muscular, stone-faced—looked like Ken ninjas in matching black slacks and long-sleeve tech shirts. They moved with the quiet assurance of jungle cats. Their body language screamed professional; the same workmanlike fluidity that caught Carter's eye in Attleboro when he spied Vickers. It was difficult for Carter to make out weapons at this distance, but even money said they were carrying. These weren't people he felt like messing with unless he absolutely had to.

Satisfied that Carter was gone, the trio clustered around the back door. Vickers waved a key card to open it and the three disappeared inside. Another five minutes passed. Then Carter's phone buzzed with a call from an unfamiliar number. He let it go four rings before picking up.

"Carter," he said.

"Mercury Carter?"

Carter gambled. "Scott?"

A long pause.

"How do you know my name?"

Bingo.

"Not important. What can I do for you?"

Another pause. "You're the one who asked to talk. Where are you, anyway? Aiden made it sound like you were waiting outside."

Aiden. The big guy with the beard and the wheeze.

Carter weighed a gambit, went for it. "I asked to talk to Randy Carmichael," he said. "Not an errand boy."

An intake of breath, like a blindfolded man unmasked at the edge of a steep precipice.

"Listen, asshole. I don't know who you are. Or what you're up to. But here's the deal. I represent Mr. Carmichael, so I'm the one you'll talk to. If you're still around, walk up to the back door and we'll go from there, one-on-one."

"One-on-one. Right. And your two buddies will do what while we chat? Play euchre?"

"You are still here. Where—"

"Carmichael," Carter said, and cut the call.

Carter had a pretty good idea how things might transpire. Vickers was a guy who carried himself with the bearing of someone used to getting his way. Controlling the state of play. Maybe with his pals, maybe not. Therefore, the idea of Vickers explaining his and Carter's brief conversation to Randy Carmichael meant acknowledging that he, Vickers, had failed in his emergency fact-finding mission. Failed despite coming in person and with reinforcements. Meaning if Carter was right, Vickers would call his boss, but not immediately. He'd need to craft his message first.

When a minute passed, then two, then three, Carter figured he had his answer. Vickers was weighing the alternatives, crunching the numbers, by himself or with his compatriots—but not, Carter guessed, in consultation with Aiden—before breaking the bad news to Carmichael.

When Carter's phone went off five minutes in, he wondered if he'd been off base. Then he saw it was Gus Papaleonardos calling.

THIRTY-THREE

"You're working late," Carter said.

"Where the hell are you?"

Carter looked around. "Someplace in Providence."

"I thought you were in Attleboro? What happened to helping out with Donny?"

"Would you believe things got complicated?"

"Not really. Those names you gave me. Shaun Volpe. Jason Schulte. This new one. Chuck Gibbons."

"What about them?"

"Did you detect a pattern? Is that why you passed them on?"

"That, and it felt like the right thing to do," Carter said. "I'm really not trying to make your life difficult."

"Could have fooled me. What's your best guess?"

"Sorry?"

"The pattern you detected." Papaleonardos sounded about as patient as a man in a sinking boat.

Carter raised his binoculars and examined the parking lot at the rear of Second Act Staffing Solutions. No activity. Pushing ten minutes since he hung up with Vickers.

"If I had to guess, those guys met up with prostitutes. Maybe same woman, maybe not. At some point, the men were drugged and robbed. The fact that all three died suggests whoever drugged them didn't want them to wake up." Carter thought about the duffel bag missing from the Attleboro apartment.

"Go on."

"Whoever drugged them—or whoever was calling the shots about drugging them—was less concerned about them dying than them waking up and realizing they'd been robbed by someone they could later identify."

"Which is it?"

"What do you mean?"

"Get to the point, Carter. A prostitute on her own, or someone calling the shots?"

"If I had to guess, the latter. Probably the same guy I tussled with after I found Linda Stauch. Donny LNU."

Papaleonardos was quiet for a moment.

"Detective?"

"We think that sounds about right."

"We?"

"A small, unofficial task force I'm putting together on the fly, not that it's any of your business."

Before Carter could reply, the detective said, "These three—they're the only victims you came across?"

Carter confirmed it. "There could be others, I suppose. Guys who survived, maybe not inclined to report they were robbed under those particular circumstances."

"This girl you're looking for, Terri Watkins. Is it possible she was in the room with any of these guys when they died?"

"I would say it's possible, yes. Like I said, I don't think she's a shot caller."

"Why not?"

Carter considered the security video, the look on Terri's face as Donny marched her into the Narragansett Get 'N Go. The glimpse he'd caught of Terri in Attleboro: a painfully thin, shrunken figure in a rumpled flannel shirt, stained gray sweats, and ladies' sneakers with the laces untied. "She's too far down on the food chain to be a sole operator. At best, she's a dog on a leash."

"Next question, as long as you're being so cooperative. We're trying to find Chuck Gibbons's widow. Stacy. She's not answering the door. One of her neighbors thought she heard a disturbance earlier today. Any idea where she might be?"

"Yes."

"Where?"

"I can't tell you."

Carter had to hold the phone away from his ear as Papaleonardos expressed his displeasure.

"Finished?"

"No. Do you have any idea—"

"Somebody's looking for her," Carter interrupted. "She's in danger. Reference that disturbance you mentioned. If it's absolutely crucial, I could connect you by phone. Even then I'm wary."

"Who was looking for her?"

Carter hesitated. "One of them is a guy named Jimmy, who's connected to Donny."

"Donny Tollman."

Now it was Carter's turn to be surprised.

"Who?"

Papaleonardos sighed. "Donny LNU. Full name Donald Clifford Tollman."

"Okay. Appreciate that info. Who is he?"

"He's not what you'd call a stand-up guy."

It took two minutes of back-and-forth before Carter persuaded Papaleonardos the world wouldn't end if he gave Carter until tomorrow morning to fork over the ring and the envelope, especially given the hour. Like the detective had any choice, although Carter didn't say that.

Call ended, Carter punched out a text message to his uncle with Donny Tollman's name and the background Papaleonardos had come up with. A résumé that included assault, theft, robbery, drugs, and trafficking. Two stints inside, both in Massachusetts, the last time four years earlier. Not a stand-up guy, indeed.

Roger, his uncle replied.

Carter was about to call Rhonda to check on Stacy, and to warn her of Papaleonardos's interest, when his phone rang again, this time with a blocked number. Fifteen minutes had passed since Carter's call with Vickers. The timing was right.

Carter gambled again. "Randy Carmichael?"

Two seconds of silence.

"What do you want?"

"Thanks for calling. I'll get right to it. I'm looking for someone. I think that person is under the control of someone *you're* looking for. I'm wondering if we could trade information."

"Who are you looking for?"

Carter told him.

"Terri Watkins? Never heard of her. What's your interest?"

"I'm a freelance courier. I have a delivery for her."

"What kind of delivery?"

"Confidential, sorry."

"Sounds like bullshit to me. Who's the person you think I'm looking for?"

"I'm guessing he's a beefy dude with a beard who runs women, and possibly drugs, out of a run-down brick apartment house in Attleboro. One of those women is Terri Watkins. I think the reason you're looking for him is because he has a laptop that belonged to someone named Chuck Gibbons, who works for you. Worked, sorry. I don't care about the laptop, by the way."

After a moment, Carmichael said, "How the fuck do you know all this?"

"I put it together. How isn't important."

"Why should I believe you? Didn't you used to be a cop?"

"Being a cop and being believed are not mutually exclusive." Before Carmichael could respond, Carter added: "That doesn't matter, because I'm not a cop now. I'm a mailman trying to make a delivery and looking for some help."

Another two seconds of silence. "Got a name for this beefy dude?"

"Depends," Carter said. "Can you help me out? To repeat, I need Terri, not the laptop."

"I need the name of this individual first."

"Then what?"

"Then my colleague, Scott Vickers, whom I'm sorry to say you've already met, escorts you to me so we can do business in person."

Carter was about to respond when he stopped, caught up by Carmichael's phrasing, plus the fact he had dropped Vickers's name. As if he expressly wanted Carter to know it, not realizing he already did. What was Carter missing here?

Carter said, "I can find my way to you just fine by myself."

"Is that a threat?"

"A point of information."

"Maybe you can. But I have to take precautions. Which is why I sent Mr. Vickers. He's good at what he does, when he follows instructions. You and he will be just fine."

There it was again. *When he follows instructions?*

"You mean, me, him, and the two gorillas with him."

"I'm sorry?"

"You heard me."

"Pretend I didn't."

Carter said, "I said, me, him, and the two gorillas with him."

"The three of them. Right," Carmichael said.

The hesitation in Carmichael's voice gave Carter pause. It sounded like Carmichael didn't know Scott Vickers brought company until Carter told him.

Whatever was going on, Carter didn't relish the thought of going anywhere with Scott Vickers and Co. It bore all the hallmarks of a one-way trip into a forest where sound didn't carry well.

"All right," Carter said. "The name of the man you're looking for is Donny Tollman."

"Donny Tollman?"

"That's right." In that moment, Carter heard a voice in the background. A woman's voice, saying something. Monica, Randy's wife?

Which meant his and Carmichael's conversation wasn't private. Did that explain Carmichael's tortured comment. *Whom I'm sorry to say you already met*? He had to speak in code because he couldn't speak plainly?

Carter shook his head again, and said, "Carmichael?"

"Yeah."

"I gave you Donny Tollman. What can you give me?"

A pause. "Nothing, asshole," Carmichael said, and the line went dead.

Carter wasn't surprised. Disappointed? Yes. But from what he could tell of Carmichael, he wasn't a two-way street kind of guy. Maybe the hint that something was off about Vickers was all Carter was getting.

Or all Carmichael could risk giving him with Monica listening in.

Carter pondered what to do next. He couldn't take on Vickers and crew here, on their territory; that was already established. These guys were apex predators even compared with Jimmy, Club Tijuana, and Hoodie. Maybe Carter could run down Carmichael's address and visit him personally, assuming he got there before Vickers. Or see if his uncle found a better address for Donny Tollman than an abandoned apartment in Attleboro. Carter even thought about seeing if Rhonda and Braden Rausch would let him park in their driveway and catch forty winks in the back of the Suburban.

As sometimes happened, the decision was made for him. Not at all what he expected. Carter was using an address-finder app to look up Randy Carmichael when he glanced over and spied movement in the Second Act parking lot. He lifted his binoculars and studied the action. *Okay. This was not good. Inexplicable, but definitely not good.*

Scott Vickers and his buddies were frog-marching the heavyset, hairy man named Aiden across the parking lot toward the SUV that Vickers arrived in.

Correction: The buddies were frog-marching Aiden. Vickers had his gun to Aiden's back.

THIRTY-FOUR

Randy sat back, panic icing his insides. He thought about what was happening. About the fact that, according to Monica, Vickers had just spirited Aiden away to God knows where.

"Seems extreme," he said.

"We can't be too careful," Monica replied. "Who knows what Aiden told this guy, Carter? You saw he used to be a fed. Postal service or something. Whoever he is, I'm calling BS on him making a delivery."

"We're dead in the water without Aiden. He's all we've got."

"He's all we've got now. Once we have the laptop back, we regroup. Chuck was the spear tip. Aiden's cannon fodder. He had to know that."

Randy recoiled inside but kept his face blank. *Spear tip. Cannon fodder.* Was she serious here?

More to the point: He needed Aiden. For now, *they* needed Aiden. Quadrant Horizons was underway. He'd sent the first phishing email. His last, best hope for Michelle. Infiltrating the networks maintained by Quadrant Horizons. Potentially millions of patient records, ripe for the picking. Personal health information out the wazoo. Like shooting fish in a barrel if your barrel, was an Olympic-sized swimming pool and your gun was an AK-47. Randy knew his way around a computer. He had the contacts. But he required Aiden a little longer to keep the engine under the hood running. And to take the heat.

Because Quadrant wasn't like the others, the low-rent nursing homes and blood labs and outpatient surgical centers with security an eighth grader could hack. Second Act's incursions undetected for months—if ever—while Chuck took the stolen PHI to market. Black market. Quadrant would be Randy's greatest grift ever. But its security protocols were on another level, and Randy needed Aiden to maintain a cloak of invisibility for as long as possible.

Except now it was going to hell, thanks to Vickers. And Monica. Who had given the order to Vickers while Randy was in the bathroom: Scoop up Aiden, see what Carter told him, try not to leave too big a mess.

And now Vickers, that wife-fucker, wannabe special-ops dickwad, had gone silent.

Randy had only one choice. He didn't like it. On the one hand, he had to agree with Monica about Mercury Carter, whoever he was. Former fed, current fed, mailman my ass, his arrival on the scene didn't bode well.

On the other hand, with Vickers unresponsive, what choice did Randy have? The plan was risky. It could backfire. But how could the risk be any greater than the order Monica gave Vickers when Randy was out of the room? He couldn't risk Vickers going rogue again and putting Aiden out of commission, temporarily or permanently.

Randy excused himself once more. He walked down the hall to the bathroom. Inside, he waited a minute, then flushed the toilet. He had no idea if this was going to work. If Carter was where he needed him to be. If Carter himself hadn't fallen victim to the same fate awaiting Aiden.

As the toilet tank filled, Randy typed out a message to the phone he'd called Carter on. Five words. Which together spelled out what was left of Randy's future. His, and Michelle's.

Save Aiden and Tollman's yours.

—∞∞—

Carter's phone buzzed. He ignored it. He kept his eyes on the two black SUVs ahead of him, staying just far enough back to hope he wasn't seen.

So far, so good. They drove five blocks. Passed a *Welcome to Olneyville* sign. Half a block up, the two SUVs turned right without signaling. Carter tapped his brakes. No one behind him. He slowed further. After thirty seconds, he made the turn. In the distance, he watched the brake lights of the trailing SUV as it slowed, turned left, and disappeared.

Carter killed his lights and came to a stop. He examined his surroundings. He was on a service drive skirting several brick buildings, many secured behind chain-link fences. Sodium lamps loomed every half block, casting oblong shadows between the road and the buildings. He was in some kind of warehouse district. He was still undetected as far as he could tell. Now or never. He pulled over, as close to a guardrail as possible. *No Parking at Any Time,* said a red-lettered metal sign with a notch missing from the upper right-hand corner. Carter took a second to view the message he received a few minutes earlier. From Randy Carmichael.

Save Aiden and Tollman's yours.

Oh boy, Carter thought. He unholstered his Beretta, ducked out of the Suburban, and headed to the corner where the SUVs had turned.

Crouching, Carter ran quickly and lightly, two notches faster than the jog to the dugout after three outs, hugging the sides of the brick warehouses on his left. He gripped his gun in his right hand, keeping it close to his thigh. He reached the corner, paused, took a breath, and peered around.

He met with a piece of good luck right away, tempered almost immediately by a setback.

The good luck: A blue dumpster sat halfway down the block, providing easy cover. Head down, Carter ran straight for it, pulling up at the last second and placing his left hand against the cool, dented metal while he slowed his heart rate. The dumpster, like any good dumpster, looked as if it had been placed there by men rolling it off a roof with sledgehammers.

The setback: Vickers and one of the operatives had hustled Aiden inside the door of a warehouse on the right, as the other operative assumed a lookout stance. The door, and the lookout, were positioned between the two SUVs.

Parking the vehicles that way made sense strategically. Carter realized it also gave him a leg up that potentially outweighed the presence of the lookout.

Quietly, Carter stood to his full five foot, ten inches and reached into the dumpster. More luck. It was a construction receptacle without a lid. He found what he was looking for, withdrew his arm, and examined his find. A chunk of concrete. A little dusty, but adequate.

Carter readjusted the concrete in his hand, took a step backward, and arced the chunk down the street. Not at the lookout, which would have required an almost perfect lob. Instead, toward the hood of the SUV on the far side of the warehouse door.

It had been a while since Carter played shortstop. Even then it wasn't as if he had to throw far; a cutoff to first base, a zinger to the catcher at home. But his aim was good then and good now. The sound the concrete made landing on the SUV's hood could not have been louder and more jarring had it been a crash-landing meteor. The lookout jumped as if he'd been hit with a cattle prod, stared at the SUV in disbelief, left his post to see what had happened.

A mistake on the lookout's part, though a natural one Carter was counting on. The guy hadn't sought the source of the object making the sound. Carter took advantage of the misstep and sprinted from the back of the dumpster to the rear of the other SUV.

He was slowed down just a little.

He had a second chunk of concrete in his hand.

This next part was trickier. The SUV's windows were tinted, making it impossible to see when the lookout reemerged from checking out the mess on the other car's hood. Carter made an educated guess based on noise from the man's footfalls. He didn't get it quite right. When Carter moved to his left and around the SUV, the lookout was already walking past the first vehicle. His eyes lit up in surprise seeing Carter and he moved instinctively for his gun. Too late. Even tossed from Carter's left hand, the second chunk of demolition debris hit the lookout in the face hard, the sound like a muted clapper striking the side of a bell. The man staggered, hunched, and dropped to his knees, hands cupping his face to stanch the blood.

Moving quickly, Carter crept to the disabled lookout, waited for him to sense Carter's approach and look up, and then swung his blackjack against the left side of the man's head. The operative fell sideways with a low grunt and didn't move.

Carter knelt, made sure the man was breathing, took his gun, removed the magazine and the chambered round, slid everything under the rear SUV, and rolled the man onto his stomach. Carter didn't have time to bind him. Instead, he pulled the man's left shoe off and tossed it toward the dumpster. Nothing throws someone off more than trying to run with one shoe on, one shoe off. Carter hoped.

Next, Carter reached into his utility vest, retrieved a box cutter, and slashed the driver's side tires of the SUV he'd hidden behind. Carter was making for the tires of the front SUV when he heard yelling inside the warehouse. No time. He pulled open the door and darted inside.

Security lights atop the building on the opposite alley provided weak illumination, along with low-level interior nighttime lamps. Still, tough to tell where the yelling originated. Carter had a choice: straight ahead, or up a set of metal stairs. Aiden could be either place. Carter didn't have time to play "The Lady, or the Tiger?" He deepened his voice and shouted, "Scott!"

Silence. Then, from somewhere in front of Carter, Vickers's voice: "Chad?"

"Wait a sec," Carter-as-Chad said, and he plunged into the room ahead of him.

Carter only had one thing going for him, not counting his track record on the USPIS shooting range. He was still Carter-as-Chad. Despite the din the concrete chunk made slamming onto the SUV hood outside, Vickers and the other operative didn't realize they were a man down.

The deceit gifted Carter exactly five seconds. Which was the amount of time it took the pair, wrestling Aiden into a chair at the rear of the large room, to glance up from their task and spot the intruder.

"Hey," Vickers shouted.

Carter glanced at the overhead panel of fluorescent tube lights casting shadows across the wide, pillared room, took aim, and shot the lights out. Glass showered the room. Return fire rang out as Vickers or the operative or both fired at Carter. Which was not actually Carter, but his last position. He was already gone, squeezed behind a support column midway down the room. Ears ringing from the gunfire, Carter tried unsuccessfully to place a weird sound coming from the direction of the shooters but didn't have time.

"Drop your weapon," Vickers shouted. "You're outnumbered."

Technically true, Carter thought, pulling a flash-bang from his utility vest and sidearming it toward Vickers. The device was a cowboy pop gun compared to the pro stuff used by law enforcement. It met Carter's needs tonight. It exploded with a flash and cloudy haze, briefly illuminating the second operative crouched in a firing stance, gun aimed in Carter's direction. Say what you will, the guy followed his training. So did Carter. He fired at center mass. A groan told him his aim was true.

"Your turn," Carter shouted. "Drop your gun and step away from Aiden."

Vickers responded with a barrage of shots, two or three of which struck the far side of the pillar. Chips of plaster skittered across the floor.

"Last chance," Carter said.

Another barrage, only one of which struck the pillar. Carter's headache, in abeyance for a while, throbbed from the volume of the salvo. Which is how, he figured later, he missed what came next.

A calm settled over the room. As the haze from the flash-bang and the gunfire dissipated, Carter's eyes adjusted to the dim illumination provided by the security lighting. Even with the dull roar in his head, he heard the odd sound again. He glanced around the pillar.

Aiden was down, on the ground, chest heaving.

Alone.

Vickers had run.

THIRTY-FIVE

Monica retreated to the patio and stared into the darkness. Something rank filled the air, as if the water from the pond beyond the pines had gone bad.

What was happening?

Had Aiden told Carter something he shouldn't have, and if so, had Vickers learned what it was?

Had Randy figured out why Monica was worried about Aiden? That Aiden might know about The Plan?

No. Impossible. Aiden couldn't.

Could he?

Except why had Randy aired their laundry in front of Carter, so to speak?

Scott Vickers, whom I'm sorry to say you've already met . . . When he follows instructions.

What the fuck was that about?

Monica was used to men failing her. Story of her life. Also, something she counted on, something she used to her benefit. Men were like those penguins that bumped into each other on ice floes until one fell into the jaws of a waiting tiger seal, warning the remaining penguins of the dangers below.

To Monica, most men were the first, unfortunate penguin. She was the tiger seal.

Tonight was different. Tonight, she needed Vickers to come through. To fix any problems with The Plan. To be the tiger seal.

To be sure Aiden hadn't betrayed them.

She needed a win, or they were screwed.

Carter thought ruefully of his last-second decision to spare the tires on the first SUV. But only for a moment. Eyeing the exit, gun in hand, he jogged toward Aiden.

"It's okay," Carter said, reaching him. "Those guys are gone."

It wasn't okay. Aiden wasn't just struggling to catch his breath. He was straining for oxygen like a lung patient disconnected from his ventilator. Asthma attack, Carter figured, not that it mattered. He dug his hand into Aiden's right pants pocket, then left, praying for an inhaler. Nothing. Desperate, he patted down the rest of his pants, one leg at a time. He found it in a plastic baggie safety-pinned to the left-leg cuff of Aiden's sweatpants. Not an inhaler, though. Something else.

He palmed the bag, wrapped his arms around Aiden, and heaved him into a sitting position. Aiden's gasping lessened slightly.

"Inhaler?" Carter said.

Wild-eyed, Aiden glanced at the door Vickers had exited through.

Vickers had taken it.

Why was Carter not surprised.

Carter retrieved a burner phone from his utility vest and called 911. He described his location as accurately as possible. Olneyville, Eil Avenue, disabled black SUV outside the warehouse, first floor.

"A man's been shot and a kidnapping victim is experiencing an asthma attack. He doesn't have an inhaler."

"Who shot the man?"

"There's no current threat, but the man having the attack needs help immediately."

The dispatcher asked again who shot the man.

"Please hurry," Carter said.

The dispatcher reluctantly confirmed that an ambulance and police were on their way. She asked for Carter's name and requested that he stay on the line. Carter cut the call and held the baggie up for Aiden to see.

"Is this what they were looking for?"

Gasping like a man who had just sprinted up a hill, Aiden shook his head *no.*

"They didn't know you had this?"

Nod.

"They wanted something, though."

Nod.

"What was it? Why did they take you?"

A new round of gasping and wheezing.

Carter made an educated guess. "Is the information that's on Chuck Gibbons's laptop also on this thumb drive?"

Nod.

"They didn't know about this?" Carter held up the thumb drive.

Aiden shook his head.

Carter thought.

"Did Randy Carmichael know about this?" He gestured at the thumb drive again.

Nod.

So many missing pieces. If Vickers worked for Randy, why would Randy know about the thumb drive but not Vickers? Was Randy hiding something from his employee? What? From what Carter could put together, someone in this operation—Vickers? Maybe Randy's wife?—hadn't trusted Aiden and dragged him here to find out what was up.

Dragged him here after Carter encountered him back at Second Act Staffing Solutions.

A dark thought occurred to Carter: *This is my fault.*

Carter recalled the text message he'd seen from Carmichael right before running for the warehouse.

Save Aiden and Tollman's yours.

Carter glanced at the second operative. Between the blood pooling on his chest and the red bubbles forming on the man's lips, Carter did not think the paramedics would make it in time for him.

He looked into Aiden's eyes. "It's going to be all right."

"*Msh*," Aiden said.

"What's that?"

"*Msh*," Aiden wheezed. "Michelle."

"Michelle?"

Aiden nodded, breathing raspy.

"Michelle who?"

"*Two thousand two . . .*"

Carter studied Aiden's face. He was familiar with shock in such situations. Was Aiden naming a girlfriend? Sister? Mom? A number that meant something to said person?

No matter. He couldn't waste time figuring it out. Carter found the operative's gun, a standard Glock 17, and kicked it across the warehouse floor. It spun, slowly rotated to a stop a few dozen feet away. He searched the operative's pockets, coming up with a set of keys. Carter cast a last glance at Aiden, saw that his eyes were still open, and headed for the door.

Outside, Vickers, the first operative, and the forward-facing SUV were gone. Not ideal. But which also meant that Carter's gamble searching the second operative's pants pockets had paid off. A gamble that boded well for Aiden.

Pausing, hearing sirens in the distance, Carter dug out the second operative's keys and pressed the fob's car alarm. Lights flashed and the vehicle's klaxon filled the alleyway. It was as close to a billboard emblazoned with a digital *THIS WAY* sign for the first responders that Carter could conjure on short notice.

He looked around, found the piece of concrete that he'd lobbed at the SUV hood, and used it to prop the warehouse door open. Satisfied, he pocketed the SUV keys, loped down the alley, and headed back to his Suburban. Willing his racing heart to slow, Carter performed the world's calmest K-turn and steered onto the main street just as the first round of rescuers roared toward the sound of the SUV alarm. Carter drove in the opposite direction like a man on the way to the library after church.

Back in city traffic, the warehouse district safely behind him, Carter pulled over and parked opposite a restaurant advertising the best Hmong food in the city. Carter wasn't into spicy cuisine, but Tomeka would enjoy testing that claim. Some other time.

After assuring himself he hadn't been trailed from the warehouse, Carter pulled out his phone, found Randy Carmichael's number, and dialed. It went to voicemail after five rings. One minute later, Carmichael called back.

"Well?" Carmichael said, voice low.

"Aiden's okay."

A pause. "Vickers?"

"His numbers are diminished. How do I find Donny Tollman?"

"There's a meetup. He'll be there. That's all I can promise."

"He's bringing Chuck Gibbons's laptop?"

"Yes."

"I need him to bring Terri Watkins, too."

"What?"

"You heard me. Terri Watkins, or the deal's off."

"Deal? What deal?"

"The deal where I don't give the thumb drive that Aiden just handed me to the authorities." Another gamble, but Carter had to believe Randy hadn't gone to all this effort to preserve a bunch of digital family photos.

"You double-crossed me."

"Not at all," Carter corrected. "A double-cross almost by definition involves calculation. Preplanning. I stumbled across this thumb drive less than twenty minutes ago. Pure happenstance. I don't mean to be a hard-ass. All things being equal, I'd give it to you in a heartbeat. First, though, I need you to do me a favor and get Tollman to bring Terri Watkins to the meet."

"If he says no?"

"Sweeten the pot."

"Why should I stick my neck out for you, Carter?"

"Thumb drive. Also, I saved Aiden. Like you asked. By the way, is that his first name or last?"

Randy cut the call without responding.

Sweeten the pot, like hell. With what? He'd already gambled away his only leverage with his threat to expose Donny Tollman's sloppy drug handling.

Randy was half convinced to call the whole thing off, laptop be damned, fuck the thumb drive, call it a day.

Except, as long as that laptop was out of his control, the possibility existed that someone could hack it and find out the truth about Second

Act Staffing. The laptop didn't have the full picture of what was going on. It didn't, for example, have the evidence Randy had compiled of Monica and Vickers's affair, evidence he'd instructed Aiden to stick onto the thumb drive just in case. But the laptop had enough, especially when it came to Quadrant Horizons. If that deal went south, if the feds or someone in law enforcement figured it out, Randy's plan for helping Michelle was going down the drain. He could do some things for her from prison. But not what the revenue from Quadrant's Personal health information bonanza promised.

Randy was girding himself to call Donny back and beg, insist he bring some girl named Terri with him, when his phone buzzed. Pauley Carnevale.

We still on for tonight?

Randy was about to reply when he remembered their meeting at the mall after the Chamber of Commerce dog-and-pony show. The way Pauley, who hadn't worked a single honest day in his life, flashed a wad of bills like a toddler pleased with the crap he just took.

A businessman who likes his Benjamins.

Randy had already baited the hook for Pauley with the promise of a duffel bag full of drugs tonight. Maybe he could bait a similar hook for Donny Tollman related to the money Pauley carried around. The two could square off while Randy took the laptop and ran. With or without Monica.

Randy returned to his phone.

Yes, he replied.

Then Randy called Donny Tollman to make a new offer.

THIRTY-SIX

Something was happening.

Something not good.

Terri dozed most of the afternoon, occupying herself when awake by trying to remember nursery rhymes she learned as a kid. *Little Miss Muffet . . . Humpty Dumpty . . . There was an old woman . . .* She didn't get far. Her headache was blinding. Her stomach was cramping. Her joints ached like a woman twice or three times her age. She was withdrawing. She figured Donny knew, too, but didn't give a shit. She thought long and hard about reaching into her pocket and retrieving the lint-covered leftover she found earlier, use it to take the edge off, but stopped when she remembered what happened when men like Jason Schulte took something similar. The edge went off permanently.

Things were quiet until a couple of hours ago. Then all hell broke loose. A door opened and slammed shut, she heard Jimmy's voice, then the voices of two other men. One of them Terri thought she'd seen before. Scary-looking son of a bitch with mirror sunglasses, biceps like melons, and tats on his tats. Who was he? No clue. With Donny, it didn't matter. He didn't have friends. He had aiders and abettors.

Whoever they were, they were upset. Pissed. Even locked in the room, chained to a radiator, Terri sensed the anger pouring out of them like blood from a gutshot. Whatever they were telling Donny was upsetting him. Soon Donny was roaring right back at them. After the shouting died down, she heard lots of conversation, the low rumble of men's voices, urgent and angry, like the idling of diesel trucks at a construction site.

Night fell. People moved through the house. Heavy steps up and down the stairs. She had a pretty good idea what was going on. They were leaving, and they weren't taking her with them. Terri called out, her voice weak and hoarse, but no one came.

The departures should have relieved her. Alone, wherever she was, without the threat of Donny and his fists. Instead, she squeezed her eyes shut as fear flooded her brain. What if they didn't come back? She had no idea where she was. She was sure no one else knew either. Or cared. She hadn't been a good girl. Donny had made that much clear. Also, Terri knew he could always find other girls to do what she did. She'd learned that much in life. There were always more girls because the supply of men who wanted them was inexhaustible.

What if Donny was leaving her to die?

Terri screamed for help. Nothing in response. Terri tugged madly at the chain but the radiator didn't budge, firm as a boulder. She tried to pull her ankle free, but the edge of the crimped straight brace was too sharp and she gasped as the metal sliced her skin. She stopped. She wept.

Nothing.

Then, the sound of the downstairs door opening and, a minute later, slamming shut. A car engine starting.

Oh my God. They really were leaving her.

"Please, no," Terri whispered aloud.

Five minutes passed. Ten. She might have passed out. She dreamed of London Bridge falling down, of her grandmother, of the ruby ring.

She woke to the sound of thudding up the stairs, the noise as loud and rhythmic as gunshots going off.

The door to the room was flung open. Donny walked in, disgust on his face as if he'd been force-fed fresh fruit. He raised a pair of bolt cutters and shook them angrily at Terri.

"No," Terri croaked, raising her arms in supplication.

"It's your lucky day, bitch," Donny said, leaning over and snapping the chain. "You're coming with us."

Midnight.

Why do these meets always have to be at midnight, Carter thought. Whatever happened to high noon?

And why this location? The back patio of PC Seafood & Chops, a bayside restaurant on the outskirts of Warwick. A short hike down the coast from Providence. Secluded, for sure. After events earlier in the evening, Carter was happy to ditch the warehouse scene. But this choice for a group rendezvous was random enough to raise all kinds of new questions. He'd texted the address to his uncle to see what he could find but hadn't heard back.

Carter was parked across the street and down the block. He was ninety minutes early. He sat in the middle seat of the Suburban, a blackout curtain pulled over his head to hide the glare of the laptop propped on his knees.

He encountered trouble right away, as soon as he inserted Aiden's thumb drive into his laptop. A row of dots autopopulated the username field. But his cursor blinked with futility in the empty password field; the existential heartbeat of the modern world. No problem. He was only looking at, worst-case scenario, ten gazillion possibilities.

SecondAct123

Nope.

Randy123

Nope again.

Aiden123

Same answer.

Carter sighed and leaned against the middle-seat headrest. He had lowered the front windows of the Suburban an inch to keep it from growing too stuffy inside and to track approaching cars. Carter could smell the salt water. Hear swells kissing the pilings of the patio and a narrow dock he'd spied jutting into the bay, a few small boats lined up on either side. He processed the random cry of an ocean bird—a gull? a tern?—roused from sleep by dreams of French fries or crab shells. He felt himself on the verge of dozing off. As he did, he wondered idly how the Red Sox–Guardians game turned out, the one he did his darndest not to glance at while babysitting Stacy Gibbons at O'Malley's.

He raised his phone to check the score. He caught himself at the last second. *Focus.* He thought back to the chaotic scene in the warehouse. Aiden, propped against the wall while one of Scott Vickers's operatives bled out next to him. Aiden's panicked rambling.

Msh. Michelle. Two thousand two.

Duh.

It took him one try.

Michelle2002

Bingo.

Who was Michelle? Aiden's girlfriend? Wife? Daughter? Why had Aiden given up the password like that? The last gesture of a man who thought he was dying to the man who'd tried to rescue him?

Carter would get to that eventually.

For now, he was inside the thumb drive and studying the root directory of folders. His eyes widened at what he saw.

Okay. This was interesting.

THIRTY-SEVEN

Squinting, Carter tried to make sense of what he was seeing. The labels on the folders in the directory didn't equate with the inner workings of an employment staffing service.

Kauai Shores. Koloa Landing. Outrigger Reef. Prince Waikiki.

Carter activated the Suburban's hot spot and Googled Kauai Shores. A moment later, Carter was staring at photos of white beaches, blue water, orange and blue and green iced drinks, and freshly made beds the size of heliports. Ah. He got it. The folders were named for resort hotels. Stacy Gibbons's comments at O'Malley's earlier in the day came back to Carter, when she was talking about Chuck's IT work.

The money's good, I'll give him that. He took me to Hawaii every year . . . A week ago, my biggest concern was figuring out what hotel to book on Maui this November.

The guy was being cute with his folder names. Fair enough. Carter decided to go alphabetical and opened the Kauai Shores folder first. Inside he found a spreadsheet titled *SPCC.* Meant nothing. Launching the spreadsheet, he examined the first sheet, labeled simply *Contacts.* Looking closer, Carter saw that three dozen rows were populated with information: names of people, followed by a job titles such as administrator, human resources, and business manager, followed by what appeared to be facility names—either Green Gardens, Sunrise Care, or Daybreak Nursing. Each row also contained a contact email and phone number.

Carter moved to the second tab. *Jobs.* Here, less than twenty rows contained a name, an occupation (LPN, janitor, medical assistant), one of the three facilities, dates of employment, and each employee's work email at their respective placement. *Huh.* Carter sat back and considered what he knew of Second Act's business model.

Randy Carmichael placed ex-offenders in low-level jobs in medical facilities desperate for workers. An admirable enough enterprise. *Second Act Staffing. Because There's Always a First Time for Second Chances.* Which would explain the first two tabs. Administrative contacts and jobs that Carmichael's temp workers were filling. Straightforward. The height of routine. Call him crazy, but Carter didn't think the information was important enough for Vickers to kidnap Aiden, steal his inhaler, and drag him into a warehouse under threat of torture and maybe death.

Carter clicked on a third tab, labeled *PHI.* This was a bigger sheet, with what appeared to be a few hundred rows. Beginning with name after name after name.

Not just names. Or names and facilities, as with the first two SPCC tabs. Carter raised his eyebrows as he made out not only people's full names, but middle names and—in the case of the women—maiden names as well. More troubling, their Social Security numbers. The names of their insurance companies. Their insurance company account numbers. Then: billing information. Credit card numbers. Expiration dates. Security codes. Even more: bank routing designators and account numbers, checking and savings. Column after column of information.

Okay. Vickers's decision to abduct Aiden and take away his inhaler was making more sense now. This was an insane amount of personal information. Information that in no shape or form a temp staffing agency should have access to.

Carter backtracked. He Googled *SPCC*. Somehow he didn't think South Piedmont Community College fit the bill. He added *Green Gardens*, the name of one of the facilities from the Contacts tab. That did the trick. *SPCC* was Sign-Post Contingent Care. A small, Massachusetts-based long-term care company. Green Gardens and the others were the names of facilities owned by Sign-Post.

The information on the various tabs started to make sense. If Carter was interpreting things correctly, Randy Carmichael's temp agency had somehow gained access to the personal medical records of multiple patients from those three facilities. Protected health information. PHI. Highly sensitive. Also, as Carter recalled from his days on the job, lucrative if stolen and sold on the black market.

Carter couldn't envision a scenario where an ex-con like Carmichael, no matter how reformed, had a productive reason to be in possession of so much PHI. It was like assuming the best of a "vegetarian" fox holding the keys to every chicken house in the county.

What was the play here? Was Carmichael using the credit card numbers and banking information for himself? It didn't seem likely. The volume of information suggested otherwise. Carter knew for a fact that bad actors swimming in the cesspool of the dark web were willing to pay a lot for such information.

He closed out of Kauai Shores and opened the Koloa Landing folder. Inside, he found another spreadsheet, this one named *NEMCS*. He searched the acronym first. Carter scanned the Google results, none of which were exact. He stopped on the fourth link down. *New England Med-Care Services*. He clicked on the link and studied the website. The company was a regional health-care facility operator. Mostly urgent care centers, with a few physical therapy facilities and outpatient surgery offices. Based on a quick review, most if not all the businesses were in Rhode Island or Massachusetts. Small, but bigger than Sign-Post.

Carter returned to the first tab on the NEMCS spreadsheet. The results on the Contacts tab were about the same, with a few more administrators' names and emails. The list of people on the Jobs tab was slightly longer than Sign-Post, but that would make sense: NEMCS owned nearly twenty facilities. The big difference was on the PHI tab. Carter was staring at more than 2,500 rows of personal health information. Because New England Med-Care was a bigger company than Sign-Post, there was more data to be had, however Carmichael was obtaining it.

Getting a bad feeling, Carter closed out and opened the third folder. Outrigger Reef. Inside he found another spreadsheet, this one labeled *QH*.

That took no time at all, now that Carter knew what he was looking for. A quick online search turned up the fact that *QH* was Quadrant Horizons, a company headquartered in Des Moines. *A Health Care Consortium*. Whatever.

Nevertheless, this outfit was a far cry from Sign-Post or New England Med-Care. Quadrant Horizons was big. Nationwide. Owned lots of small medical facilities, sure, but also major hospitals coast-to-coast. Infiltrating a company this size—if that's what Carmichael was up to—might compromise millions of records. A treasure trove of personal health information.

Carter opened the Contacts tab and found the biggest listing yet of company employees, more than two hundred rows. Names, job titles, and email addresses that ended with the domain @quadranthorizons .com. All positions related either to human resources, accounting, or payroll. Exactly the kind of emails, Carter thought, that you'd want handy if your job was coordinating the work schedules of temporary employees you'd placed in a corporate environment. Oddly, the Jobs tab contained about the same number of placements as New England Med-Care. Then Carter realized the individuals only worked at facilities in Rhode Island or Massachusetts owned by Quadrant.

When Carter opened the third tab, for PHI, he frowned. The sheet was empty. At first he wondered if he'd opened the wrong tab. Then it came to him.

Carmichael hadn't gained access to Quadrant Horizons' personal health information yet. But if and when he did . . . *Jackpot.*

Despite the hour, Carter was about to call his uncle and enlist his help in processing the find when he paused. What, in fact, did any of this have to do with him? Or, more to the point, with delivering a ruby ring to Terri Watkins so he could complete his assignment for Jim and Valerie Watkins, make his other delivery to Lenny Pellegrino, and be on his way? Wasn't all this just background noise complicating the task at hand?

Carter checked his watch: 11:05 P.M. Less than an hour to go. For all he knew, Randy or Donny were already in the restaurant, biding their time. Same as Carter was doing, parked across the street. As long as they didn't know he was here, he wasn't going to sweat it.

Carter was about to close out and call his uncle when his eye drifted to a fourth folder. Prince Waikiki. He double-clicked on it. Inside sat two other folders. One was named *Michelle*, the other *Monica*. Recalling Aiden's mumbled clue in the warehouse—*Msh . . . Michelle*—Carter opened that first.

A second later he hunched down below window level. A car was approaching on the street running past the restaurant. After a few moments it continued on, tires smacking softly on the roadway , which was growing damp with evening dew. False alarm. Carter sat up and examined the documents inside the Michelle folder. He puzzled over the information, then slowly made sense of it.

Michelle was Michelle Carmichael. As far as Carter could tell, she was Randy's adult daughter. She was also severely handicapped, confined to a hospital bed. Carter skimmed medical documents and correspondence with a long-term care facility in Albany. He looked at a list of staggering care cost projections. If those were true, the scope of Randy's personal health information grift made more sense. The guy needed money if he was going to pay his daughter's health-care costs. Carter almost felt sorry for him. Then he thought of the millions of Quadrant Horizons patients facing financial disaster if their PHI was sold on the black market. He brushed away his sympathy. Being a criminal with a heart didn't make you less of a criminal.

Outside, the sound of another car approaching. Carter clicked out of Michelle's folder and opened the one labeled *Monica*, presumably for Randy's wife. Inside nested a series of photographs. Carter clicked the first one open and stared.

My, my.

The picture was of Monica—Carter recognized her from Second Act's website—lying half dressed atop what looked like a thick end-grain butcher block kitchen island.

Mounting her was a man who, even from behind, Carter could tell was Scott Vickers.

Suddenly, Randy's desire to keep Aiden alive—or more to the point, keep the thumb drive that Aiden had out of Vickers's hands—made a lot more sense.

Carter didn't have time to finish the thought. The approaching vehicle had turned into the parking lot of PC Seafood & Chops.

THIRTY-EIGHT

Monica shouldn't have let Randy drive. Not after how upset he'd gotten when Scott finally called. The radio silence up to that point had been excruciating. Especially during what was supposed to be the simple task of determining whether Aiden had double-crossed them in his interaction with Mercury Carter. Then, ensuring that Aiden couldn't jeopardize the future operations of Second Act Staffing.

Or, more importantly, Monica and Vickers's own plan.

Goddamned Chuck. This was all his fault.

It was past ten thirty when Monica's phone buzzed with Scott on the other line. Randy climbing the walls because they were supposed to be on the way to the designated meeting place. Some seafood joint down in Warwick. Monica wondered why, but Randy said he had his reasons.

Meanwhile, the fact that Scott chose to call her and not Randy spoke volumes. The message unmistakable: *We're still in this together, right?*

For now.

Monica connected the call, told Scott she had it on speaker, and told him to talk. He talked. While Monica and Randy listened in disbelief and growing horror.

An abandoned warehouse in Olneyville. Scott and two of his private security gunners. "Top-of-the-line guys," he said at least twice. *Right.* Things going fine until suddenly they weren't. Somehow Carter got the drop on them. One of Scott's guys was down, possibly dead. The other temporarily out for the count after Carter clocked him. Not to worry, though: The man was coming to and mad as hell. Ready for revenge.

"Not to worry?" Randy said, his already gravelly bass down to bathysphere levels. "Are you out of your mind?"

Monica interjected, unable to help herself: "Did you at least take care of Aiden?"

A pause, during which Monica felt her heart sink.

"Not exactly."

"Meaning?"

"He was having one of his attacks. I grabbed his inhaler. I doubt he made it."

"You *doubt*?"

Randy said, "His inhaler? Seriously?"

"Let's assume he's out of the picture," Monica interrupted, sensing that Randy was spiraling in a way she couldn't handle just now. He wasn't seeing the bigger picture, that Aiden was a liability for all of them.

"Did anybody see you?" she demanded of Scott. "Is there anything tying you to the scene?"

Another pause.

"Scott?"

As Scott explained what happened next, Monica's sinking heart was replaced by a chill creeping spiderlike up her spine. One of the two SUVs they'd arrived in had been disabled. Tires slashed. Scott thought—no, he was pretty sure—he heard sirens as he and the other guy pulled away.

"It's okay," Scott said. "That license plate won't come back to us. I made sure of it."

"You made sure of it," Randy said.

"How in the hell," Monica yelled, and stopped. She collected herself. She forced herself to lower her voice when all she wanted was to scream at the top of her lungs as she reached through the fiber-optic cables and ripped Scott's throat out. "How in the hell did this guy, Mercury Carter, whatever, get the drop on *three* of you?" she said. "He doesn't look much bigger than me. He said he was a mailman, for fuck's sake. *A mailman.*"

"Mailman, my ass," Scott said, doing his best to telegraph bravado even though he sounded as if he were pausing at the top of a long flight of stairs to catch his breath. "He's a fed, right?"

"Former fed. Not that it matters."

Scott started to say something but Randy interrupted.

"What's your status?"

"My what?"

"You heard me. Thanks to you, we're already late for this meet. The one where we get the laptop back that was your whole fucking job to keep safe. Literally, your one job. And now we've got your mailman to deal with."

"What?" Scott said.

Slowly, as if speaking to a child on the cusp of a tantrum, Randy explained that Carter had added a new demand: Donny had to bring a girl named Terri Watkins with him tonight. That Randy, like he was some kind of goddamned King Midas, had to sweeten the pot to get Donny on board.

"Donny?" Scott said. "That's his name? How do you know that?"

"Forget how I know. Are you two girls, you and whoever the hell let a mailman get one over on him, up to this job or not? Because if you're not, I've got to make alternative arrangements with no time left."

Monica fought the panic rising in her. Tonight was the best opportunity to wrap everything up in a nice bow. She couldn't handle alternative arrangements.

"We're still doing this?" Scott said.

"Of course we're still doing it," Randy said. "Like we have any choice, thanks to you."

Monica couldn't help herself and chimed in with the obvious. "If we don't get that laptop, we're screwed. All of us." She drew out the last three words as much as she dared to get her point across to Scott.

Monica figured that was it. That Randy's taunt and her needling would push Scott over the edge. She braced for the explosion on the other end of the line.

Instead, after a moment, Scott calmly asked, "You're sure that guy, Carter, is coming?"

"Of course I'm sure," Randy said. "Like I said, he's got a hard-on for some junkie whore working for Donny."

"I'll be there," Scott said. "I'll make sure we get the laptop back, I promise."

"Big of you—" Randy said.

"And once I do," Scott interrupted, "I'm going to chop that motherfucker Carter into a thousand pieces and chum the bay with him from here to Block Island."

Carter closed the laptop and slipped out from under the blackout curtain.

Just in time to catch the taillights of the car, whoever it belonged to, disappearing around the side of the restaurant. Headed for an employee parking lot? Either way, it was now out of view, of Carter and of anyone driving past on the road.

As Carter kept watch, a second vehicle rolled down the road and turned into the parking lot. The second black SUV he'd seen at the warehouse, the one whose tires he hadn't managed to slash. It parked to the left of the restaurant's entrance in a clearly marked handicapped space.

Nothing happened; no one emerged. Carter had to assume Scott Vickers and the surviving operative were inside, the latter with a king-sized headache thanks to the concrete Carter hit him with, so not at full strength. Not that it mattered, with the number of total forces lined up against Carter at this point.

Carter calculated the distance from his Suburban to the right-hand corner of the building around which the first vehicle disappeared. Sixty yards from where he sat. Maybe sixty-five. A long way to go accompanied by Terri Watkins, assuming she was still alive and in any shape to walk, let alone run. Assuming they made it five feet before Vickers or the other operative shot them in the back.

Movement by the front of the restaurant. The doors of the SUV parked in the handicapped spot opened simultaneously, like a giant black bird about to take flight. Difficult to make out the faces of the two black-clad figures who moved swiftly to the left and around the restaurant. But not to guess who they were.

Carter texted his uncle. Gave him a quick overview of what he'd found on the thumb drive and what his next move was. Pocketed his phone before a reply came and opened the Suburban's metal utility box. Carter found the object he was looking for and tucked it into a vest pocket. Next, he felt around for the six-pack of motor oil he kept in case of an emergency. Six-pack in hand, he slowly opened the car door.

And froze in place.

A blue van was pulling into the restaurant parking lot.

THIRTY-NINE

Terri still wasn't sure why she had it.

It—the extra pill.

Donny was careful distributing the blue jobbers to her or to Sheena ahead of time, that was for damn sure. But there it was in her right pocket, next to a condom and a stick of gum, covered with lint but intact when she found it hours earlier.

She worried Donny would search her after snapping the chain and freeing her. She realized after a second that she was flattering herself. All he cared about was getting her out of the apartment—she'd been right, glancing around once she was outside, it was South Providence—and into the van. For some reason he wouldn't explain.

Now that van was tearing through the night, headed south. But where? Donny driving, white-knuckled fists gripping the steering wheel, eyes pinned to the road like an engineer on a runaway train. Jimmy beside him with his head buried in his phone. The other guy, the one behind her, the one with his sunglasses pushed off his forehead, sat silently, staring out the window, clenching and unclenching his hands, which freaked Terri out most of all.

She knew she had to act soon. With no idea where they were going, or what was happening, she might not get another chance. Except now she was stuck. Donny's Monster Energy can—fifth of the day? sixth?—was sitting unopened in the cup holder beside him. Just her luck. The one time she needed a break was the one time Donny decided he wasn't thirsty.

Thirsty.

"Hey," she croaked, her voice like sandpaper on unplaned wood in her dad's workshop. "I need something to drink."

"Shut up," Donny said.

"Please," Terri whined. "Kept me locked up in that room all day like a fucking dog."

"I said, shut up."

"*Pleassse*," she said, drawing out the word as far as she dared.

"For fuck's sake," Donny said, reaching to his right.

Pssst went the can as he popped the tab.

Without taking his eyes off the road, Donny picked up the can and took a pull. He belched, long and loud, and angled the can toward Terri.

"Here."

She leaned forward eagerly, her thirst not entirely faked. The room they'd held her in had been so dry, so hot. As she shifted in her seat, Donny shook the can in his hand three times, like a man jerking off, emptying half its contents into Terri's face.

"Fucker," she screamed.

"Bitch," he said, laughing, placing the can back in the cup holder.

Now or never. She strained forward, clawing at Donny's meaty right arm. He roared at her, angling his arm to hit her, just as Jimmy finally snapped to and grabbed her by the waist.

She ducked as Donny backswung, yelling as loudly as her parched throat allowed. Jimmy swore, pulling at her with his surprisingly strong, skinny arms. Terri yelled again, summoned her last ounce of strength, and bent her hand toward the can of energy drink. As she did, two things happened almost simultaneously.

Donny's right arm, unyielding as a truck axle, connected with her chin, rocketing bursts of lightning through her head so painful she nearly blacked out. Nearly. Because the second thing that happened was that Terri's hand reached the can of Monster Energy drink. Her fingers, feeble from the pain, almost fumbled the pill. Her vision narrowed into a cone of darkness pinpricked by shape-shifting blobs of light. At the last moment, she dropped the pill into the open can.

Terri wasn't sure how long she was out. Time enough for Donny to exit the highway and hit a city street. She couldn't tell where they were between the darkness and the fog clouding her eyes. Story of her life. The only thing she saw, in fact, was Donny reaching over, grabbing the can, and draining the last of the energy drink before he belched again, the sound like a dog farting off its breakfast ahead of a morning snooze.

"Drink this," Donny said, crumpling the empty can in his right fist and chucking it behind him.

There's always windows, Cupcake.

"Fucker," Terri whispered as the can bounced off her forehead.

Carter kept his eyes on Donny Tollman's van. Watched it stop on the right side of the restaurant door, occupying the mirror image handicapped spot that Scott Vickers took on the left. A moment later, the driver's side door opened and Tollman emerged, looking if anything more angry and menacing than the night Carter first encountered him. Carter's view of the right side of the van was blocked. The passenger door opened and closed. Carter held his breath, then released it as he heard the side door swing open, followed by a sound that might have been a woman swearing, or weeping. A second later the woman came into view. *Terri Watkins.*

Carter waited another minute. All clear. Except a good chance existed that one or the other of the late arrivals had parked a lookout inside their vehicle, assigned the job of keeping an eye out for Carter, or whoever. He'd have done the same. Question was: What to do about it?

He went for Vickers's SUV first. Less of an unknown. Carter had direct knowledge of Vickers's recently diminished force strength. He also knew you didn't summon new comrades at the drop of a hat, especially after a debacle like the Olneyville warehouse. Carter left his SUV, leaving the driver's side door ajar by an inch to avoid the sound of the door clicking shut. He darted left, six-pack of oil hanging loosely in his left hand. He arced in a parabola that took him behind a trailered boat parked on a gravel berm to his left, across the road, into a thin grove of trees. Carter watched the SUV for a full minute. Satisfied it was empty, Carter tiptoed out of the woods, into the parking lot, twisted the cap off the first bottle of oil, and dumped it in a shiny pool by the SUV's driver's side door. He opened the second bottle, painted a curve around the rear of the SUV, then drained a third bottle by the passenger door. Finished, he peeked inside the vehicle.

Nothing.

No one.

Assured, Carter crept along the front of the restaurant. Past a weathered sign that read Fine Dining Since 1972 and had a faded painting of an angler battling a marlin. He tucked himself against the left side of Donny's van. He held his breath and waited another minute, tamping down panic at how much time was passing. Hearing nothing inside, he emptied another bottle of oil. He snuck to the right, paused, and used the third and fourth fingers of his left hand to *tap-tap* the van's sliding door. And made a mistake. By not emptying the next bottle of oil.

The sliding door flew open. The van wasn't empty after all. Club Tijuana—the man from Stacy Gibbons's house—found his bearings and pointed a gun at Carter.

Except Carter wasn't there. A second is hardly any time at all, but the interval during which Carter heard the door click open was long enough. He ducked around the back of the van and once more considered his options. Better than a three-legged cat cornered by a junkyard dog, but not by much. He raised his right foot onto the van's rear bumper and vaulted atop the van. He landed with a thump on the roof, which buckled with a metallic pop. Not loud enough to attract the attention of the already assembled meetup attendees around the corner. More than enough to give his location away to Club Tijuana. Which was somewhat the point.

Carter spun himself around in time to see his foe's head appear as he hoisted himself up on the rear bumper. The man used his left hand to gain purchase on the van's roof. Which made sense because the gun was in the man's right hand. Which never made it level to the roof because Carter scissored his right shoe into the side of Club Tijuana's head as hard as a soccer corner kick, if Carter played soccer.

The man grunted and disappeared. Carter didn't hesitate. He swung himself off the roof and onto the back of the man, who was hunched over as he cradled his head and cursed in Spanish. Carter curled his left arm around the man's windpipe and jammed his Beretta into his right ear.

"Drop the gun," Carter said.

The man swore and swiveled, backing Carter hard against the rear of the van.

Carter winced, took a breath, and ground the Beretta a few degrees each way into the man's ear, clockwise and counterclockwise, as if mulling a lock's combination.

"*Suelta el arma*," Carter said, channeling his barebones USPIS Spanish.

The man dropped the gun.

"On your knees."

Instead of complying, the man grunted, reared back, and slammed Carter against the van again. He made a better show of it this time. The impact emptied Carter's lungs and he whooped for air, feeling his grip around the man's neck loosen. He tried to keep the Beretta in place but his gun hand dropped as his feet hit the pavement. Fighting to remain standing, Carter used his left hand to grab the first thing he could find—the back of Club Tijuana's belt. The man swore and took two steps forward, dragging Carter with him. The man swiveled, balling his right hand into a grapefruit-sized fist, and arced his arm for a punch.

The fist found air. Carter, behind the man, pivoted in time with the gunner's movements, gripping his belt for dear life as he mirrored the man's turns like a firefighter reining in a thrashing hose. They danced like this alongside the van, closer and closer to the driver's side, for half a minute. Each time moving up. Another foot. Another six inches. Almost there.

There.

Carter released the belt and shoved Club Tijuana forward like a man done with the lawn mower for the day. The man's left foot skidded on the pooling motor oil and he windmilled his arms for a long three seconds before yelping as something in his back twisted. He fell backward, grunting when his head bounced off the van's front bumper, rolled over and went silent. Carter glanced around, found the man's gun by the van. He examined it while briefly pondering the need for a thirty-round magazine, tucked the weapon into his waistband, and beelined for the rear of the restaurant.

Rounding the corner, Carter reached into a lower right-hand pocket of his utility vest and withdrew the object inside.

Hopefully, this will work.

Like he had any choice.

FORTY

Where the fuck is Pauley? Randy thought, staring at the six people gathered on the back patio of PC Seafood & Chops.

Everyone was spread out in a space the size of a small bandstand, a boundary created by shoving the round outdoor dining tables to one corner and piling the chairs in two precarious towers by the steps to the restaurant's narrow dock. Everyone's eyes—with the exception of the half-dead-looking girl next to Donny Tollman—bright with rage.

Randy did his best to hide his frustration while silently searching out his quarry.

Absolutely no sign.

Really? After all this? After all that talk of sweat equity? *Of* conformity? *What the actual fuck*?

Carter knew a little about grenades. Had handled a couple. Thrown one. He knew the effect they had on people, the sight of one in a hand, finger through the firing pin. The way such a small object made time stop and noise disappear. For sure, this one accomplished its purpose, freezing the circle of seven people standing on the back patio as Carter stepped into view, grenade in his left hand.

He hadn't exactly lied to the Pawtucket patrol officer who asked him what was in the box inside his Suburban the night of Linda Stauch's accident.

Hadn't exactly told the truth, either.

"*Fuuuck*," said a woman on the far side of the circle, eyes widening at the object. Monica Carmichael. Carter tried not to think of the photo he'd just seen of her.

"Evening, everyone," Carter said.

Seven pairs of eyes drilled into him. The only reply came from waves splashing the shore by the dock.

"All right, then," Carter said. "Point one: The shrapnel from a grenade is deadly, but some of the worst injuries come from the percussive blast. Especially in close quarters. It's not something you walk away from."

The small crowd flinched in unison as Carter wiggled his left forefinger within the firing pin.

"Point two." He focused on Randy. Carter recognized his photo from the Second Act website. A big guy, exuding toughness, but also with an odd expression of anxiety on his face that Carter sensed wasn't entirely related to Carter's weapon.

Carter said, "As some of you may know"—he stared at Randy—"I am in possession of a thumb drive of some importance."

Randy didn't react. Admirable. But it was hard to miss the panicked, puzzled look that Monica and Scott Vickers shared.

"The thumb drive contains some interesting details about Second Act Staffing, along with certain other information." Now Carter looked at Monica and Vickers. They glared at him uncertainly.

"The thumb drive is safe but it's not here," Carter continued. "It's not on me or in my car." A bluff, but it's all he had. "I walk away with Terri"—he nodded at the haggard woman, who looked like something left on the beach after low tide—"and you'll have it back in hardly any time at all. But."

Left forefinger wiggle. A collective recoil.

"But," Carter said, "if something happens to me, it's not like the thumb drive's in the wind. It's on the desk of the US Attorney in Providence twelve hours later. Believe her office is on Kennedy Plaza. Understood?"

No one spoke. Each of the seven stood frozen in place, staring at Carter as if he were an apparition that emerged dripping wet and draped in seaweed from the bay behind them.

Carter glanced from side to side, eyes stopping on Terri, her left arm immobilized in the grip of Donny Tollman's right hand.

Carter cleared his throat, raised the grenade half an inch, and said, "The thumb drive is going on that desk, if anything happens to me or to Terri." He nodded at the young woman he'd been hunting for three days. She looked at him in confusion but stayed quiet. "Understood?" he said again.

Still no sound. The scene like a play from hell where everyone simultaneously forgot their lines. Finally, Jimmy spoke, twitching like a squirrel on a live wire.

"Who the fuck are you? First last night, and now tonight?" Rocking from foot to foot as his eyes darted from Carter to Donny and back.

Donny, eyes glassy, appeared about to reply but instead shook his head, as if bothered by a fly. Carter took the opportunity to assess the situation.

On Carter's left, beside a servers' station for the patio, Scott Vickers and the surviving operative, the one who took the concrete to the face. Vickers held his gun on Carter, cold eyes following his every move. The surviving operative, gun raised, blinked slowly.

To their right, their backs to the bay, Randy and Monica Carmichael, the latter looking like a pent-up hellcat that hadn't eaten in a week.

To their left, closest to the employee parking lot, Donny Tollman and Jimmy.

Between them: Terri Watkins.

"Deal's a deal, Carter." Randy, speaking at last. "Girl"—dismissive nod at Terri—"for the thumb drive. You don't have it, you don't get her."

Monica and Vickers traded glances again at the word *deal.*

Carter said, "You'll get it once Terri and I are safe."

"*Once Terri and I are safe,*" Jimmy mimicked, cackling like a witch. A witch on a two-day meth bender.

Donny, slurring his words, looked accusingly at Randy. "You promised me ten large, plus the duffel bag, if I brought her. Where is it?"

"It'll be here," Randy said. "I just need to deal with this idiot first."

"Careful who you call names," Carter said. "I'm not the only one who knows what's on that thumb drive. All the stuff about Sign-Post Contingent Care and New England Med-Care Services. Oh, and Quadrant Horizons. And your daughter." He made eye contact with Randy. "And other stuff that's on there."

"Fuck you," Randy said.

"I only mention this so we have an understanding," Carter said, grenade still upraised. He took a step toward Terri and held out his right hand.

"The hell with this," Donny said, slurring his words again as he raised his gun and slowly waved it back and forth between Carter and Randy. "I want my fucking drugs back, and I want my money."

"Laptop first, asshole," Vickers said.

"*Laptop first,*" Jimmy said.

Guns rose all around.

Crap, Carter thought.

At that moment, the rear door to the restaurant burst open.

"Freeze," said the man standing before them. "Don't anybody move."

Carter, inching toward Terri, stopped and stared.

What the heck?

FORTY-ONE

Standing in the door stood a man—a kid, really—wearing what appeared to be thick red pajamas and holding a Desert Eagle so big he was having trouble lifting it. The do-rag on his head looked as natural as if a tern had built a nest there. He stepped out and was flanked a second later by two other men. One—who couldn't have been more than five foot six in the shower—was dressed in full Boston Celtics regalia. The other, looking like a refugee from *CSI: Atlantic City*, was decked out in a sport coat, electric-blue golf shirt, pleated trousers and black loafers, and wearing enough gold chains around his neck to bind a racehorse. Both were similarly armed.

"Jesus, Pauley," Randy said. "You took your fucking time."

"You should talk," the man called Pauley said. "Now, which one of you lovely dipshits has my drugs?"

Randy pointed at Donny.

"Drugs? Where's my money?" Donny said.

Randy pointed at Pauley.

Donny and Pauley aimed their guns at each other.

"Fire in the hole," Carter said, lobbing the grenade in a short arc toward the middle of the deck.

"Shit," Vickers said, scrambling to his left.

"Fuck," said Monica, scrambling to her right.

Carter darted to Terri, wrapped his arms around her waist, backed himself against the rail and without hesitation flipped both of them over the side as gunshots flew left and right above them.

They landed hard, the drop a good four feet. Terri's weight drove Carter's back into a scattering of crushed gravel and broken shells. Carter groaned involuntarily just as the grenade hit the patio floor. Solid plastic, $17.99 for eight on Amazon, so Carter hadn't totally lied. He heard it bounce twice as the toy's LED light emitted a small flash. Carter pegged Pauley for the squeal that followed.

Time to go. He shifted out from under Terri, grasped her right arm, and lifted. And paused. A sound above, from the patio. Carter looked up in time to see Donny Tollman leaning over the railing, gun in hand, aiming at Terri's back. Carter reached for his Beretta as he pushed Terri to the side. Too late. Tollman sighted on Terri. Carter rolled atop her to shield her and shut his eyes.

Nothing.

Hearing a sound above him, Carter looked up. Donny grabbed the railing with his left hand to brace himself, snorted as if finding something funny in the situation, snorted again, and collapsed backward onto the patio.

"Where's my drugs?" the man called Pauley screeched. "You promised me drugs!"

"Want my money," Donny mumbled from the patio floor.

Carter rolled, grabbed Terri, dragged her upright. He briefly considered jumping into the bay, then realized he had no idea if Terri could swim. Or if she could, whether she was in any condition to make it farther than the end of the dock. Instead, he wrapped his left arm around her waist and hauled her up the driveway as more shots went off.

"It's okay," Carter said. "Keep going. That's it."

"I can't," Terri sobbed.

"You made it this far."

"I don't know what's happening."

"Makes two of us."

They reached the front of the restaurant. Shouts and curses filled the air behind them, but no more gunshots. Carter had maneuvered them as far as Donny's blue van, pulling Terri around the spreading pool of motor oil as fast as she could move, when he heard footsteps. He turned and saw Vickers charging up the driveway, gun hand extended.

"You fucking little—"

Carter released Terri, swung his right arm behind him without looking, and fired off three shots. He grasped Terri again and half dragged, half whipped her around the back of the van just as a right-side window shattered from Vickers's return shot. A moment later, an intake of breath followed by a thump and a curse as Vickers reached the oil and went down hard. Carter grabbed Terri and pulled her toward the Suburban.

They crossed the road. The SUV was thirty yards away. Twenty. Ten.

"Stop."

Carter and Terri turned in unison. Monica stood before them, someone's gun in her hand. Hard to know whose, with all the players back there.

"Enough's enough," she said, catching her breath. "That thumb drive you're talking about. Did Aiden give it to you?"

"No comment."

She pointed the gun at a spot between Carter's eyes. "Where is it?"

Carter tried not to focus on how badly Monica's gun hand was trembling. He swallowed and said, "Where's Randy?"

"Shut up. Answer the question."

Carter's mind raced. He said, "Randy knows about you and Scott."

She froze, pinned in place like a mannequin on a display pole.

"What?"

Beside Carter, Terri stiffened. Carter glanced at her, concerned, then followed her gaze up the road. After a moment, he returned his attention to Monica.

"You heard me. He has pictures of you and Scott. They're, well, graphic. I'm guessing based on your reaction that you didn't think he knew."

"You're lying."

"Negative. Give me your number and I'll text you the photo I found."

"Stop talking. Now."

"Did you know his daughter's name was the thumb drive password? Or maybe not?"

Monica shook her head. "Shut the hell up and tell me where the thumb drive is before I kill you both."

Carter looked over Monica's shoulder, then directed his eyes back to her face. He said, "It makes sense you wouldn't know the password. That's more the operational side of things. The side where actual work gets done. You're more, what, marketing and communications?"

"Fuck you."

"Director of synergy?"

"Last chance." She raised the gun.

"Look out."

"Nice try."

On Monica's right, Randy limped into view. Monica turned, mouth opened wide in surprise. Randy stared back, his expression someplace between disgust and despair. The fact their attention was on each other was enough for Carter. Beretta trained on a space between Randy and Monica, Carter dragged Terri to the Suburban, deposited her inside, and ran around to the driver's side door. Gravel kicked as he pulled away fast. And stopped, just for a second, looking in his rearview mirror.

Monica was pointing her gun at Randy.

Randy had produced a handgun from someplace and was pointing it at Monica.

"Get down," Carter yelled, using his right hand to press Terri's head below window level. He lowered his own head, pushed hard on the gas pedal, and roared away.

Behind him, the sound of gunshots.

FORTY-TWO

Carter thought about separate hotel rooms but rejected the idea immediately. He wasn't about to let Terri out of his sight, not after all that. Not after the last three days. Nevertheless, he sensed her discomfort as he made the arrangements for a single room with the night clerk at a Comfort Inn off Route 2. It was 1:15 A.M. Only a single king-sized bed available.

As soon as they were in the room, Terri rushed inside the bathroom. Carter heard the door lock.

"You okay?"

"I'm not sleeping with you."

He sighed. He thought he'd satisfied her on that point as they drove away from the mess at PC Seafood & Chops, passing a line of cruisers and ambulances headed in the opposite direction. Right after Terri asked him for the third time what was happening and who he was.

"My name's Mercury Carter," he'd told her, keeping his eyes on the road. "I'm a friend of your parents."

Her bloodshot eyes widened. "My parents?"

He nodded. "They thought you were dead. When it looked like you weren't, they hired me to find you. Well, that's not exactly true. To deliver something to you."

"What?"

Carter hesitated. "Something important. I'll explain later, once we've gotten some rest. I'd like them here when that happens."

"I'm not sleeping with you," she said, fumbling at the passenger door lock.

"No worries. That was not my expectation."

Now, back in the hotel room, he repeated his assurances through the bathroom door and added, "As long as you're in there, go ahead and grab a shower if you want. I'm going to leave clean clothes right outside."

Carter hoisted his go bag onto the bed. The one he stored in the Suburban's trunk, that held a decent mix of men's and women's clothes. He reached inside and made some selections. Satisfied, he placed the items on the floor and knocked lightly on the door.

Nothing happened for a second. Then, the door opened barely wide enough for Terri's hand. She reached out, grabbed the clothes, shut and locked the door. Carter waited until he heard the spray of shower water and Terri's feet hitting the bathtub floor. Satisfied she was all right, he laid out his sleeping mat and sleeping bag on the floor beside the bed. Next, he microwaved two cups of instant ramen from his emergency supplies. Finally, he texted a summary of the night's events to his uncle.

Carter was stirring the ramen cups when Terri emerged from the bathroom, drying her stringy hair with a towel. She was wearing jeans, pink Hello Kitty socks, and a purple-and-orange Nazareth College sweatshirt. In contrast to her appearance a few minutes earlier, she looked a solid ten feet—no, fifteen—from death's door.

"Hungry?" Carter said, handing her the ramen.

Two minutes later, as she slurped down the last of the noodles, he handed her his cup as well. He'd be fine with a granola bar.

She slurped down the second cup more slowly, but not by much.

Finished, she said, "Are you a cop?"

"Ex-cop. Now I'm a mailman. Freelance."

He could tell from the confusion on her face the information wasn't computing. Before he could explain further, she said, "How'd you even know about me?"

"I know about you because your . . ." He stopped. "Because Donny Tollman and I ran into each other a couple of nights ago. Near the Narragansett Get 'n Go. We had a, sort of, altercation." Carter shrugged. "One thing led to another."

Terri shook her head, disbelief etched in her eyes. "Those people back there. The one lady and the other guy." Voice hoarse as an emery board scraping against sandpaper. "The one dressed weird as shit in those red sweats. Who were they? Why were Donny and Jimmy there? And what about the thing you said you had?"

"Thing?"

"A thumb thing."

"Thumb drive." He patted his utility vest, assuring himself the drive was there after he'd transferred it from the Suburban's metal box. He suppressed a yawn and checked the bedside clock. Almost 2 A.M.

"It's a long story. Might be better to wait until morning."

"It is morning."

"Like, when the sun is up."

Hesitantly, as if captured in slow motion, Terri twirled her right forefinger in a tight circle. Universal signal of Get on with it.

"Well," Carter said, when his phone buzzed with a call. He glanced at the caller ID.

"One sec."

Terri shook her head in disgust and ran her fingers around the inside of the second ramen cup. Carter reached into his go bag and handed her a granola bar.

"Hello?"

"Where the hell are you?"

Gus Papaleonardos.

"I'm safe."

"What about the girl? Terri Watkins?"

"Safe as well."

"Where?"

"Safe, like I said."

"Enough's enough, Carter. She's officially a person of interest. There's a line of people waiting to talk to her about those three guys, the names you gave me. Shaun Volpe. Jason Schulte. Chuck Gibbons. Whether she was acting alone or not, she's got to answer questions."

"At 2 A.M.?"

"No, smart guy. The 2 A.M. talk is for you."

"Me? Why?"

"Because there's a separate line of people waiting to interview you about the mess you left at Carnevale's. Several of those people have three letters on the back of their windbreakers."

"Where?"

"Carnevale's—the restaurant."

Carter thought for a second. "PC Seafood?"

Papaleonardos paused for a moment, and when Carter didn't reply, he said, "You have no idea what I'm talking about, do you?"

"I'm sorry. It's been a long few days."

"Ever heard of Paul Carnevale?"

Carter told him he hadn't.

"Rhode Island mob boss, back in the seventies and eighties. Ran half of New England and a chunk of Philly. Him and Raymond Patriarca split things up."

"Who?"

"Jesus. Never mind. That restaurant, it was Carnevale's. He cleaned money through it. Despite that, the clam chowder was supposedly decent."

Confused, Carter said, "What's that guy have to do with any of this?" He turned and glanced at Terri. She was flat on her back on the bed, half-eaten granola bar in her right hand, sound asleep.

"Carnevale died in prison a few years back. His son's a piece of shit but no mobster. Just ran a fish restaurant his dad left him, as far as anyone knows. But *his* son is a real piece of work. Goes by Pauley. Fancies himself a comeback mob kid, like that's a thing."

Slowly, like a self-sorting Rubik's cube, pieces of a puzzle clicked into place. "Let me guess," Carter said. "Gangster sweatpants? Designer do-rag?"

"That's him. You see him tonight?"

Carter held the phone away from his face. He probably should have given Papaleonardos one of his burner numbers, not his actual phone. Not the one he called Uncle Dean on. The one he used to text Tomeka accountant memes, of which there existed a surprising number. Not the phone whose screen lock was a photo of his mom and his late father.

Carter knew from experience that cops tracing calls in real time wasn't like the movies. But it wasn't unlike the movies, either.

Carter said, "I did see him. I'm not sure why he was there."

"Surprise, surprise, we're trying to figure that out too. We've got seven question marks right now, thanks to you."

Now Papaleonardos had Carter's attention. "Sorry. What?"

"You heard me. We currently have in custody Pauley Carnevale and a buddy of his who has a thing for the Celtics. We also have a couple named Randy and Monica Carmichael. Ever heard of them?"

"Possibly. They're alive?"

"Yes, they're alive. Why would you ask that?"

"No reason."

"Right. Well, they've heard of you, trust me. Next we've got some half-conscious big dude who's on the way to the hospital with a concussion. Not to be confused with another big dude who's also on the way to the hospital."

"Was one of those guys on the patio? Trouble breathing?"

"The second one, yeah. They think he overdosed."

"That's Donny Tollman."

"Okay. That's actually useful."

"Anybody else?"

"An ex-cop, last name Bouton, who got shot in the thigh. Works for a security company. He clammed up pronto."

The operative who took the concrete to the face.

"All right. What about the other three?"

When Papaleonardos didn't answer right away, Carter peeled back the covers of the bed, shifted Terri onto the sheet, and covered her up. She didn't stir.

"Detective?"

"Don't know about three. We've got two DOAs. A skinny guy with a bunch of tattoos who got shot in the chest on the back patio, and one of Pauley's guys, dressed up like he was going out for cocktails. Took one through the eye. That's it."

Carter ran the numbers. Randy and Monica. Club Tijuana, Jimmy, and Donny. Pauley and his two lieutenants. The operative with the rearranged nose.

"You see another ex-cop type?" He described Scott Vickers.

"Nobody like him."

"How many vehicles on the scene?"

"Two that we could find. Randy and Monica's SUV, and what I assume, thanks to your intel, is Tollman's blue van."

"No black SUV? Parked in a handicapped spot on the left as you face the restaurant?"

Papaleonardos confirmed no such vehicle was found.

Perfect. Scott Vickers is on the run.

"Carter. What's going on?"

He was so tired. He just wanted to sleep.

Carter said, "Earlier this evening, an incident got called in, in Olneyville. Gunshot victim, plus somebody named Aiden in respiratory distress."

"What are you talking about?"

"The guy, Aiden. I'm not sure if that's his first or last name. He might be in trouble. I need you to check on him."

"Check on a guy whose full name I don't know? Plus, what's any of this have to do with Terri Watkins? You're not making sense here, Carter."

Carter was inclined to agree. He was about to explain when his phone buzzed again. This time with a text.

"Hang on."

"I'm not hanging on, Carter. We need—"

"I said, hang on."

Carter pulled up the message from an unknown number.

A moment later, he stared at a photo of Aiden, gagged and blindfolded, with the barrel of a gun kissing the left side of his head.

The message that accompanied the photo was simple—an address, followed by eight words:

Thumb drive. One hour. Come alone. Otherwise, bang.

For the love of Mike.

"Gotta go," Carter told Papaleonardos, and cut the call.

FORTY-THREE

Carter's first attempt went to voicemail. As did his second. And his third.

Two rings into the fourth try, Jim Watkins finally answered. Groggy, barely awake.

"Hello?"

"It's Mercury Carter," Carter said. "I have a bit of a situation."

To Watkins's credit, he went from dead asleep to coherent in under half a minute.

"Okay. I'm awake. What's going on?"

Thumb drive. One hour. Come alone. Otherwise, bang.

Fifty-five minutes to go.

"I found Terri. She's safe. She's with me. I was going to—"

"What? She's alive? Where are you?" Watkins was now fully awake.

"Don't interrupt. We don't have much time. I was going to bring her by in the morning, but something's come up. I need you to come to me, ASAP, and stay with her until I sort something out."

"Come where?"

"I'll tell you in a second—"

"Do the police know? There was a detective—"

"The police only know I have her. I assume you're talking about Gus Papaleonardos. He's on our side, but we have to go slow. Terri's fine, but she's in trouble. If the police get to her first you can kiss a reunion goodbye. Understand?"

"What kind of trouble?"

"The kind I can't get into right now. I think it's something we can manage, but we can't go to the authorities yet. Can we agree on this?"

Silence on the other end. Then: "Yes, okay. What should I do?"

"Like I said, I need you to come to me. Like, immediately. Without being followed. Can you do that?"

"Sure."

"Before you do anything, though, can you look outside real quick? See if there's any cop cars sitting by your house?"

"Are you serious?"

"Please, Jim. I'm running out of time."

A minute later, Watkins confirmed he wasn't being watched.

Carter checked his watch. "This could be a long day, just so you know. Those frozen meals you mentioned you've been getting? Since Valerie stopped cooking? Maybe grab a couple."

"Um, okay."

"I'm texting you the address. Get here as fast as you can."

Carter cut the call before Watkins could reply and sent him the hotel information. He thought for a second and sent a second text, this one to the phone that had relayed the picture of a bound and gagged Aiden.

Need more time. There's cops everywhere. Assume you don't want me bringing them along?

Nearly five minutes passed. Then Vickers responded:

4 A.M. That's it.

Thirty extra minutes. Okay. Carter could live with that. Would have to.

He glanced over at his sleeping bag and mat laid out next to the bed holding an unconscious Terri Watkins. A king mattress at the Ritz-Carlton with a chocolate on the pillow couldn't have looked more inviting. For twenty seconds, Carter entertained the notion of stretching out until he heard Jim Watkins's knock on the door. Just resting his eyes, as his father used to say after a long day schlepping mail up and down Rochester streets.

Fantasy concluded, Carter picked up his phone, thought for a minute, and sent another text to a new number. To a woman he knew in Indianapolis. Hopefully she slept with her phone muted, given the hour.

Finished, he retrieved Aiden's thumb drive from his vest, plugged it into his laptop, opened it, and studied the root directory. He'd only have one shot at this. He had to get it right. He thought about Vickers, his close-cropped blond hair, his black operative uniform that was meant to be intimidating but instead brought to mind an extra from a *Star Wars* movie. He considered the compromising photos of Vickers and Monica he'd found. He went back to the Monica folder and copied the most graphic. Okay. This could work.

Better work.

RIDOC's Gloria McDonald Women's Facility wasn't even twenty years old, but had always struck Monica as looking like one of those brick boxes from the nineteenth century where they sent women to die of tuberculosis, leprosy, or the crime of being poor and female. She'd had plenty of time to make such observations going in and out of the building during her stint as a night nurse at the women's medical clinic before she transferred to the men's side of things, where she preferred to operate. Personally and professionally.

Now, Monica stared numbly at the snot-colored cinderblock walls of the intake cell where she was being held, along with a woman picked up for soliciting who stank of vomit and a woman with crossed eyes arrested for drunken driving who stank of pot. Monica had no idea where Randy was, though she assumed he was someplace in the same RIDOC complex. They'd been driven in separate police cars after what felt like the entire Rhode Island law enforcement community descended on PC Seafood & Chops, the cruisers' blue-and-white lights painting the trees and the front of the restaurant like concert strobes.

Monica went back to the armed standoff with her husband. She wasn't sure how she missed. She damn sure wasn't sure how Randy missed. All she knew was they were staring at each other in disbelief, and rage, when the first cop roared up and ordered them to drop their weapons.

Which they did, slowly and reluctantly.

The knock came twenty-eight minutes after Jim Watkins answered his phone at his house in Cranston, roused from a dead sleep. Carter gripped his Beretta and crept to the door, standing to the side.

"Who is it?"

"It's Jim Watkins. Jim and Val."

Carter said, "Mother's Day, two years ago. Where did you and Val and Terri and your mom and"—he hesitated, straining to make his exhausted brain cooperate—"and Nate go to lunch?"

Without hesitating, Watkins said, "Marchetti's."

Good enough. Carter pushed back the door's security latch, flipped the dead bolt, and opened the door. Carter grabbed Watkins by the front of his shirt before he could speak, pulled him inside, repeated the drill with Valerie, glanced up and down the corridor, and shut and secured the door.

Valerie gasped, seeing Terri in the bed. "Is she . . ."

"She's asleep," Carter said. "She's been through a lot. I wouldn't advise waking her right now, but it's up to you. Did everything go all right? Getting here, I mean?"

Jim looked at Valerie. "As far as I know. Nobody followed us—the streets were empty." Valerie nodded her agreement.

"Do either of you have the Find My app activated? It lets people track your location."

They shook their heads.

Carter asked to see their phones to be sure. Satisfied, he instructed both to set their phones to airplane mode.

"Why?" Jim said.

"We can't have anyone tracing you here. Use this if you have to contact me—my number's the only one programmed in." He handed Jim a burner phone. "Like I said"—Carter glanced at Terri—"she's in trouble. I can help her, but we need time."

Watkins repeated the question he asked earlier. "What kind of trouble?"

"I'll get to that. I need to move. Once I'm gone, bolt the door and flip the security latch. Do not open the door under any circumstances unless you're sure it's me. For God's sake, don't let Terri leave if you can help it. I'll pay for a second night to be safe, in case I'm gone a while. All set?"

Watkins glanced at Valerie.

"Not really." He looked at Carter. "But I trust you." Another glance at Valerie. "We trust you. You found her, like you said you would."

"I said I'd get the ring to her." He almost left it at that, then added: "I've never missed a delivery."

Carter couldn't decide if Vickers was being cute by choosing Stacy Gibbons's empty brick Colonial for the meetup or was just desperate. He settled on diabolical, a word he'd always felt was underrated. There was a better than even chance that Vickers expected to find Stacy there and planned to incriminate her, and/or eliminate her, as part of his final act. In an abstract sense, Carter wished he could have been there when Vickers discovered that Stacy was gone.

Carter opted against stealth. While he felt good about his plan, it was a one-hit wonder and a lot depended on it. Starting with Aiden's life. He couldn't risk jeopardizing everything by storming the castle.

Stacy's street was quiet when he pulled up. No surprise: it was quarter to four in the morning. No sign of Vickers's SUV. He opened his door, held in place as his phone buzzed with an incoming call. Papaleonardos. They were both pulling all-nighters. Carter weighed his options. It wasn't ideal, but he settled on distraction, the way magicians drew your eye away from the trick. Better here than the Comfort Inn. He texted Papaleonardos Stacy's address without comment, set the phone to silent, and placed it back in his utility vest. Time to launch his plan, such as it was.

He left the Suburban, strode up the street with an air of confidence, bearing erect—*Lived here all my life, folks, nothing to worry about*—then turned right into Stacy's driveway. Doing his best impression of a man who had every reason to be on a stranger's property before dawn. Surprise, surprise, Vickers's SUV was parked in front of the garage. Carter turned to unfinished business. What he'd run out of time for at the warehouse, which had likely added to the mess at PC Seafood & Chops. He used his box cutter to slash the two tires on the SUV's right side. He listened for the whistle of escaping air, crouching as the SUV tilted to the right like a beast of burden overcome by the sun.

Satisfied, Carter crossed the yard to the landscaping stones encircling beds of asters and mums he remembered from earlier in the day. He studied them for a moment and made his choice. Not too big, but not too small. Medium, the way Carter liked things. He palmed the stone, tossed it up, and caught it, liking the feel in his hand. He took three steps toward the house, aimed, and hurled the stone through the window to the left of the back door. The sound of exploding glass and the accompanying *thud* of the rock as it struck the kitchen floor wasn't as loud as Carter hoped for, but loud enough. No one awake within half a block would mistake it for an errant raccoon knocking over a bottle in the recycling.

Without waiting to see what happened, Carter returned to the front of the house, mounted the steps, and rang the doorbell.

FORTY-FOUR

Nearly two minutes passed. No answer. About what Carter expected.

It wasn't hard to work out what was happening. The crash of the rock through the window. Vickers, already on edge, roused to action by what he assumed was Carter's assault from the rear of the house. A rush through the kitchen, gun drawn, to encounter . . . nothing. Then, maybe the last thing Vickers expected, the sound of a doorbell. Like a neighbor was dropping by to sell Girl Scout cookies. Except at 4 A.M. Carter pictured Vickers inside, deciding next steps. He was a trained operative. Accustomed to hair-trigger reactions to a variety of violent, volatile situations. But, best guess, he probably wasn't as good at deciphering a simple doorbell. Which hopefully had him off his game.

Carter rang the bell again.

Thirty seconds later, the door opened halfway. Carter peered inside and saw himself staring at a gun barrel. Not for the first time.

Before Vickers could speak, Carter said, "I got here as quickly as I could. Everything okay?"

"Inside, asshole."

Carter walked into the house, palms up in supplication, and stepped to the middle of the living room. Aiden was slumped on the couch, hands bound behind his back, still gagged and blindfolded. He was drawing deep breaths through his nose but didn't appear to be suffering a full-blown asthma attack. Yet. How he ended up here was anybody's guess. For now.

"Gun," Vickers said, closing the front door and waving his own weapon at Carter.

Carter looked around like a painter checking out a prospective interior residential job.

"Stacy's not here, is she?"

"Why do you care?"

"I care because I know where she is and you don't. Which is par for the course for you, isn't it, Scott? Always one step behind?"

"Fuck you. Gun."

"Clock's ticking."

"What?" Vickers said.

"That rock through the back window, however that happened, was kind of loud. I might have seen a light go on next door. I'm thinking we don't have a lot of time."

Vickers shook his head. "Gun—take it out slowly and set it on the coffee table."

"Neighbors can be so nosy."

"*Gun.*"

Carefully, Carter reached inside his vest, removed the Beretta grip first, and set it on the table.

"Anything else?" Vickers said.

"Pepper spray. Oh, and a flea bomb."

Vickers waved his gun from Carter to the table and back.

Carter removed the items and set them beside the Beretta.

"Thumb drive."

"In my vest."

"Take it out. Slowly."

Keeping the gun in his right hand trained on Carter, Vickers held out his left hand, palm open.

Carter extracted the thumb drive from a middle vest pocket on the left. He stepped to his right, reached over, and placed the device between his gun and the flea bomb.

"I said—"

"You got what you wanted. Let Aiden go and we'll be on our way."

"Right." Vickers lifted his gun and pointed the barrel between Carter's eyes.

"One point," Carter said quickly.

"What?"

"It's possible I came here with a dummy thumb drive. Eight bucks at Staples. Good deal, though it's cheaper to buy packs of three. A bargain like that, maybe I had a trick up on my sleeve and figured I could prank you and get out of here safely."

"Shut up—"

"I'm not saying I did that. But if that's a fake, and you kill me, guess who's never going to find out where the real one is? Remember what I said about the US Attorney, back at the restaurant? Also, did I mention I thought I saw a light go on next door?"

"You're bluffing."

"Laying out a scenario is all."

Vickers blinked. "I'll kill you both. I will."

"I don't disbelieve you."

Vickers and Carter stared at each other in the dim light of Stacy Gibbons's living room for almost ten seconds. At last, Vickers said, "Chair. Sit."

Carter turned and saw a wide blue tufted armchair two feet from the end of the coffee table. He took a breath, backed up, and sat.

Gun never leaving Carter's chest, Vickers stepped across the room. He moved slowly, with a limp. It occurred to Carter that Vickers hadn't escaped unharmed from the fray at PC Seafood & Chops. Possible he'd been winged in the barrage of bullets shortly after Pauley Carnevale made his appearance.

Now that, as his uncle would say, had been a shit show.

Vickers found what he was looking for, a tablet on the dining room table, and carried it into the living room. He fired it up, hunting and pecking with his left hand as he worked. The movement looked awkward and inefficient. Carter didn't move, watching the barrel of the gun he was facing, the way it bobbed up and down, just a bit, but remained pointed dead center. Carter's center.

Finished, Vickers switched hands, moving the gun to his left, the barrel never leaving its target. Ambidextrous gun-handling skills. *Impressive.* Carter stayed put. Best not to test that capability. Vickers leaned forward and picked up the thumb drive with his right hand.

"You better not be fucking with me."

"You're the one with the gun."

Vickers inserted the drive into the USB port on the right side of the tablet. Carter held his breath for what he knew was the approximately 2.5 seconds it would take for the root directory to appear on the screen. He exhaled as Vickers's eyes scanned the directory before stopping. Carter had only one play left. A play that gambled that a lone file sitting in the directory by itself, one that hadn't been there before, tucked between Koloa Landing and Outrigger Reef, and labeled, all-caps, *FBI—SCOTT VICKERS*, would be of interest to his captor.

It was. Vickers, eyes flicking up at Carter and down at the screen, used his right hand to double-click on the file.

Carter waited, doing everything he could to calm his pounding heart.

"The fuck?" Vickers said, staring at his screen, distracted for the first time since Carter entered the house.

Carter reared back and kicked the end of the coffee table. The far end skidded into Vickers's knees with a crack like a dinner plate splitting in half. Vickers fell backward with a yell, gun pointed at the ceiling. Carter launched himself across the table, reaching in vain for his Beretta, watching it fall to the side instead. No matter. He threw himself at Vickers.

First priority, the gun. Carter gripped Vickers's left arm with both hands, forcing the gun hand up and back. It wasn't easy. Vickers rained blows on Carter's head with his right fist. It was like being struck by a rubber mallet on automatic repeat. Carter's grip on Vickers's left arm loosened. He could feel the strength pulsate through Vickers's toned, muscular body. This was ridiculous. Like a meerkat battling a hyena. He winced, realized his left cheek was bleeding. Carter squeezed his eyes shut and snapped his head forward, butting Vickers's nose. The crack was louder than the coffee table hitting Vickers's knees. Vickers jerked back with a roar. Carter butted him again. *Okay, that one really hurt.* Turned out that seeing stars was a thing.

Carter felt Vickers's hand relax, grip lessening for a moment like a man readjusting his hold on a trowel. Carter grabbed Vickers's gun with his right hand and brought it down hard and fast against the right side of Vickers's face. No crack this time, just blood gushing from a crease running the length of Vickers's face from jaw to ear. Red to match the blood pouring off Carter's face.

"Don't move," Carter said, hopping backward on one foot as he stood, struggling to keep his balance.

"Little shit," Vickers managed, levitating more than leaping off the couch in Carter's direction. The movement rocking the coffee table enough that the tablet spun, screen briefly facing Carter before it crashed to the ground. The screen sporting the image of Vickers atop Monica on the kitchen island that Carter discovered in the Monica folder. The picture Vickers found in the *FBI—SCOTT VICKERS* folder.

Timing was everything. Carter had used up his last allotment with the photo trick. Vickers, bleeding face and all, struck him like a linebacker whose scholarship hung on a single tackle. For the second time that night, landing hard on the floor on his back, Carter *whoop-whoop*ed for oxygen as air emptied from his lungs. Arms trapped beneath him under Vickers's weight, which was almost all muscle. As Carter struggled to gain his bearings, wriggling like a beached whale, he felt something cold scrape his forehead. He had just enough time to see the incongruous sight of an inhaler before instinctively squeezing his eyes shut as Vickers ground the device into Carter's left eye. The device—Aiden's inhaler.

Carter's stomach turned as pain flooded his insides. Vickers's grasp was inexorable as he threw his arm strength into the effort. Exploding pinpricks of color flooded Carter's brain as the device's sharp plastic edge fought its way toward his brain despite how tightly he was squeezing his eyes. The colors faded as darkness crept around the edges of Carter's consciousness.

A final glint of color. Red. Ruby red. Terri's ring. She still didn't have it. Carter had never missed a delivery.

Carter relaxed, caught his breath, did what he hoped would be the last thing Vickers expected. He pushed *into* the inhaler. Attacked instead of retreated. Directed all his weight onto it. All his remaining strength. Vickers, caught off guard, fought briefly for purchase. Difficult because of how slick the inhaler was. Slick with blood. Vickers's or Carter's. Vickers's hand slipped. That was enough. Carter freed his right arm, grabbed the inhaler, fought briefly, yanked it from Vickers's hand. Without looking, he jammed it up, hard and fast, into Vickers's mouth, a punch like the whip of a ball to first base. Vickers gasped, went quiet. Gray clouding his vision, Carter smacked the inhaler as hard as he could with the base of his palm, forcing it deeper inside. Vickers bucked and fell to the side.

Carter rose to his knees. Cleared his head. Saw Vickers, eyes bulging, the inhaler jammed halfway down his throat. Face turning red. Chest heaving. Hands scrabbling in vain to pull the device free. Carter dried his hands on his cargo shorts, leaned forward, pushed Vickers's hands out of the way, reached for the inhaler.

Mad for oxygen, eyes glassy with panic, Vickers flailed, shoving Carter away. Carter tried again, took a fist to the eye. He blinked, saw those stars once more. He shifted forward, grabbed Vickers's right arm, pinned it beneath his left knee, and reached for his left arm. Once, twice—hand whipping back and forth out of reach—third time the charm. Carter pinned Vickers's left arm. Reached again toward Vickers's mouth—

Too late. Vickers lurched back and forth violently, like a man walking into an electric fence. His chest bucked again, twice more, the movement so violent Carter was knocked back, losing control of Vickers's arms. As Carter collected himself, Vickers's eyes rolled into his skull white as bleached bones. Blood oozed from his nostrils.

Carter reached forward, tried three times to grab the slippery device, finally yanked the inhaler free.

Vickers didn't move.

FORTY-FIVE

Terri stirred, rolled over, opened her eyes. Terror gripped her for a moment as she realized she had no idea where she was.

Slowly, like figures growing close on a foggy day, things came back to her. The one-room prison in South Providence, where she was chained to the radiator. The bat-out-of-hell ride in the van to a restaurant by the bay. The standoff on the patio, the sound of water lapping the dock jutting into the bay behind them. The appearance of the man in the vest with the ball cap, the same one who'd been in Attleboro, holding a grenade, of all things. The bizarre arrival of a clown-like guy in red pajamas and two other clowns from inside the restaurant. Donny and the clown's strange two-sentence conversation.

The clown first: *"Where's my drugs? You promised me drugs!"*

Then, Donny: *"Want my money."*

The man in the vest with the ball cap wrestling her over the patio railing. Donny's gun pointing at her, followed instead by his collapse. A confused drive in the dark to a hotel. A shower, clean clothes, cups of warm noodles.

She blinked. The room was dark except for a thin band of light from the slightly parted curtains. In front of the curtains, two chairs. In them, two people, sitting silently.

Her parents.

Terri gasped, but the sound was so quiet it might have been the faint shifting of a blanket. She stared for a moment, deciding if she was seeing straight, if it was really them. She tried to speak, but her lips were too dry, too cracked. By then, it was too late.

Sleep overtook her once more.

Carter used his box cutter to free Aiden's hands, then removed Aiden's blindfold and the duct tape from his mouth. Aiden took two long, shuddering breaths, leaned forward, and threw up. Carter moved to the side just in time.

Carter left the living room for the kitchen, opened drawers until he found a hand towel, soaked it in cold water. He poured a glass of water, and returned to the living room with both, carefully sidestepping Vickers's body as he handed them to Aiden. He pointed at the bloody inhaler lying on the floor, eyebrows raised. Aiden shook his head. Hard to blame him.

"Thanks," Aiden said at last. "Twice, I guess."

"Not a problem." Carter looked at Vickers. "He get you at home?"

Aiden nodded. "Stupid. I was out of it—just got home after talking to the cops. It never dawned on me that he'd try that, after everything that happened at the warehouse."

"Desperate times. He wanted that thumb drive."

"Yes and no." Voice raspy and halting.

"Meaning?"

Instead of replying, Aiden said, "Who are you, anyway?"

"Like I told you before, at Second Act. Mercury Carter. I'm a mailman. An independent courier."

"You're not a cop?"

Carter assured him that he wasn't.

"A mailman?" Aiden looked skeptically first at Carter, then at Vickers's remains.

"Long story."

"What's a mailman have to do with any of this?"

"Forget that part. Why did you say 'yes and no' about the thumb drive?"

"You looked at it?"

Carter confirmed it.

"You figure out what Randy was up to?"

"Stealing PHI? And selling it? Something to do with that temp agency he founded?"

Aiden nodded.

"How'd it work?"

Aiden hesitated. Carter didn't say anything. Silence was golden in situations like this. In his experience.

"You're really not a cop?"

"Really."

Aiden looked around the room, settled on a spot to Carter's left.

"Randy placed temp employees in medical places," he said. "Once they started, he'd send the employees emails with scheduling information and copy all the office administrators at wherever they were employed. The schedule was a phishing link. One or two administrators always clicked on it. Like clockwork. Once they did, we were in."

"We?"

"Chuck, mostly. Chuck Gibbons. But me too."

"They fell for it that easily?"

Aiden rubbed his right hand over his left wrist, working on his circulation. "Health care's the worst when it comes to IT security. Systems on systems that don't communicate with one another. Plus, so many third-party vendors with their own systems. Like Swiss cheese."

Aiden's voice took on a note of confidence. He was on a roll. *Got a live one*, Carter and his USPIS colleagues used to say. You could always tell.

"Every year there's all these breaches," Aiden continued, "followed by all these reports warning how bad the problem is, and it just keeps happening. Randy looked at that, took the Trojan horse approach, voilà."

"Nobody detected the thefts?"

Something like pride crossed Aiden's face. "Some of these places, their security was a McAfee subscription. In those cases, no. A few caught on, but usually months later. By that time the damage was done. In those cases, we fell on our swords fast. Told them we'd both been scammed."

Carter rolled the details around in his head. He had to admit, putting aside the illegality, the system had an elegance to it. What better way to override warnings about phishing than to embed the phishing link in a legitimate email from a known person?

He thought about the rows of personal health information he'd seen from the first two companies—Sign-Post Contingent Care and New England Med-Care Services. "How much PHI did Randy steal?"

Waiting for Aiden to respond, Carter had a thought. *By that time the damage was done.* Carter said, "How much did *you* steal?"

If Aiden was offended by the question he didn't show it. "Enough to keep the operation going, set some reserves aside. Like I said, not enough to attract a lot of attention. That was the beauty of Randy's plan."

"Of your plan," Carter said.

Now Aiden looked uncomfortable. But he didn't deny Carter's statement.

Carter said, "The PHI was on Chuck's laptop. Which Donny Tollman stole after Chuck overdosed with a prostitute. That's why Vickers wanted the computer back so badly."

"Like I said about the thumb drive, yes and no," Aiden said.

"And like I said, meaning?"

Aiden stared briefly at the ceiling. "Vickers cut a side deal with Chuck. Chuck was helping them with some kind of new operation." Aiden rolled his eyes. "They called it 'The Plan.' Randy didn't know about it."

"Them. Monica and Vickers?"

"That's right."

"Is that why they were having the affair?"

Aiden smirked. "You saw the photos?"

Carter confirmed it.

"Maybe? All I know is that Monica and Vickers knew that Second Act was close to a jackpot, and they wanted a bigger cut than Randy would ever give them because of his daughter."

"Jackpot—Quadrant Horizons?"

Aiden nodded.

Carter considered this. If Carter were still a cop, Aiden would have been writing his own sentencing memo at this point. But there was no mistaking the relief on his face. Carter saw it often in his USPIS days. The perps stopped lying through their teeth and decided to confess. Visibly relaxing as they finally told the truth, like men having splinters removed after years of limping. Live ones, indeed.

Carter said, "I'm guessing the information about Monica and Vickers's plan was on Chuck's laptop? But Randy didn't know about that part."

"That's right."

"You mirrored the laptop on the thumb drive?"

"Right again."

"How'd the photos of Monica and Vickers get on that?"

"Randy took me aside a couple of weeks ago, told me what was happening and what he had. He'd installed webcams everywhere. He said to keep the photos safe in case anything happened to him."

Carter thought about the scene outside the restaurant parking lot, Randy and Monica facing off, guns in hand.

"Anything like what?"

"I didn't ask. It wasn't hard to figure out, though, given the affair. Vickers was a scary dude." He pursed his lips. "Almost as scary as Monica."

"And you're in the middle, playing both sides?"

"Me?"

"Sure. You knew about Monica and Vickers, how they were planning something behind Randy's back. And you knew Randy knew about them, at least about the affair."

"I guess."

"Okay. Quadrant Horizons."

"What about it?"

Outside, Carter heard a car stop on the street outside the house.

"That hadn't started? The phishing, I mean?"

Aiden shook his head. "It was about to go live before Chuck died. Randy decided to go ahead anyway."

"Quadrant's a whole other level than those other places. Randy didn't worry about getting caught?"

"Chuck told him he could cover their tracks. I'm not so sure, but Randy was hyperfocused on his daughter."

Carter heard a car door open and shut.

"What about you?"

"What about me what?"

"Were you worried you'd get caught? You're in this up to your eyeballs."

Another smirk crossed Aiden's face. "I'm just a cog. Cogs cut deals."

"Wonder if Quadrant Horizons will see it that way?"

Aiden laughed dismissively. "My guess is, they'll be too grateful that you came along to care about me."

Their conversation was interrupted by someone pounding at the front door. Carter instinctively reached for his Beretta, then relaxed as he saw flashing lights illuminating the street.

Carter said, "The thumb drive. You kept a copy of everything."

Aiden nodded.

"Insurance?"

"Something like that."

"Randy and Monica didn't suspect you were onto them?" Carter said.

He shook his head. "Not until tonight. Until you came by. They were worried I told you something. Vickers and Monica were worried, I mean."

Sorry not sorry. "Why'd you tell me the password? At the warehouse?"

"Thought you were a cop. Guessed the gig was up. Figured it was better to cooperate."

"You kept that secret until now. How?"

Aiden shrugged. "I'm the big, ugly guy in the corner wearing sweatpants with crumbs in his beard. Nobody ever suspects us."

FORTY-SIX

Carter admitted it this time. He was lucky. Had officers come to both doors of Stacy's house, front and back, his morning would have been cut dramatically short. Instead, he safely slipped out the rear a minute later, crept to the far side of the backyard, vaulted awkwardly over the wooden fence, and worked his way back to his Suburban. He was three blocks down when Papaleonardos rang. He declined the call.

Carter used the door by the Comfort Inn's rear parking lot to re-enter the hotel. The precaution didn't matter; he knew every inch of his movement was covered by a camera someplace. Hopefully no one was watching too closely at 5:30 A.M.

"It's Mercury," Carter said, after Jim Watkins demanded to know who was knocking. He added the only confirmation he could think of. "Terri's wearing Hello Kitty socks."

Terri was sitting up in bed when they entered. Valerie was beside her, holding her hand. Jim stayed standing. So far, the reunion was hardly cinematic. Carter saw the pain in everyone's eyes. A lot of damage had been done. You didn't repair that overnight, or with a derring-do rescue.

Carter's phone buzzed. Papaleonardos again. He didn't have a lot of time. The fact Carter could have slept twelve hours uninterrupted, maybe where he stood, notwithstanding. He checked his phone. Nothing back from Indianapolis. Not a surprise. It was early for normal people.

Carter pulled a chair beside the bed and sat.

"Terri. I need to ask you some questions."

She kept her eyes pinned on her hand in her mother's.

"Terri?"

"About what?" Terri said.

"About Donny Tollman. And your customers."

Her face hardened.

"What about them?"

"Does the name Shaun Volpe mean anything to you?"

Confusion clouded her eyes. Carter described him as best he could from the open casket and photos he'd seen at the funeral home.

She shook her head.

"What about Chuck Gibbons?"

This time, Carter's description hit home. Slowly, she nodded.

"Did you give him a pill?"

Terri whispered something Carter couldn't make out.

"Terri?"

"Yeah," she said.

"Do you know what that pill was?"

"Is this really necessary?"

Jim Watkins, leaning over Carter, anger in his eyes.

"Yes," Carter said, meeting his gaze. "Terri?"

She nodded.

"What about Jason Schulte? Did you give him a pill?"

Tears streamed down her cheeks as she nodded again.

"Did Donny make you give them those pills?"

She nodded once more, sobbing.

"That's enough," Jim Watkins said.

"Jim," Valerie said, looking up at her husband. "Don't be a fool."

Valerie reached out and pulled her daughter close. Terri stiffened, then relaxed into her mother's arms.

Carter's phone buzzed with a call.

Indianapolis area code.

Carter answered.

"Rachel?"

"Mercury—is everything all right? I just saw your message."

"Things are interesting. I'm sorry to message you so early. I'll get right to it. I'm guessing you're not admitted to the bar in Rhode Island?"

"I'm afraid not," she said, the lawyer's voice still hoarse with sleep. "Indiana, Illinois, and soon Ohio. And DC, but I'm letting that lapse. Why?"

"I have a situation and I'm not sure how to proceed. I need your help."

"Anything. What's going on?"

Carter felt a little guilty hearing the willingness in Rachel Stanfield's voice despite the hour. He supposed it made sense. Not all that long ago, she and her husband had nearly been murdered by home invaders. Carter's fortuitous arrival at the door of their suburban Indianapolis home with a delivery for Rachel saved the day.

Luck?

He blinked the thought away and told Rachel about Terri Watkins, the blue pills that weren't Viagra, and the dead johns.

"Hoo boy," she said when he finished. "That is a mess."

"I was afraid you were going to say that."

"Not insurmountable, though. This is why there's pandering laws. It puts the onus on the pimp. These women are basically prisoners. Let me make some calls, rustle up counsel who can help."

"I appreciate it," Carter said, pausing as his phone lit up with another incoming call from Papaleonardos. "Oh, and Rachel?"

"Yes?"

"It's a time-sensitive matter."

He cut the call and put the phone on his thigh, screen down. He looked up and saw Jim, Valerie, and Terri staring at him.

"If it's all right with you, I'm going to make a donut run," Carter said.

He found a Dunkin' half a mile away open early for the commuter crowd and loaded up. Six coffees in case people wanted extra, plus a large tea for himself; bag full of cream and sugars; a bunch of donuts—glazed, apple cinnamon, blueberry, others—and then four bear claws for good measure. It was a risk leaving the three of them alone, but the look on Valerie and Jim's faces suggested they understood the stakes and the downside of them leaving. Sure enough, everyone was in place back in the hotel room. Jim, Valerie, and Terri were looking at each other like a family that had barely survived a small plane crash. An accident for which each bore equal responsibility. But now both Jim and Valerie were sitting on the bed, each holding one of Terri's hands, so Carter counted that as progress.

As Carter laid out the coffee and doughnuts and blew the steam off his tea, Valerie said, "What now?"

Carter's phone buzzed again. Papaleonardos. Carter couldn't put him off much longer. It wasn't fair. Or smart.

Carter didn't answer the phone.

Carter looked at Terri as he replied to her mother's question. "I'm getting you a lawyer. Once that happens, he, or she, is going to make contact with the police. You'll be arrested. I'm guessing you know the drill?"

Terri nodded, eyes dull as spring mud.

"Arrested?" Jim said. "Is that necessary?"

"Yes." Carter turned his attention back to Terri. "After that, we'll have to trust the system. Donny's the villain here. But villains sometimes win."

With that, he took a sip of tea and reached for a Boston Kreme.

"That's it?" Jim Watkins said. "That's the best you can do? 'Villains sometimes win'? Are you serious?"

"I said sometimes."

"That's outrageous. This is our daughter we're talking about here. You can't just—"

"Jim," Valerie interrupted.

"What?"

"We thought she was dead. Now we're sitting here with Terri safe." She nodded at Carter. "Listen to what he's saying."

An hour passed. Conversations started and stopped. Terri was having a hard time staying awake. Eventually, Carter turned on the Weather Channel to lighten the mood. Compared to what he'd just been through, he found it oddly calming to watch wind-whipped correspondents in Tampa Bay broadcasting tropical storm updates.

The call came at 9 A.M. Carter identified himself, answered some preliminary questions, asked a few of his own. He shifted the phone to his left ear as he pulled a notebook the size of a deck of cards from a pocket on the right side of his utility vest, dug a pen out of his pocket, and made notes.

"Thanks," he said at the end of five minutes, and cut the call.

"Who was that?" Jim demanded.

Once again, Carter addressed Terri. "That was your new lawyer. Her name is Diane Menashe. She'll be here in thirty minutes. She'll make arrangements for you to surrender. On your terms, not the police's. You'll still be arrested, though. Do you understand?"

Terri nodded.

Jim said, "Can I speak to you for a second?"

Valerie, Jim, and Carter retreated to the far side of the room while Terri stirred five sugars into a second cup of coffee.

"I'm sorry I snapped. Valerie's right—we never thought we'd see Terri again. But—we can't afford a lawyer. We almost bankrupted ourselves trying to get Terri clean. I don't mean to put it like that, but it's the truth. I'm grateful beyond words that she's alive. But we're tapped out."

This time, Valerie didn't interrupt. She placed her right hand on Jim's arm and nodded.

"You don't need to worry about payment," Carter said.

"Why not?" Jim said.

"You just don't."

Carter recalled Nelson Ramos's irrefutable logic outside the house where they rescued his kidnapped sister. His intuition about what Terri might need. The tackle box currently sitting in a locked metal utility chest inside Carter's Suburban.

I bet she could use it as much as us.

Carter read the skepticism in Jim Watkins's eyes. He was about to say more, fudge something, when his phone buzzed again. Papaleonardos. Grateful for the interruption, he connected the call.

"This is Mercury."

"Finally—"

"Hang on," Carter said, lowering the phone.

"I need to take this," he said to Terri's parents. "Can you help Terri clean up a little? Get ready?"

Valerie nodded, eyes bright.

"I'm here," Carter said, as the couple returned to their daughter.

"What the hell's going on? I've been trying to call."

"Sorry for the confusion. Here's what's happening. Stand by for a call from Terri Watkins's lawyer. She'll take it from there."

"Take it from there? What's that supposed to mean? You can't hide this girl, Carter. That's breaking the law. We had a deal."

"I know we did. Do. What it means is, Terri's turning herself in."

"When?"

"As soon as her lawyer calls you. Which will be soon."

"What about you?"

"What about me, what?"

"When are we going to see you?"

Carter thought about it. "Once I've made my delivery, I guess. My original one, I mean."

"Delivery? We're so far past you making your delivery, we might as well be in Beijing. The priority is Terri, and you, getting your asses down here."

"The delivery is my first priority," Carter said, ending the call.

Menashe arrived twenty minutes later. Carter let her inside after verifying her identity. She was dressed professionally in a white blouse and dark blue pantsuit. If anything about the unorthodox nature of this appointment fazed her, she didn't show it. She might have been meeting with a prospective plumber.

Interview over, they were packing up, preparing to leave as a group, when Carter said, "One sec."

"What?" Menashe said.

"Back to business," Carter said. He removed the small ring box from a pocket inside his utility vest, where it had periodically bumped up against his Beretta for the past three days, faced Terri, and handed her the box.

"This is yours, I believe. Your parents hired me to deliver it to you."

Terri opened the box. Her eyes brightened as she spied the ring. Even in the dimly lit room, the ruby seemed to glow.

"I thought it was lost."

"Not lost," Carter said.

Slowly, like a woman handling a fragile glass ornament, Terri slid the ring onto her left ring finger, where it covered a faint band of pale skin. She examined it as if seeing it for the first time. Carter looked more closely and saw how beautiful the piece of jewelry was. But also how modest. The ruby wasn't much bigger than a sunflower seed. An unpretentious item to have triggered so much chaos.

"We should probably go," Menashe said.

Terri extended her hand, fingers splayed, the gesture of a newly engaged fiancée showing off the hardware. Except her expression was that of a woman who's just learned her fiancé is dead. She brought her hand back, slipped off the ring, returned it to the box, and handed that to her father.

"Can you keep this for me while I'm gone?"

"Of course—"

"It might be a while," Terri said.

FORTY-SEVEN

In the dream, Randy was at a park.

He couldn't remember the park's name, just knew it was someplace in Albany. He was standing at a swing set, pushing Michelle. Three years old, maybe four. Tiny jeans with elastic waist, Mulan sweatshirt, brown hair pinned back with pink barrettes. The dirt below each swing gouged deep from years of big kids scuffing their shoes as they slowed themselves. Randy with three hours of court-permitted unsupervised time. Same amount of time the trip took from Providence—one way. "The triple nine," Randy called the long out-and-back days.

No matter. Randy would take what he could get. Just the two of them. The cool touch of Michelle's tiny hand slipping into his meaty paw. Father and daughter. Who cared how frustratingly short the visits were? The brief one-on-one time was a harbinger of a brighter future, regardless of the mess Randy made of things in the past. In his dream, he permitted himself a glimpse of himself, years later, pushing a granddaughter on a swing. Michelle's own kid. A nice thought. Circle of life.

"Again, Daddy," Michelle crowed each time the swing's arc brought her back toward Randy. "Again."

In the nightmare, three days after the disaster at PC Seafood & Chops, Randy was in an interrogation room.

The room was crowded with players whose roles he recognized, if not their names.

The guy with the red cheeks, Tom Selleck mustache, and a dad bod stuffed into business-casual khakis and a button-down shirt: local detective. Probably Providence.

The woman in the Macy's pantsuit and beige blouse, gray-flecked black hair cropped short, CVS cheaters hanging around her neck: Rhode Island State Police, Detective Bureau.

The two guys and one woman in bespoke suits droning on in flat, Midwestern accents: feds.

Their rat-a-tat questions were a confused jumble, with references to "thousands of records" and "dark-web criminals" and "millions in fraudulent payments." Another constant, annoying phrase, like a mosquito in his ear: the Identity Theft and Assumption Deterrence Act.

Millions. Right. He never saw millions.

Would have, with Quadrant Horizons.

Not now.

Now, everything was in the toilet.

Again, Daddy. Again.

"No comment," Randy said to no one in particular.

"Listen, Carmichael—"

"No comment!" he roared.

Hands on his knees, studying a watercolor of trillium creeping along the edge of a forest, Carter sat in the business office of a nursing home on the outskirts of Albany and resisted the temptation to look at his watch. On the other side of a desk, the Autumn Crossing Skilled Nursing Facility director reviewed the paperwork in front of her. Her name was Angie. She seemed young to Carter, but that was happening more and more these days.

"Looks as if everything's in order, Mr. Carter. Given, I mean . . ."

Carter let three beats pass. "Yes?"

"It's a little, unorthodox, is all. If I'm being honest about it. You not being a relative of Ms. Carmichael."

"I believe corporate explained all that?"

Just for a second Angie panicked, as if eyeing an unexpectedly large credit card bill.

"Oh, yes. For sure. Yes, they did."

A week had passed. The inmate population of the Rhode Island Department of Correction facilities was not shrinking. Donny Tollman had joined the ranks of the pretrial incarcerated along with Pauley Carnevale, sans the red sweats. And Carnevale's surviving lieutenant with a thing for the Boston Celtics, and several other individuals. Including Aiden—Aiden Mabry, it turned out—in a protective custody cell, for now. *Cogs cut deals.*

Jim and Valerie Watkins visited Terri every day, was Carter's understanding. As they probably would for a while. They had a long road ahead of them. But Carter had seen longer roads. Ironically, like the one Stacy Gibbons was facing, broke and widowed, and she wasn't even in jail. At least she was safe.

On his way out of Providence, before driving to Albany, Carter completed his original delivery. The one he'd been on his way to make before encountering Linda Rausch trapped in her car in the pouring rain on Armistice Boulevard in Pawtucket. Stopping by the Providence home of Lenny Pellegrino, who'd recently turned ninety-one. Carter's mission: to deliver a vintage 1951 baseball card signed by Cleveland Indians turned Boston Red Sox shortstop Lou Boudreau.

As a kid, Pellegrino had seen Boudreau play, had once possessed such a card, and had spent a certain amount of money on another when it came to auction outside Cleveland.

Carter didn't normally get too excited about deliveries. In this case, he was looking forward to seeing the look on Pellegrino's face when he handed him the relic. Anticipating the moment, he limped toward Pellegrino's door, feeling the last few days.

A young woman who bore a passing resemblance to Fernanda Ramos, Nelson's sister, answered the door in blue scrubs. Carter explained why he was there.

"That's right. You're the one who called?"

Carter confirmed it.

"Mr. Pellegrino's expecting you. He's right in here."

Carter stepped inside the house, which smelled of mothballs, coffee, and overcooked marinara sauce. The woman led Carter through a dining room with the curtains drawn to an adjacent living room, nearly as dark, illuminated mostly by the glow of the TV. Opposite the TV, in a green wingback recliner with frayed upholstery, sat a man Carter mistook first for a boy, he was so small and frail.

"Mr. Pellegrino? I'm here with your card. Sorry I'm a little late."

Pellegrino cleared his throat. "I was starting to wonder," he said, voice low and hoarse as if he'd finished a coughing jag a moment earlier. "I'm glad you're here now."

Carter glanced at the woman, whose name badge—*Filomena S.*—gave her away as a health aide. She nodded. Carter approached and handed Pellegrino the plastic ziplock bag holding the Lou Boudreau card, along with one of Carter's business cards.

Pellegrino slowly opened the bag and removed the baseball card. He turned it back to front and back again several times, a smile growing on his face. At last, satisfied, he placed it back inside the plastic bag, set the bag on the brown throw blanket covering his legs, and examined Carter's business card.

"Mercury," he said. "Like the messenger of the gods."

"Yes," Carter said.

"You came a long way to deliver this."

"Six hundred and forty-one miles. Not so bad."

"That far from Cleveland?"

"A suburb called Lakewood. But yes."

"I'm grateful. Did I mention I'm the founding member of the Providence Lou Boudreau fan club?"

"You did."

Pellegrino nodded, lifted an envelope from his lap, handed it to Carter. For a split second Carter thought about declining the money. He changed his mind as he read the gratitude in Pellegrino's eyes. Sometimes charity was nothing more than doing what you said you'd do. In Carter's experience.

"Thanks," Carter said, pocketing the check.

"I was about to watch a movie, if you're interested." Another smile crossed Pellegrino's face. "The greatest baseball movie ever made." He looked at Carter expectantly.

Carter thought. "*The Pride of the Yankees*?"

Pellegrino shook his head. "Too hokey. Gary Cooper was old enough to play Miller Huggins by the time he was cast, let alone a rookie ballplayer. Try again."

"Um, *The Natural*?"

"Same problem with Redford. He practically had his AARP card when they made that."

"*Field of Dreams*?"

“Getting closer.”

Carter snuck a glance at the grandfather clock to the right of the TV, thinking about his drive home.

“Give up?”

“Afraid so.”

“*The Bad News Bears.* Seen it?”

Carter grinned in spite of himself.

“Not today.”

“Filomena says she’s never watched it, if you can believe that.”

Filomena smiled shyly.

“You’re welcome to watch with us,” Pellegrino said. “I’ll throw in lunch.”

Carter thought about the trip home to Rochester, with the pit stop in Albany along the way. His promise to Tomeka that this time, for sure, he’d be home for dinner. His desire to put Rhode Island in his rearview mirror for a while.

“It’s a deal,” Carter said, muting his phone and settling on the couch beside Pellegrino’s chair.

Back in Albany, Carter couldn’t restrain himself. He looked at his watch as he processed Angie’s response about corporate. Pushing 1:30 P.M. Later than he wanted to be on the road thanks to watching Walter Matthau and company with Lenny Pellegrino. Followed by several YouTube videos of Lou Boudreau afterward that Carter dialed up on his phone.

Carter said, “Since you spoke with corporate, then . . .”

“Boy, did I ever,” Angie said. “I was on the phone with them all day yesterday. Might have been easier if I’d just flown to Des Moines.”

Carter didn’t say anything. He pictured Quadrant Horizons’ headquarters in the Iowa capital. Big, gleaming, and landscaped to within an inch of its life. He was due to go back to Des Moines one of these days. Catch another Iowa Cubs game.

"It's just . . ."

Carter waited.

"I've never seen corporate take an interest in a case like this. Especially with a resident with Michelle's . . . special needs. She'll be very well taken care of," Angie added quickly. "I can assure you of that."

"Good to hear," Carter said.

What he didn't say: He wasn't sure he'd heard of a corporation taking that kind of interest either. He was glad they did. It had taken some doing, and some additional help from attorney Rachel Stanfield in Indianapolis. But making Aiden's offhand comment a reality hadn't been all that difficult.

They'll be too grateful that you came along to care about me.

Carter said, "If there's nothing else, then?"

"We're all set," Angie said, rising from her chair and extending her right hand. Carter shook it. Firm and professional. He took that as a good sign.

"Contact me with any questions," he said. "Well, contact the guardian ad litem, then me."

"Of course. Have a good day, Mr. Carter."

"You as well."

Carter had just exited onto I-90 West headed for Rochester when his phone buzzed. Marcus Washington. The USPIS agent who investigated his father's murder. And who now, late in his career, was chipping away at the back-burner task of finding Earl Madden.

"News?" Carter said, preliminaries out of the way.

Washington paused and said, "Possibly. A man matching Madden's description used an ATM in Phoenix two days ago."

"Matched how?"

"Facial recognition software."

"That's unreliable at best."

"I don't disagree. I've seen the photo. It's him."

"Okay."

"I've got agents in Phoenix pursuing the lead. I'm sharing this information with you in the interest of full disclosure. I'm advising you strongly not to do anything with it, other than telling your mom and your uncle. You're not planning any deliveries out west anytime soon, are you?"

Carter tucked the Suburban behind an Amazon truck and set his cruise control at sixty-eight miles per hour. "Generally speaking, my deliveries are confidential. However, also in the interest of full disclosure, it is possible I'll be in Los Angeles next month on a previously scheduled trip."

"But not Phoenix?"

Carter flashed back to the day in college that his mother called about his father's murder. The killing that Madden's wrongdoing made possible. His mother's sorrow and shock so incapacitating that Carter couldn't understand her at first.

"Your father. He's, he's . . ."

"Mom?"

Carter ticked the cruise control down to sixty-seven, and said, "As you probably know, I rarely fly. So, transit wise, it's hard to say. Last time I checked, Phoenix was on the way to LA."

"Beg to disagree," Washington said.

"Objection noted," Carter said.

After saying goodbye, he turned on the radio, surfed over to SiriusXM, and found the second game of a Jays–Royals doubleheader. The game probably wouldn't take him the entire three-hour drive to Rochester, but close.

It would be good to be home, he thought, settling back. Rest up for a while. See Tomeka after too many days on the road. Catch a couple late-season games on the tube. Grab a drink with his uncle.

Do all that, before it was time to set out again. To make another delivery. To head west, to Los Angeles. With a couple of stops along the way.

ACKNOWLEDGMENTS

I'm grateful to several people who made Mercury Carter's second outing possible, including Philip Eil, Phil Gentile, Bill Kole, Adam Nemann, and Pawtucket, Rhode Island, Detective Sergeant Theodore Georgitsis. They answered many questions and provided valuable information; any mistakes in the book are mine. Deep appreciation goes to the team at Mysterious Press, namely founder and CEO Otto Penzler, publisher Charles Perry, and publicist Julia O'Connell. Special shout-out to Luisa Cruz Smith, Mysterious Press editor-in-chief, for her hard work—and hard questions—on early drafts that helped dramatically improve the final product. As always, big thanks to my literary agent Victoria Skurnick of LGR, and thanks as well to my TV and movie rights agent Sylvie Rabineau. Of course, a tip of the hat to my publicist, Wiley Saichek, for his many efforts helping get the word out about my books. Finally, as always, thanks to Pam, my life and literary correspondent for more than four decades.